BOUND BY FATE!

A collection of short stories
OAK 2022

KEPRESSNG

NIGERIA | UK
First Published in 2022

The moral rights of the authors has been asserted.
Individual contributions ©2022

This book is sold subject to the condition that it shall not, by way of trade or otherwise, be lent, re-sold, hired out, or otherwise circulated without the publisher's prior written consent in any form of binding or cover other than that it is published and without a similar condition including this condition being imposed on the subsequent purchaser.

Kemka Ezinwo Press Ltd (KEP) has no control over or responsibility for any author, third-party websites, or articles that may be referred to in or on this book.

A CIP catalogue record for this book is available from the Nigerian National Library & the British Library.

978 978 790 465 7 (Paperback)
978 978 790 469 5 (Ebook)

This novel is entirely a work of fiction. The names, characters, and incidents portrayed in it are the work of the author's imagination. Any resemblance to actual persons, living or dead, events or localities is entirely coincidental.

Typeset by Kepressng Ltd
Cover design by Agnes Kay-E

To

All who have tempted fate.

All the writers who made this book possible.

CONTENTS

FATE AND FURIES 7
BADE'S INTERCESSORS 51
MY HEAD IS MY INTERCESSOR 71
TRAUMA 95
PURPLE JADE 129
YEWA'S IN-DWELLING 219
SCENT OF A FLOWER 256
DON'T FIGHT TODAY! 282
DEATH DIDN'T DO US PART.. 307
Bonus Story 331
THE WANDERER 332
OTHER KEP SHORT STORIES COLLECTION 339
CONTACTS 340
ABOUT US... 341
2026 COMPETITION 342

Can fate be altered or changed?

No one really knows if they can redefine their destiny, but some writer attempted to in their short stories following the theme, BOUND BY FATE. The final Kepressng Anthology Prize competition of the year 2022 celebrates the fatality and intrigues of fate as well as explores our divergent ideologies of the word.

Welcome to the JUVENILE version of the KepressNG Anthology Prize 2022, and these were the judges:

Efe Ogunnaiya is otherwise known as @bookreviewbymo on Instagram. She started her literary career reviewing e-books. So far, the books she's edited have gone on to be bestsellers.

Titi Oyemade enjoys reading and listening to music. She is currently a book reviewer for the Businessday Weekender newspaper, and her reviews have also appeared on The Newcastle Review website in the United Kingdom. While browsing the bookstore for books by Nigerian authors, a memoir, biography, or autobiography will almost certainly entice her into a reading binge. She owes her reading addiction to the book clubs, The Book Club Lagos and the Sunshine Book Club Lagos.

Agnes Kay-E is a Nigerian in the United Kingdom and the author of nine books, including Something New & Blossom in Winter, bestsellers. She writes contemporary women's fiction, fantasy, and new-age fiction. Her latest is Unexpected Complications. She is presently working on another Contemporary Fiction. In her spare time, she sings and writes music and hosts African and African by Descent authors every weekend on Instagram.

FATE AND FURIES
Adam Sunus

It was almost nightfall. The sun sought refuge past tall brown hills and behind the mountains beyond the city's capital, its receding luminous orange rays tainting the blue skies. The skies were flecked with fat, fleecy clouds, whose pure white was illuminated by night's arrival and the day's departure - twilight.

Overlooking the great expanse of the horizon was a dark figure. Dark, not in the sense that one would associate with nightfall, but dark complexioned. With skin the colour of charcoal, Kismet stood atop a fairly large hill draped in a thick woollen blanket around his shoulders; his arms were crossed over his chest, pulling the blanket tighter around himself as the wind grew stronger and colder.

Living on a hill wasn't always favourable, especially when night descended. The cabin in which he lived stood behind him, emitting creaks of protest as the wind grew stronger. Kismet wasn't the only one who disliked the cold, blistering wind at this hour, but it was at this hour that one could enjoy the view of the whole dryland and the city beyond it. His mother had gone to the city.

Kismet could picture his mother now, garbed in her black cloak, her black hair pulled back into a tight bun on her head, her lips widening in delight at the sight of Kismet, warm burnished brown hands clasping his arms and hugging him. Her skin would be silky and soft, and her brown eyes would be creased excitedly, just like his own. Kismet felt a bubble of warmth and love as he thought of his mother.

'Where was she now?' Kismet thought, his eyes skimming over the forest below and the path that she had passed some hours ago.

Kismet usually remained outside the hill whenever he wanted to see his mother from a distance, and when he did, he would run down the hill to meet her, feeling the cold winds blowing past his face, through his black hair, whistling into his ears, tickling him. Kismet loved that feeling -- like he was one with the wind.

It seemed today that he wouldn't be getting that feeling. Mother wasn't anywhere in his line of vision, and the sun's receding rays which gave off light, were extinguished by night. Kismet could no longer see farther than his black fingers. Night had finally descended.

Kismet finally went inside, chased by the cold that seeped through his woollen blankets and into his pores, causing goosebumps to erupt all over his skin. Inside, the cabin was pitch dark, and even the silver crescent outside couldn't lighten the room. Kismet was somewhat accustomed to the dark, so he used his mind's eye to navigate through the room and soon, he lit a match for the oil lamp in his hands. He was too young to start a fire in the fireplace and could risk burning his hand if he wasn't careful. Mother had told him so. Mother never lied. So, Kismet steered clear of the fireplace.

A soft orange flame grew from the enclosed oil lamp, bringing the cabin's interior to light. The floor was carpeted by brown and dusty fur roughened by overuse. The walls were bare and wooden, save for two nails for hoisting a night cloak, one of which was absent; Kismet's cloak hung limply on the nail in varied patches, coloured ones that suggested wear, tear, and patch. A fireplace was situated at the other end of the cabin, where a chimney rose up and outwards the cabin's exterior.

The only pieces of furniture were three long stools, a table, and a long battered old couch which Kismet and his mum squeezed together to sleep at night. Those were the only pieces of furniture that Kismet had to remind him of his late father.

Dropping the lit lamp on the wooden table, Kismet laid his woollen blanket onto the couch and laid himself on the couch to rest. The couch creaked under the weight of his body, but Kismet ignored the sound and adjusted his weight fully onto the couch. Tucking his legs together for comfort, Kismet fixed his gaze on the slow hypnotic dance of the fire and zoned out the howling winds outside; his eyes drooped shut, and he fell asleep thinking of the warm bread and milk that he was going to devour when Mother arrived.

Half an hour later, the wind ushered a presence up the hill -- Kismet's mother, Elna. She climbed up the hill with her cloak billowing behind her, her hands cradling warm bread and milk to her bosom. She had spent three hours working as a scullery maid in the city, doing menial chores. Elna finally got away from her job with a few coins that were provided for dinner.

The door to her home came into view, and Elna was more than happy to be in the comforts of her home. She closed the door behind her and was surprised to be met with darkness and, no less, with Kismet inside. Her son was more afraid of the dark than of her. He feared what lurked in the unknown crevices of the dark and never slept with the lights off unless with her beside him. Seeing as her son was asleep in the dark, Elna realised that the lamp must have gone off, which meant they had run out of lamp oil.

'I would have to get more oil next time,' Elna thought as she manoeuvred her way through the room and behind the couch, where the light snores of Kismet could be heard.

She swiped her hands under the couch for one of the candles she reserved for moments like this. She hid those candles from Kismet because he had a habit of lighting every corner of the room. She lit the candle in her hands, and after some seconds of steadying the fire, Elna poured some melted candle wax onto the table and pressed the candle unto it before the wax solidified.

"I expect you must be hungry," Elna said as she hoisted her cloak.

She turned to face Kismet, who had pretended to be sleeping. He had heard her enter the room but had been too scared to call unto her, in case it was one of the imaginary 'friends' that he feared.

"So hungry," He sat up with a yawn and walked over to Elna, hugging her as a sign of greeting.

"Come here," Elna bid as she pulled him to the couch.

Kismet's eyes went wide as he caught sight of his night meal. With a word of thanks, he pulled his share of the warm pastry and ravenously bit into it. For the next minutes, both of them sat in companionable silence as they feasted on warm bread and downed it with milk, after which they cuddled on the couch.

"Mom, would you tell me a story?" Kismet asked. It was his nightly request.

"A story? What tale do you want to hear?" Elna queried, knowing fully well that he was going to request the same story he requested every other night.

Kismet cuddled into his mother's warmth. "Tell me about the Furies."

"Furies?" Elna's brows were furrowed. She didn't recall telling him about the Furies; this wasn't a tale she had ever told him.

The Furies were a past that she had prevented herself from thinking about. She had made sure never to indulge her child in anything that would provoke him to ask about her past. That was one of the reasons why she lived here, on a hill where she was blanketed by the clouds and away from prying eyes.

"Where did you learn this word?"

"A woman in my dreams told me,"

His dreams? A woman? Elna couldn't believe it;

her son had started his divination at such an early age. He was only ten and could already be communicated with via dreams. The woman was probably from Elna's coven; they were still trying to find her, which meant that the magic seal she had placed on her son to enshroud his location had broken. Elna knew her coven was bound to search for her, especially after defying their customs and running away, but she didn't expect it to be so soon. It had only been eleven years.

'Calm yourself, Elna,' she thought. 'You have been expecting this, just reinforce the spell, and everything should be okay,'

Out loud, Elna said, "Are you ready?"

"Always!" Kismet affirmed in a chirpy voice.

Elna pried herself away from the couch and got up to sit on the stool. Kismet had sat up straight; his eyes fixed on his mother.

"Hope you won't fall asleep," Elna teased as she braced herself to tell the tale. Kismet shook his head and wrapped his blanket over his shoulder. The wind howled outside, rattling the windows, and the candle's fire flickered.

Elna exhaled, "Long ago...."

Six Years Later.
Kismet heaved as he dropped the last bundle of firewood into the fireplace of his home. He wiped off the sweat from his forehead and swiped his hands on his khaki shorts. The firewood should be sufficient to keep

his mother warm for the period that he was away. Elna was seated on a rocking chair that Kismet had made for her; her hands were occupied with a ball of yarn and a pair of thin rods she used for knitting. Elna was knitting a head wrapping for her travelling son.

Today, Kismet would set out to seek his fortune in the world. In these times, it was customary for every child who came of age to seek his fortune away from the comforts of his home. The idea was to give the child an outlook of the world and let him make decisions on his own. The child was to travel far into the desert, and if he were ever chanced to meet another settlement of people where he was accepted, then that would be his new home; and his new family.

There were also scenarios when the child would travel to gain new experiences and return to his home as a changed person. Elna hoped that this was the case with her son. It was Kismet's turn to journey the great plains of the desert with nothing more than a jar of water and his clothing; food could be foraged from animals. It was a Pilgrim's Test

Elna hadn't been opportune to seek her fortune, but she heard tales of people travelling the great plains of the desert only to come across different oddities. Some claimed to have been captured by wild animals who understood human dialect, others were reputed to have fought creatures of inhuman strength, and a lot of people insist on having seen a moving oasis that only appeared at night for travellers to drink from, only for it to disappear at the break of dawn--taking along with it, the people who had drunk from it.

Whatever contrasts each tale held, they all came around with a resounding clarity of how dangerously compelling the desert could be. Elna believed that all that would befall a person in the desert was known only to the fate that spun the destiny of every living creature.

Elna also believed in divine beings and the powers they possessed. Divine beings were seen as the parent to all living creatures and sometimes bestowed gifts on their children. Elna was one of the gifted ones. She was a witch. Nearly all of her life was spent worshipping them until they decided to forsake her, making her lose her first child in the same desert that her son was to journey upon.

Elna was convinced that she wouldn't be a bad parent and forsake her child to an uncertain fate in the desert. Thereupon, she prepared supplies that would prepare him for the outdoor life, especially her son's favourite--bread.

"Are you ready?" Elna adjusted the straps of his bag.

"Always," Kismet replied excitedly.

"Your knives?" Elna asked,

"Packed," Kismet answered abruptly.

"Water bottle?" She queried, to which Kismet

replied with an affirmative.

"Are you sure?" Elna insisted,

"Yes, mom. I assure you, I have packed everything," Kismet affirmed. He could see that his mother was having a hard time saying goodbye, he was too, but Kismet couldn't help but feel excited to be going somewhere. After years of being restricted to the hills, he felt positive that it was going to be a memorable adventure for him.

"I guess this is goodbye," his mother sniffed.

"Not goodbye mum. I will be seeing you soon." Kismet hugged his mom.

"And when will that be?" Elna asked,

"In two weeks," Kismet assured.

Elna nodded in comprehension. "And if you ever lose your way?"

"I'll run towards the sun," Kismet recited,

"Run towards the sun," His mother repeated, and they shared another teary-eyed hug.

Elna sobbed as they bid each other farewell. She stood by her cabin door, her eyes trailing the back of her son's head, watching as he descended the hill and strolled towards the great expanse of land behind her cabin. It was the same plains that she had been lucky to have survived after running from her past.

After spending hours navigating through the desert, Kismet realised there was no seeming end to the sandy plains. The barren land stretched on for miles with nothing to show for it except dry and hot sands. There was also little to no vegetation, and no landmarks could mark how far he had gone; for all Kismet knew, he had been walking in circles all day.

"The sun will guide you," Elna had said, but the sun only worsened Kismet's ache when he breathed.

Kismet squinted his eyes at the radiant ball of fire in the sky. The sun was relentlessly flaunting its light without any regard for whatever walked beneath it. Kismet was grateful for his mother's thoughtfulness in providing him with long, loose-fitting robes, preventing his sweat from evaporating quickly and aiding easy airflow.

'Fortune seeking was hard,' Kismet realised as he adjusted the white head wrapping on his head and continued onwards into the unknown.

A few weeks prior, when his mother introduced the idea of him embarking on a customary journey into the desert, Kismet had felt elated. Having lived his life restricted to the hills with no peers and nothing to sustain his curiosity about the world, he was ecstatic to finally have a chance to explore. However, Kismet was barely through half a day and was already exhausted. He had a line of complaints: the desert provided no shade against the sun, there was no point of rest, and he had already gone through half his water supply.

'This was all folly,' His mind seemed to be telling him. Kismet knew that having been coveted all his life had made him ignorant of the world, making him easy prey to the harsh elements of the desert; not having a particular destination infuriated Kismet even further.

'Was he just expected to navigate through this endless maze of sand and find his fortune?' Kismet wondered.

'If this fortune is anywhere, it might as well be everywhere.' Kismet muttered to himself.

Miniature dust devils twirled ahead of him, and the wind blew residues of hot sand into his mouth. Kismet coughed and spat the sand particles that invaded his mouth, but that only worsened the ache he felt in his chest. Each breath he took burned and required even more effort than the last; his eyes were slightly clouded by dust, his lips were parched, and he craved water to quench his thirst.

Time passed with Kismet scouring the plains for something that could give him a sense of direction, and it wasn't until near sunset that Kismet spotted two black stones protruding from the singe-brown sands. The black rocks stood out like a sore thumb, or in this case, sore thumbs.

The black stones were considerably large; they rose from the ground from two opposing points on a level plane and converged at the tip, some meters apart; it looked like an overturned 'V'. The arched stones were surprisingly protruding at a slope that backed the direction of the sun.

"It could provide shade!" Kismet exclaimed to himself.

Feeling a sense of purpose and direction, Kismet changed his trajectory and bolted toward the arched stones. They weren't as far as he expected, and before he knew it, he was pulling off his bag, tossing it aside and settling in between the arched stones.

The sands were just as Kismet expected, warm and less likely to burn him. The winds were slightly cooler, and the shade was exquisite; the sun's rays were still burning his outstretched feet, but that hardly mattered when Kismet tucked his legs beneath him.

'Problem solved,' Kismet thought before positioning himself on his side to sleep.

No sooner had Kismet fallen asleep did he feel a repetitive sting on his foot. Being as exhausted as he was, Kismet ignored the pain. However, he soon realised that the more he ignored the pain, the harder it was for him to enjoy his nap.

Kismet awakened in sharp panic, bewildered by the sight of a black scorpion with its tail poised to strike him again. Shock geared Kismet into motion, and he kicked sand in the direction of the scorpion; the scorpion retreated.

Taking care to examine the area for lurking scorpions, Kismet got up and dusted himself. His foot had swollen up, and he felt a throbbing ache in the affected foot. Kismet grabbed his bag of supplies and was about to rummage for an anti-venom when he heard the loud growls of some creature.

Kismet paused midway; the sound didn't seem to have resonated around him, and yet, he could have sworn he heard a loud bark-like growl.

'Could I be hallucinating?' Kismet pondered, trying to discern the sound.

"Get back!" A voice cried out desperately. This was human.

Momentarily forgetting his troubles, Kismet grabbed his knife and ran up the slope where the sun's rays could be seen. It seemed someone was in danger, and there was a possibility that someone was also searching for their fortune. Kismet reasoned that if he were also in need of help, he would want anyone to help him. Kismet scrambled up the slope without further thought.

Upon reaching the top of the slope, Kismet burrowed his feet into the sands to steady himself, and on the other side, the sight that met Kismet's eyes caused him to falter in fear. Three grey-coated wolves had surrounded two men and had them enclosed in a tight-spaced circle that forced them back-to-back. One of the men held a bleeding arm, and the sight of the blood was sending the wolves into a frenzy; the desert wolves were rabid-looking and were sure to attack--even if both men held weapons.

Kismet felt his blood boil at the spectacle before

him. He unsheathed his knife, hopped off the top of the slope and ran towards them while yelling at the top of his lungs. Both men and wolves turned, startled to see a young boy approaching them with a knife. The wolves spaced away from the two men and let out menacing snarls at each other. They regrouped and changed their trajectory for a new target: Kismet.

Kismet was charging at the wolves with a knife and no backup. The wolves regarded him as easier prey and bolted in his direction. They probably wondered what good it would do for them to attack the former duo when they could attack a lone figure who didn't seem capable of fighting and was also willingly throwing himself at them.

Adrenaline rushed into his veins, and Kismet felt an extra spurt of energy. The pangs of hunger within the wolves spurred them. They formed a triangle around him and, with their leader, bared fangs in anticipation of a sumptuous meal.

A whooshing sound cut through the air, preceding the fall of the leading wolf. An arrow had lodged itself into its head and ended its ascent. The other two wolves bolted in two opposite directions with their tails between their legs, disoriented by the fatal attack that met their leader.

Kismet staggered to a stop, just as confused as the wolves. 'Where had the arrow come from?'. The man with the injured hand dropped his bow to the ground and gave Kismet a salute. Kismet smiled and was about to return the salute when he felt all the energy within him fizzle out; he could feel every strain on his body.

Black and white spots clouded Kismet's vision before his legs gave way beneath him. Feeling dizzy, his breathing forced and the world spinning around him, Kismet collapsed and fell into peaceful unconsciousness.

~~~~

Kismet woke up with a gasp. He was perspiring from the nightmare he had just had. It was one of those dreams from when he was younger, the dream about Furies. The dream felt like it meant something crucial to his life, but Kismet couldn't tell what it meant; the more he tried to remember, the more he seemed to forget.

The area around him was dark, and Kismet felt like he was inside some kind of tent. The tent-like enclosure also seemed to be moving. Kismet paused and looked around; he was in a kind of convoy. His mother had home-schooled him about convoys like these and how only the extremely wealthy could own one. Kismet wondered how he got into one, and the preceding events flashed through his mind; he had collapsed after his encounter with the wolves.

Those two men must be merchants, Kismet thought as he tried heaving himself off the floor. In the dark, Kismet couldn't navigate through, and his legs kicked at some object that drowned the enclosed space in a loud bang. Kismet paused as he heard whispers coming from somewhere in front of him.

Shuffling sounds followed the whispers, and Kismet tried reaching for his bag when he remembered that he had left it at the arched stones. A lit lantern passed through a partition of a curtain ahead of him before a figure entered the enclosed space along with it. The lantern was hung on a nail near the ceiling, and the features of the figure were brought to light.

The entity was a dark-skinned man with equally dark hair that framed his head in a buzzcut. The man was lightly-built and had a warm, cheery smile that made him look strikingly handsome in the orange light. It was the man who had shot the wolf.

"How are you feeling?" The man's voice was baritone.

Kismet wasn't sure whether to answer or not. This was his first time seeing someone besides his mother, and this person appeared to be a good person, considering he had saved him from what could have been a gruesome death.

"You saved me," Those were Kismet's first words, and up until he spoke, he didn't realise how thirsty he was.

The man noticed. "You saved us. It was only right that we returned the favour," The man said as he handed Kismet a cup of water, and after Kismet had drunk, he motioned towards Kismet's bitten leg.

"We?" Kismet intoned,

"Kwame is the other man. He is my assistant but has settled into moving us out of the desert,"

Kismet watched his movement. The man raised a hand in surrender. "I only want to examine your wound," Kismet nodded his head, to which the man began untying the cloth around his ankle.

"You don't seem apprehensive of me," The man said by way of question.

Kismet shrugged, "If you wanted to hurt me, you'd have done it already,"

"Ah, that's a good logic, and yet a terrible one," The man said as he placed Kismet's leg on a slate.

"And why do you say so?" Kismet winced at the man's touch.

"Well, there could be multiple scenarios; I might be a cannibal nurturing you back to health just so I can devour you. I might also be a trafficker transporting you to unknown lands for slavery, a drug dealer in need of an errand boy, or a fetish priest looking for an uninjured human sacrifice. I could be anything out here, just lying in wait to ensnare you." The man applied a cold, slimy ointment on his wound.

Kismet exhaled deeply; this man could be any of those things he mentioned, which would explain his accessibility to a caravan. Yet, Kismet couldn't help but feel some degree of trust towards him.

"Could you be all those you mentioned?" Kismet asked, unsure and seeking to trust his instinct.

"Not all at once. I couldn't," the man chuckled.

"Then I guess that's fine by me," Kismet said with conviction.

The man stared at Kismet for a moment, shook his head and laughed. "Tola." He said with an outstretched arm.

Kismet clasped his hand in a warm shake. "I'm Kismet."

Tola grinned. "Well then, Kismet, you and I are very alike."

"In skin colour?" Kismet's eyebrows were furrowed in confusion.

"No, silly. We are both too trusting," Tola chuckled at the boy's obliviousness.

"And that's a bad thing?"

"Not necessarily, but this world is filled with people who would manipulate trust, and that's bad," Tola explained.

"I see," Kismet remarked.

They both stared at each other for some seconds before sharing a smile.

"So, tell me, what is a boy of …" Tola trailed off.

"Sixteen."

"What is a boy of sixteen doing in the desert alone?" Tola queried. Was this boy sixteen? He couldn't believe it. The boy must have lived a sheltered life somewhere.

Tola could tell that the boy wasn't a city boy; he was too innocent and happy that it seemed infectious. The boy reminded him of a younger Tola.

"I'm searching for my fortune," Kismet responded honestly.

"Fortune? You don't mean the Pilgrim's Test?" Tola rolled his eyes.

"You know of it?" Kismet queried.

"Know of it?" Tola scoffed. "I once journeyed myself."

Kismet was awed; he was in the presence of someone who had gone on the journey. He couldn't believe it. How lucky was he to be sitting beside an actual voyager?

"What did you find?" Kismet asked curiously.

"It was all a waste of time," Tola responded.

Like an air balloon deflated, Kismet paused to stare at Tola. "There was no fortune, just sand, snakes and more sand." Tola laughed mirthlessly.

"However, I did meet a pregnant woman," Tola reminisced.

Kismet was silent. He could sense a story.

"She was lying in a pool of blood when I found her. I remember examining her for wounds, and when I found none, I realised that she was bleeding her child away. She was having a miscarriage and had fallen unconscious. The situation required immediate attention, so I carried her to a nearby cave where I tended to her and nursed her back to health."

"When she awakened, it was with the hostility of a tiger that she spaced away from me; she was a beautiful young lady, but her growls made her look menacing, so I kept my distance. I only drew close to her when I wanted to dress her wounds, feed her or adjust her sleeping position," Tola chortled.

"Soon, I had to leave and return to my family. I didn't know what to do with her. We spoke that day, and she surprisingly obliged to follow me back home. On the way home, she divulged to me that she had been on the run from some people who were after her. We grew close, and soon we reached my hometown, but she chose not to stay." Tola finished.

"Did you ever see her again?"

"No, it was goodbye," Tola stated somberly.

"That's a bad love story." Kismet laughed.

"I know," Tola said amidst a shared laugh.

"Your majesty!" A voice called out.

"I'll be right back," Tola said to Kismet before he leapt to his feet and went out.

Kismet stared transfixed in the direction where Tola passed; he couldn't believe what he had just heard. Tola had just been referred to as 'majesty', which meant that Kismet had been speaking with someone of royalty, and he hadn't known.

The next few days passed in a flash, with Kismet and Tola getting to know each other better. In a short time, they realised that they had much in common and could relate to most occurrences in each other's lives.

Despite having lived in isolation, Kismet could sympathize with the travails of a leader trying to balance his personal life with the duties and obligations expected of him. In his opinion, Tola ruled an entire kingdom and was accountable for every denizen and their actions. He was burdened with expectations weighing him down. Kismet had never experienced such and couldn't help but wonder how it felt to meet a set standard.

"I grant you. It's not easy," Tola told him.

Tola was faced with the need to provide an heir to the throne but had instead only borne girls--one of whom was a year younger than Kismet. It was hard to maintain a parental role with any of them when he had diplomatic events to cater to. As a result, Tola and his children were estranged from each other. It wasn't like Tola didn't delegate responsibilities, but there were some who didn't favour his rule for reasons known only to them. They made every success and failure of his administration seem like a failure anyway.

It was for administrative reasons that Kismet was able to meet Tola in the desert. Tola and Kwame had been returning from a diplomatic visit to a settlement in the desert. This settlement was known as the Savage clan. They lived in a region of the desert which was rarely ever journeyed to, but Tola had sought them for their technical know-how and bizarre agricultural skills. The people of the savage clan were reputed for their skills in nurturing plants in the harshest of weathers; their ways were secret and closed off from the world, yet they seemed to be doing great despite being in the desert.

Tola sought them to seal an alliance that would be mutually beneficial, and the terms were that the savage clan disclosed some of their bizarre planting techniques, and in exchange, Tola provided them with able-bodied men who would develop their infrastructure and introduce better facilities in their lives. The result of the visit was uncertain, as they requested the king visit them in a week's time.

"Strange and fetish" was what Tola described their nature to be. He also termed them as rudely inquisitive and creepy enough to query about his offspring. Tola frowned when he said this because--according to him--they seemed pleased that he didn't have an heir, but he also said that he might have imagined it; his emotions were all over the place.

The borders of the kingdom soon came into view, marking the end of their journey. Kismet could spot the wooden outline of his home on the mist-clouded hill, and he could already imagine what his mother would be doing on an afternoon like this. For some reason, Kismet didn't feel too excited to be back in the hills.

BOUND BY FATE

He might have felt nostalgia for his home and longed for his mother, but that paled in comparison to the feeling of freedom he felt in the desert--the aching feeling of freedom.

Tola noticed the downcast look that had blossomed on Kismet's face, and he realised at a glance that the boy knew the end of the journey marked his return to seclusion, and that was a damper on the boy's excitement. Tola wished he held some sort of jurisdiction over the boy's freedom, but he wasn't the boy's guardian, nor was he Kismet's parent, so he couldn't influence the boy. The only thing Tola felt he could do, was to suggest in the most subtle way possible.

"Kismet," Tola called.

Kismet turned to look at Tola. They were seated in the driver's compartment, with Tola riding the caravan because Kwame was exhausted from riding it all night. The sun was of moderate temperature as they drew closer to the kingdom and farther from the desert.

"Anything the matter?" Kismet asked concernedly, the wound on his hand wasn't fully healed and Kwame warned that there could be an infection from the wolf's bite, but Tola insisted on riding back.

"No, nothing at all. I was just thinking about how far we've come and how it is a pleasure to have met you." Tola's eyes were trained on the distance uncovered, but his face held an infectious warmth.

Kismet smiled."It was a pleasure meeting you too, your majesty."

Tola chuckled, "I have told you not to call me that."

Kismet gave a mocking salute that made Tola laugh even further.

"But, I was pondering the details of my deal with the savage clan, when I realised that I would be bored if I ever lost the deal, so I was wondering if you'd love to accompany me in a week," Tola requested,

Kismet paused with an incredibly bright smile on his face. "Would I? I would like that!"

Tola chuckled as Kismet wrapped his arms around his body in gratitude.

"Are you sure?" Kismet asked. This meant another journey to a new location.

"A king never reneges on his word, and if you don't believe me, I can ask your mother for permission. That should be binding enough," Tola promised,

So it was with that promise that Tola steered the caravan towards the direction of the hill while wondering what could have prompted someone to live so high up on a hill, far away from everyone. It felt like an intentional attempt at seclusion. However, Kwame had woken up and overheard the discussion between his friend and the young boy, and he wasn't pleased with the king's promise.

Kwame felt it was too forward of a king to pick up

an absolute stranger from the desert, give him a ride home, and promise him a spot on their next journey, and now, he was planning on meeting the boy's mum. What was next? An adoption? Kwame sincerely hoped Kismet didn't thwart the king's plans in any way, for his sake. If he did, Kismet would regret ever seeking his fortune-- Kwame would make sure of that.

I'm getting ahead of myself. Let's see what happens at the hill first, Kwame thought. The convoy jerked to a halt, signalling their arrival at the base of the hill.

The convoy grounded to a halt at the bottom of the hill. Kismet and Tola hopped off the caravan, after which Kwame got off too. Kismet breathed in the 'hill air' and felt a sense of peace resonate. His mother would be surprised to see him, he had only spent half the weeks that were expected of him, and he was back home, alive and well, with the king at her doorstep.

Elna was in for the surprise of her life.

"Come on!" Kismet's excited voice carried over the winds as he set himself on the path uphill. Tola followed with an ever-present smile on his face. Kwame trailed behind them, he didn't want to go into a stranger's house, but for his king, he would do anything.

The motion uphill was strenuous to the two men,

but Kismet clambered up with the agility of a monkey and would only pause to check how the two men were faring. Eventually, he turned his agile pacing to that of a turtle's trot. Both men kept wondering what on earth could have influenced a person to build a house so high and without fear. Tola had forgotten that he had a fear of heights and had to be steadied by Kwame.

Before the marching men could reach the front of the door, Kismet had beat them to it and rapped his hand on the door before he heard the patter of running feet and the door gave way to reveal Elna.

"Kismet!" Her eyes were wide in shock and awe. Then her eyes slid to the approaching men, and she froze at the sight of the dark-skinned man. It was him. The man who had saved her in the desert. The man who was responsible for...

"Elna?" Tola asked. It was a face he hadn't expected to see.

"Tola," Elna stated, her heart pounding.

Kismet stared between his mother and the king. "Wait, you know each other?"

Minutes after being ushered in, Kwame was seated beside his master on the couch. Kismet sat on the stool while Elna insisted on standing.

"I didn't know that you lived so close to the kingdom and yet very high away from the world," Tola stated.

"What can I say? It deters visitors," Elna replied, holding Tola's gaze.

"Still antisocial, I see," Tola remarked with a smile.

Kwame frowned. The woman looked vaguely familiar, like the priestess from the savage clans and yet somewhat different.

"I am sorry. I did not know that Elna was your mother." Tola said as he faced Kismet.

"And why should you be sorry?" Elna's attention was piqued.

"I told him of how we met in the desert."

Kismet's eyes widened in surprise. That meant his mother was the woman Tola met in the desert. That also meant that his mother had lost a child before giving birth to him.

"Oh," Kismet gasped.

Elna frowned. She couldn't wrap her head around how her son came to know Tola. It felt like fate was trying to mess with her.

"So, why have you come here?" Elna asked, folding her arms.

"Oh, yes. We almost forgot," Tola explained. "I am visiting a clan in the desert next week, and your son has proven to be an excellent companion, so I was wondering if you'll permit him to follow me."

Kismet looked expectantly at Elna. Elna froze when Tola said the word clan. It reminded her of a place that she fled years ago. Tola recognised the conflict within her. "You don't have to decide this moment, we'll drop by next week, and if you agree, we'll take him with us and if not..."

Elna simply nodded. Kismet frowned; his mother had been acting strange ever since they had arrived. It was weird seeing his mother so ruffled and odd.

"I guess our job here is done then." Tola rose to his feet, and Kwame imitated. His eyes were still on Elna.

"Kismet, I'll see you then," Tola bid, with a smile more akin to a grimace. "Elna. It is a pleasure meeting you again."

Elna forced a smile in return. Kwame and Tola were about to leave the room when Kwame whispered something in Tola's ear, to which Tola nodded in assent.

"Miss," Kwame turned to face Elna. "Do you by any means know of the savage clan?"

Elna inhaled, and her whole body stiffened, but she replied quickly. "No,"

Kwame looked at her with narrowed eyes.

"That will be all," Tola said.

"Yes, your majesty," Kwame said as he retreated towards the door.

Elna's heart pounded, and she blurted out before she could control herself. "Majesty?"

"Do you have a problem with the title?" Kwame asked.

"No, no, it's just –"

Tola helped her out. "When we met, I didn't tell her I was a prince. She's probably shocked to know I now rule the kingdom."

"Yes. Yes, that's it," Elna spoke abruptly.

Kismet narrowed his eyes at his mother.

The moment both men were gone, Tola faced his mother. "Are you alright?"

Elna sat on the couch, her hand fanning her face. She looked faint.

"I'm alright. I'm just a little bit faint from seeing him again," she said.

"You never told me that you knew a king," Tola accused.

"It was a meaningless period. I didn't see the need to indulge you," Elna dismissed.

Kismet paused and examined her. He was certain that something was bothering her, and it had something to do with the king. Knowing that his mother wouldn't tell him if he asked directly, he decided to use another approach.

"What do you think about the king's proposal?" Kismet asked as he sat beside her on the couch.

Elna remained silent.

"No." She faced Kismet. "You mustn't go. I forbid it."

She'd spoken with way too much emotion that Kismet's heart sagged. Yet, he felt a sort of defiance and anger at her.

Kismet snapped back for the first time. "Why?"

"Excuse me," Elna exclaimed, her face wrought

with shock.

"Why?" Kismet reiterated. "Why can't I go with him?"

"Because I said so. And because it's bound to be dangerous," Elna stated in a tone that dismissed an argument.

"Oh! More dangerous than sending me into the desert alone?" he scoffed sarcastically.

"Yes, and -"

Kismet cut her off. "No! Don't tell me to trust you on this. You are always doing that."

Elna paused to look at him; her son had never been so resolute before.

"That desert didn't do you any good," Elna stated as she got up from the couch.

"So, now the desert is bad?" Kismet let out a peal of derisive laughter.

"What has gotten into you?" Elna asked in disbelief.

"You!" Kismet spat in anger. "All my life, I've turned a blind eye to your orders and carried out all your wishes in love for you. I didn't go to the city to make friends, I never disobeyed you, and I made sure not to bring up your background or the fact that I've had the same dream all my life."

"And now you deny me a simple adventure because you want to?" Kismet stared his mother in the eye. "I want answers, and I want them now." He demanded,

Elna paused and stared at her son. "Very well, I guess it's time then."

"This story I'm about to tell you explains everything in detail and should provide answers to your recurrent dream." Elna sighed.

Elna solemnly began to narrate, "Long ago, I lived far away from civilization and in an area that most people abhorred. The desert. In this area of the desert, I lived among a settlement of blessed humans who called themselves the Savage clan.

The Savage clan originated from the women of vengeance. The furies. And they were the instruments of the gods in this world. They were blessed with powers of divination, soul communication and the ability to control elements in our favour.

As the instruments of the gods, they were also instruments of fate and could turn the tides of the fate of every living being. That was our means of living.

As generations progressed, the furies took on a different name. Witches. The witches settled into the roles of our ancestors and lived happily performing our duties to the gods until the day the prophecy came.

The prophecy foretold the end of the savage clan by the son of the priestess and a king. It foretold the child would end the savage clan and bring about the flourishing of the king's kingdom."

"I was, at the time, the priestess of the savage clan

and some months pregnant. The witches of the coven were terrified. They didn't want to die. They dreaded their end and didn't want to lose all we'd worked to build. To prevent the prophecy and their fate, they decided to destroy my unborn child without consideration for me. I tried to explain to them that I had never slept with any king and that I was safe, that we were all safe, but they didn't understand because, according to them, I was a risk they couldn't afford to take." Elna sighed, and Kismet sat in silence, torn by the pain his mother felt.

"I ran away without being struck a ghastly blow."

"That was when Tola found you...." Kismet trailed, realising the pieces of the puzzle were settling in.

"Yes. I didn't know at the time that he was a person of royal birth. One thing led to another, and then I got pregnant. By that time Tola had returned home, I built a home high away from everybody and placed a protection spell around it to ward off strangers."

Kismet narrowed his eyes. Something was puzzling him. If she got pregnant again and Kismet had no brother. So....

"Tola is my father," Kismet gasped.

Elna nodded solemnly. "Yes. He is your father, but at the time, I didn't even realise that I hadn't been able to evade fate. I thought losing my home, my child, and my status as the priestess meant our fate had changed, but I now realise that we had been bound to it."

"Eventually, you began to display signs of powers, so I sealed it with a spell, but your powers were too strong, and my spell could only prevent you from using it subconsciously. Your powers leaked, and you saw the dreams of you ending the Savage clan," Elna explained.

"I didn't expect that you'll meet Tola in the desert, and I didn't even know that he was a king until now," Elna said, cupping his face. "That is why you must not go with him because if you do, the witches will see through you and kill you."

Kismet stared at her.

"Promise me! Promise me that you won't set foot away from this hill, for your sake and my sake," Elna sobbed.

Kismet stared at Elna. She had done all this for him. She had done it to save him from a terrible fate.

"I promise. It's okay. I promise," Kismet said and moved to hug his mother when she slapped him.

He stared at her in shock. "That's for speaking back to me." She chuckled amidst tears.

"I guess I deserved that." Kismet chuckled before finally being embraced by his mother.

A week later, when Tola came to their door to pick up Kismet, Kismet politely declined. Although Tola was disappointed, he obliged the boy's wishes and went his way, leaving Kismet thinking that he had evaded his fate and that Tola had an heir, unlike what everyone thought.

Later in the evening, Elna was preparing for her working shift in the city when she heard a knock on the door. Thinking it was Kismet who was expected to be returning from the woods, Elna tossed her cloak on the couch and approached the door. The sight that met Elna's eyes as she opened the door caused her to freeze in shock. The person standing on the other of the door wasn't supposed to be there.

It was a witch from the savage clan, her sister, Kemi.

"How?" Was all Elna could spew before Kemi pushed her aside and barged into the cabin.

"Do you mean, how did I find you or how did I know that you have borne the child that will end the savage clan?" Kemi asked as she settled on the couch.

Kemi was dressed in the traditional orange attire of the clan, her brown skin gleamed beneath the black chalk markings on her body, and her forehead held the tattoo of a wolf, which was one of the gods that she served.

"Both," was Elna's reply.

"Well, you do know that I was born with the ability to ferry the spirits of animals to the underworld for reincarnation. I came across a wolf spirit and was skimming through its memories when I saw that your son was among the ones responsible for its death. From there, I was able to link into his soul and pinpoint your location. However, your magic spells kept leading me astray. I was able to find you, and now here we are. A

BOUND BY FATE

sisterly reunion." Kemi grinned maniacally.

"Why are you here? We both know you are not here for a reunion," Elna urged. Kismet could be returning any minute now, and she didn't want Kemi to meet him.

Kemi laughed. "You haven't changed one bit. I'll have you know that I have been ordered here to end your son."

Elna stilled; her shackles were rising. "He isn't here. Besides, the child in the prophecy is dead. He died when you attacked me," Elna accused.

Kemi paused in thought and then scoffed, "Nice try. I may not know much, but I do know that the prophecy foretold that he would 'drench a wolf in blood', and since you have been so kind enough to let me know that the initial child is dead, I'm certain that this child is the child of prophecy."

Elna narrowed her eyes. "And what makes you think I'll let you take him?"

"Well, you won't be able to stop me if you are dead." Kemi stood up and cracked her knuckles.

They both faced each other in readiness for a magic brawl, and Elna hoped the lack of practice hadn't dulled her.

Kismet was coming out of the woods, a bundle of firewood on his right shoulder, his right hand supporting the heavy load of wood, when he heard a loud boom. The sound reverberated around the surrounding area, sending nesting birds into the sky.

'It seems to be coming from the hills,' Kismet thought and broke out of the woods in a sprint. He smelled it before he saw it. Fire. The cabin was engulfed in flames. The bright orange flame licked the wood and wrapped its orange tendrils around the cabin as if comforting. Black smoke wafted from the open windows of the cabin. At that time, it seemed someone threw a rag from the windows and fell over the peak of the hill and down to the floor.

It wasn't until Kismet neared the 'rag' that he realised that the rag was a person, and that person was no other than his mother. The shock of seeing the cabin in flames was washed away by fear and concern, gearing Kismet into motion.

"Mother!" Kismet ran towards her and tossed aside the firewood. Kismet staggered to a fall beside his mother's limp figure. Her face had grown pale, and there was blood gushing out of a wound in her stomach; her attempts at breathing were followed by a gurgled sound as she coughed blood and spit.

"Kismet. Run!" Elna gasped out in acute pain.

"Kismet?" a voice resonated from behind Kismet, causing him to whip back in shock. It was a woman who looked like his mother.

"Kemi! Please." Elna begged.

"I never knew you could plead, but pity is for the weak and you..." She drew close to Elna. "Are not weak."

Kismet stood in between them, "I won't let you lay a single finger on her,"

"Of course, but I'll lay many knives into her." Kemi cackled.

Kismet backpedalled, not daring to look away.

"Do you know the meaning of your name?" She asked.

Kismet looked at his mother, whispering, telling him to run, but he couldn't leave Elna alone.

"Kismet means Fate. Do you know why?" Kemi asked, her face drawing closer to his.

The stench of fear was so thick that Kemi felt she could cut it. This boy was terrified of her.

"That is because it's only fate that can end the furies, the witches. Your birth foretold our end, and only by your influence can we die. No mere human can go against us, but once a single part of you rises in rebellion against us, then anyone can end us," Kemi murmured before she grabbed the boy by his throat and squeezed until he blacked out.

The last thing Kismet saw was a large flaming part of the building fall from the sky and onto his mother.

Kismet woke up to the distinct smell of grilled meat and the stench of burning skin. His eyesight focused on the sight of numerous bonfires surrounding him, his arms restrained, and his legs, but his back rested on a cold, slimy substance that seeped into his clothing and was solid enough to support his weight.

It didn't take long for him to realise that he wasn't on the hills. The hills. The memory of the cabin exploding in fiery flames came to Kismet unbidden, leaving a sour feeling in its wake, the memory stirred aside, and a different memory took its place, amplifying a feeling of loss, anger, and a murderous desire to enact his revenge on his mother's look-alike. That woman had murdered his mother because of a prophecy.

Kismet hadn't entirely been concerned about ending the savage clans, but now, he was determined to end them. They had caused more damage than was necessary; their involvement in his life had only caused him pain – directly and indirectly. They were the reason for his seclusion, his mother's pain, his pain, and now his mother's death.

"They don't deserve to live," Kismet whispered to himself, and he let his tears go so he could taste them.

Shadows erupted around the surrounding area outside the circle of bonfires, appearing in twos and threes until they appeared in what seemed to be a colony or settlers. Kismet squinted his eyes at the dark figures appearing in something equivalent to a hundred. They all looked and dressed in the same attire as his mother's lookalike. Kismet realised that he was in the Savage clan. His mother's coven.

That means I'm surrounded by witches and wizards, Kismet thought.

The congregation of witches suddenly parted in the

middle, and a woman walked in their midst, holding a white staff. Kismet stared at the woman's gait and judged that she must be very old. Beside her was his mother's lookalike, staring at him with a grin gracing her lips. Kismet's blood boiled. If he ever had a chance to escape, she would be the first on his list to die before he burned the whole village.

As they reached the clearing of the bonfire, the old woman grounded her foot to a halt and rattled her staff, to which the congregation cheered and hooted in their dialect. The old woman was the high priestess of the savage clan; she sacrificed her tongue to gain the position of High priestess, and as a result, she needed someone to be her mouthpiece.

Kemi moved to the centre of the congregation and cleared her throat in readiness.

"Today, we mark a milestone for the progression of our coven and our people for having persevered centuries and managing to remain the most powerful beings on this side of the plains, even in the face of extinction by the birth of a mere child." Kemi looked to the priestess, to which the priestess nodded.

"For that, I congratulate you. I congratulate us on our victory in capturing the supposed bane of our existence!" Kemi yelled the last part, and the congregation reciprocated in a louder ovation.

"I congratulate us on our success and our recent

alliance with a king who has promised to restructure our village and bring innovations for us all!" Kemi yelled once more, and the congregation didn't fail her.

Tola was here, Kismet recalled. The agreement between them had succeeded.

"To mark this double achievement, the blood of our bane shall wash our village clean and welcome a new life for us all," Kemi stated and waved to someone in the crowd.

A tall, muscular figure parted them and towered over them, clutching a large, sharpened axe. It was the executioner. He lumbered towards the surrounding bonfires and walked through a partition where the flames couldn't reach, and he approached Kismet with his axe raised high.

Kismet felt his heart pound and his pulse quicken. 'This couldn't be the end, right?' he thought as the executioner raised his axe.

Kismet eagerly shut his eyes when he heard someone yell, "Stop!"

Kismet opened his eyes to see that someone was running through the crowd and causing discord. This discord caused the executioner to pause and stare back. Someone broke out of the crowd and into the open. It was Kwame.

"Stop!" Kwame yelled once more. It was quickly followed by hushed whispers.

Kemi looked displeased. "What is the meaning of this?"

"His majesty bid me tell you that that boy is of royal blood and that no harm is to befall him, or the deal is off," Kwame announced in his baritone voice.

The congregation hushed, and whispers of 'the prophecy' could be heard. Even the executioner let out a disgruntled groan; it seemed it had been a while since he beheaded someone. Kismet let out a relieved sigh. Tola was here to save him. His father was here to save him.

"And if we don't?" Kemi asked.

"Then there will be war."

"And how shall you raise an army on such short notice?" Kemi was infuriated now.

"We don't need an army," Kwame replied and pointed behind her.

Kemi turned to look behind her congregation and frowned as she saw them. It was the workers whom the king had promised for infrastructure. They were holding their instruments as weapons. Her victory was about to be snatched from her. The priestess whispered something into Kemi's ear. Kemi faced Kwame, who was already smiling. The workers were twice the population of the witches.

"Alright! You can take him," Kemi said.

Kwame smiled.

He turned his back on Kemi and was about to approach Kismet when Kemi stabbed him in the back. The white staff passed through his back and protruded from his chest. Kwame shifted on his feet. He turned to her, smiling in pain. With all the energy within him, Kwame let a loud war cry, and at that moment, all hell broke loose.

Kismet watched as the workers surged in from all ends brandishing their weapons and attacking the witches. Opposing sides turned against each other, and Kismet could hear their cries. From where he was tied, he saw an arrow lodge itself in Kemi's head. The night bore witness to the slaughter.

The battle ended in a matter of seconds, the witches lacked battle experience, and they bore huge losses that had more death counts than that injuries. The workers only lost a few who were fallen by magical spells.

Tola ran through the bloodbath and the space in the bonfires. He came bearing a slash on his forehead. His face was writ with concern as he untied Kismet and helped him to his feet. Together, they supported each other out of the village with the workers behind them. They then gathered to burn their dead.

The bonfires were the pyre on which the dead were placed. Kismet and Tola watched as they burned Kwame's body. He was a loyal friend to the end. Kismet stared at the pyre in thought. Despite his mother's attempt at keeping him away from the prophecy and his fate, it only seemed to flow into a perfectly woven sequence. It was bound to happen eventually. Nothing could change his destiny. He was bound to the fate he had been desperately trying to

BOUND BY FATE

avoid.

But there is nothing more fated than death, and though Kismet survived today, tomorrow wasn't guaranteed; only death is guaranteed.

BADE'S INTERCESSORS
Oluwatoyin Magbagbeola

There is an adage that says, 'a mother that her children fail to take care of has lost childbearing. But a woman that has no child, it is a child that would bury her'. All being said, the importance of having a child to call hers is the happiness of the four-letter word 'LOVE'. Also, the love a mother has for a child can't be compared with any valuable possessions of the world, either gold or diamond, and some women would go the extra mile to have one they would call with their names, and so did Yetunde Animashahun.

BOUND BY FATE

Yetunde Animashahun, a woman full of hope and desire to be a mother, is in her fifteenth year of marriage to a wonderful man, Bade Animashahun, and it has been a struggle for them to conceive. Although Bade might be chill on the issue of their childlessness, but not Yetunde; she was bent on becoming a mother.

The two met during their university days, fell in love, and married. Their expectations of becoming parents was foiled, thus making Yetunde a ridicule, especially by her in-laws.

"A woman that can't bear my son a child is not worthy of being called his wife. You better act fast on it before I allow my son to go look for one outside!" Her mother-in-law threatened her for the umpteenth time.

Yetunde's mother-in-law never liked Yetunde and didn't support their union. She wanted her son to marry someone of a higher social class. To avoid being on her son's bad radar, she grudgingly accepted Yetunde. Their mother-daughter relationship was good as long as they weren't face-to-face, but Yetunde has refused to give her grandchildren, which is unforgivable.

The pressure from her mother-in-law has made Yetunde fret so much so that every day has been about calculating her ovulating days, drinking herbal tonics, practising yoga, eating healthy, and a lovemaking marathon with her husband.

Bade, on the other hand, has lost interest in sexual activities with his wife as it's no longer for the real affection he sought. Some doctors had advised them to try other means, such as IVF. Bade feels like he was nothing to his wife but a sperm donor. He wants to reignite the connection between them to when they first got together, the love and passion that made them defy the odds. Lately, his wife's attention has been on how to make babies as soon as possible.

"I'm doing this for us. If I can't make a baby as your parents expect, I will amount to nothing in your household," she defends in another confrontation with him.

Her arguments aren't far from the truth. Most women go through the same scenario in the country, and if not mistaken, it happens all around the globe. Women are pressured to be more than enough, it doesn't matter if there is love, but as long as the woman isn't fruitful, that is always the problem. Her husband might be chill-and-relaxed. He still has a long chance of becoming a parent in the future, but not for her; she has to be counting her cycles.

"I want the same thing as you. I want children that look like us too. I want you first and foremost. You keep indulging in weird things, and as your husband, I'm not a tool!"

"A tool? But you love making love to me."

"Yes, I do and always do, but…" he shrugs, not

maintaining eye contact with her; he didn't want to make her feel bad about what he was about to say, so he kept quiet.

"So having making love to me is difficult for you?" she questioned, raising an eyebrow. She understood his meaning. She also noticed how often her husband would try his best to not have sex with her. She had also seen a change of attitude in him. It made her feel like she was the only one after their goal.

"Babe, it's not like that. I want to make babies with you, but I want it to be a natural thing... not forced!"

"Am I forcing you? So I'm forcing you to make babies with me?"

"Yes, you are! You're so crazy about conceiving that you don't even know!"

"I should be concerned, Bade. You, too, should be concerned! Or do you enjoy your family ridiculing me, calling me barren?" she screamed.

"I married you because I love you and not because I want to make you a baby factory like my parents supposed. We don't have to make babies. I'm fine with that," he said defensively.

"You don't want to make babies with me, but you can with someone else outside?" she lamented.

Yetunde has allowed her mother-in-law's threat to get a hold of her; she has no doubt that her husband has someone else outside their marriage, someone he probably would want to make a family with if she failed at her responsibility.

"Are you being real here? Are you suggesting that I'm cheating on you?"

"Well, you might, one day!"

Out of annoyance, he left his home for the bar. He didn't want to continue having unnecessary arguments with his wife. Fixing their marriage is what they should be after and not some baby parade. Both are in their early forties, it may appear late to others outside their home, but Bade believed they will have a child to call theirs one day.

He has picked up a drinking habit while trying to cope with his worries, for he thought drinking might ease his worried heart and numb his pains, but it has made him turn alcoholic. Their drifting apart is affecting not only Yetunde but also him. If she hadn't allowed the pressure into their happy home, then they could still be as happy as ever.

Bade would choose whiskey on ice whenever he was at the bar. He drank slowly until he was knocked out by it. As usual, the bar owner would flash his best friend. His friend would call Yetunde to pick him up. Before he got knocked up, multiple women who came by themselves to the bar eyed him severally, giving him the seductive looks of wanting their way with him.

As a good-looking man, is, he was forever desired by women. A young lady in a tight red dress walked up

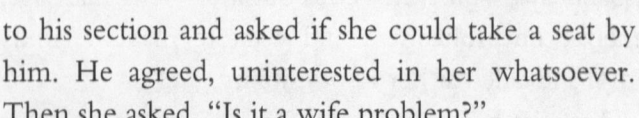

to his section and asked if she could take a seat by him. He agreed, uninterested in her whatsoever. Then she asked, "Is it a wife problem?"

"Excuse me?"

"It must be, seeing how messed up you appear," the lady in a tight red dress murmured.

"And who are you to know that?"

"Hi, my name is Carolina. You?"

"Bade! Nice to meet you," he replied, extending his arm for a handshake.

The two clicked right and spent the whole night chatting. For the time, he forgot about his worries. Bade was faithful to his wife. He only had eyes for his wife, and no other woman would equal her in his heart. Just as the devil brought temptations, the lady tried to seduce him in order to sleep with him. Even in his drunken state, Bade was sane; he resisted the temptation of being lured to a hotel by the woman in the red dress and raced out into a taxi to take him home.

Yetunde, who had been worried sick about how bad things got between them, was delighted to see him back home to her. She worked up an apology. He accepted. After he'd sobered up, both made love that night.

It was an unexpected weekend visit from Bade's mother. Bade worried about his wife and the pressure she'd put him under, especially as things had gotten better between them. Patrolling the house was what she would do whenever she was around to make sure she was doing the house chores, and with the disdainful look, she would always give her daughter-in-law, Yetunde, while reminding her of her childlessness.

"Mama, could you please stop bothering my wife with the pressure of giving me a child? We are not kids. We can take good care of ourselves. Moreover, it's God that gives!" Bade complained after seeing his mother ranting to his wife.

"My son, if you are not in a rush, I am. I also want to see my grandchildren and hold them in my hands just like my friends. I don't even know what this woman gave you to eat, that she's now controlling your life?"

"You and your superstition, mama. Don't be ridiculous. We love each other!" Bade defended his wife. If his mother did not attack them for their childlessness, she would rant about Yetunde being a witch who couldn't have children because she had sacrificed all her unborn kids.

"I'm sure she must have given you something to eat. If not, you wouldn't have resisted another opportunity that could bring joy to our lives," Yetunde's mother-in-law complained.

It now made sense to Bade what his mother was referring to. He remembered the easy rapport between him and Carolina days ago, his mother must have planned it, and he was right about it.

"Mama, don't tell me you were the one behind me meeting up with a stranger at the bar?"

"Carolina should have been a better candidate, but you foiled the plan," she replied.

"Mama, how could you set me up with another woman when you know I'm married?" Bade whispered so as not to arouse his wife's attention. Yetunde could have felt betrayed if she ever found out about her husband's encounter with another woman, which almost led to their breaking up or another misunderstanding.

"Carolina isn't a stranger. She has always had a crush on you before you got married to that one," Mama responded.

"And how do you know about Carolina?"

"She is my friend's daughter, the last child, and she always followed you around when you were younger," Mama murmured, laughing.

"Mama, don't ever try such a thing again. Never set me up with another woman, and do not interfere in my marriage. My wife and I will have a child whenever it's God's time for us," Bade said in a determined voice. Lately, Bade has been handing over his life and situation to God. He wasn't the religious type, he hardly went to church, but he still kept mentioning God's name all the time. He may have said his mind to his mother, but she isn't known as the type to back down easily. She has worked up another plan to see it through, and on her next agenda, she would make sure it works naturally without anyone suspecting it.

Mama had formulated a plan that could eradicate Yetunde completely from their lives, and to do so, she has to first be friendly with her. She called like a caring mother would, informing Yetunde to get a househelp that could help her around the house, so she could focus on getting pregnant.

Yetunde, who thought her mother-in-law had her best in mind, fell for the trick. She allowed her mother-in-law to handpick a new househelp to be living in her home, acting like an assistant but manipulative enough to make Bade fall for her. Fatima was her name, a fair-looking young lady in her twenties. She doesn't look like a usual househelp; with her beauty, she could be a model for she was tall and slender.

At first glance, Mama already knew she was the perfect one for the job, and her job required her to make Bade sleep with her, or if not, she's to make it look like it, so the blissful union between the couple could ensue into chaos.

Fatima took on the mission to destroy a happy home, for she also wanted the life Yetunde was living. She began to admire and lust after Bade the moment she came into their house. The money and *blings* lifestyle that one could live without stressing much, and having a doting husband that only has her in mind.

Fatima, who grew up without her parents' love,

BOUND BY FATE

instantly felt loved by the couple. Yetunde would always make sure she was alright and treat her like a sister. If she was shopping for new clothes, she would ensure she bought for Fatima the time of jewellery she would wear, or perfumes, or bags, or shoes. To her, Fatima was like a younger sister.

The two women got along with ease.

One night, Bade returned from work, tired and helpless, but Yetunde wasn't home; she had added night vigils to her activities. Those were nights her husband would long to hold her in his arms and sleep till morning came, but his wife, who was hungry to have a child to call theirs, would either be on the mountain praying or would be in some white garment church rolling on the floor for God's favour.

Yetunde might have gone to seek God somewhere else, not knowing her home is where the devil dwells. Fatima took the opportunity to lure Bade in. That night, she wore red lingerie, made her hair and applied makeup because she wanted him to get attracted to her. She stood by the door to welcome him in.

"Oga, good evening. I hope work wasn't stressful?"

"Good evening to you, too! Is my wife home?" he asked. He didn't glance at her but she kept trying to draw his attention to her.

"Is everything okay? Are you going out?" he asked when he did.

"I'm not going out, sir!" she replied, giving him a flirtatious look.

"So, why are you dressed as if you're about to go out soon?" he asked again, still lost.

"I did it for you, sir," Fatima replied.

"Me? Why?"

"Oga, why are you acting like you don't like what you see? Madam is not home. She's never home, so I know you must be lonely," Fatima said, trying to take a chance with him by touching him inappropriately.

Bade, still surprised, retracted, taking a step back from her.

"Why should my loneliness be your concern?" he asked.

"Bade, why are you doing this? Am I not prettier than your so-called barren wife? I can give you what she lacks; I'm still young and fresh and capable of bearing a child. So why don't you try me?"

Bade was angry at her for daring to call him by his first name, trying to seduce him, and for the boldness of calling his wife barren.

"Now I understand. You planned this with my mother. You want me to leave my wife, the woman I love, because we are yet to be parents," Bade said, nodding. "Leave my household this instant! Pack your things and leave!"

Fatima shook and quickly approached him on her

knees, begging like some sinner asking for forgiveness.

"Oga, please, don't send me away. I'm sorry for my actions. Please, I won't do it again!"

"You should have thought of that before dressing like a common *ashawo* to seduce me?"

"Sir, at least not tonight," she begged, expressing her remorse.

"Why not? So you can have your way with me?"

"Sir, it's so late and dark. If you give me the grace till tomorrow, I will leave!" Fatima begged.

Bade ordered his driver, Kasali, to assist her in leaving. He couldn't allow Fatima to spend the night with Yetunde away. God knows what she would do overnight. Kasali acted on his boss's command, and with all the pleas from Fatima insisting on not leaving, Kasali picked her up like a child and dragged her into the car without taking a single of her property. That night Bade slept with peace of mind without the worries of someone bombarding him at night.

Yetunde returned home only to discover Fatima gone. She asked her husband of Fatima's whereabouts, and he told her to have let her go the previous night.

"How could you do such a thing?" Yetunde complained.

"She isn't worth it, and she might not be the

person you thought she may be," Bade replied, and again he tried concealing his reason from Yetunde, for she may be heartbroken if she ever found out.

"You still can't do that without letting me know first. She's like a sister to me," Yetunde cried.

"Darling, that girl isn't worth your stress. I did the right thing by letting her go."

Yetunde couldn't fathom his unexplainable reasons resulting in Fatima's dismissal, but it was not something she could resolve on her own, so she waited on her mother-in-law to make a call to her own son. He has warned his driver not to mention a word to his wife.

Fatima reported to Mama that her first try didn't work out as planned, and she seemed to have something to say.

"Mama, I'm beginning to wonder if it's your son that has a problem and not your daughter-in-law!"

"Will you shut your mouth and stop spewing nonsense? You can't even get work done at once," Mama reprimanded Fatima. Only she could say something against her son; no one else.

"Mama, I don't mean to disrespect you, but your son wouldn't even give me a look last night. Mama, if you see what I wore last night. What kind of a man wouldn't see that and be turned on?" Fatima insisted.

"Shut your mouth. My own son is one hundred percent agile and able. It's just that the witch of a wife he married may have done something to him!" Mama made an uncanny suggestion. She would forever believe her son was charmed by his wife.

"I think so too. Because the way I was last night, he shouldn't have resisted that if he wasn't under a charm." Fatima also agreed to such laughable allegations made by Mama.

"I will make sure you go back into that household and unleash all the evil bonds the witch has on my son."

"Will I still get the chance? I don't think your son will ever allow me back in."

"He will. In fact, he must!"

Immediately she called on Yetunde to have a chat with her. She told her to beg her husband to allow Fatima back into the house but didn't let her know what she did wrong, instead, Mama told Yetunde that Fatima only stole something from the house, which made Bade send her packing. Furious by this, Yetunde lashed out at her husband for not being kind enough to let things go.

~~~~~~

"You still want her back in this house?"

"Yes, I do! We can't abandon her just because she stole something from us. God blessed us anyway. Why do we have to act like we owe nothing?"

"Who told you she stole something? Did she tell you that?" Bade asked.

"It doesn't matter who told me. Please, Darling,

let it go!"

In order to avoid a prolonged argument, Bade succumbed to his wife's wish. Only this time, Fatima must behave herself around him.

One Sunday afternoon, after the church service ended, Pastor Gbemileke called Yetunde aside to deliver God's message for her. Pastor Gbemileke has been on the journey with Yetunde on the quest of child seeking, and she had been of great consolation to Yetunde. She saw in a vision of seeing Bade in a pool of blood and Yetunde saving him in the end. The vision wasn't clear enough to explain better, but Pastor Gbemileke warned Yetunde to be careful of people around and not worry about childbearing, for it is her fate to be a mother.

"Something destined for someone can never be changed, sister Yetunde. It can only be delayed," Pastor Gbemileke said.

"Thank you, pastor. I hope so, too," Yetunde replied, sounding like someone whose faith was as weak as a lost soul. Yetunde began finding herself so lost that all she would ever ask for was a miracle, not hope.

Draining herself in sorrow each day, Yetunde began losing weight, her face galled in appearance, and her mind wouldn't live a day without thinking, *God when?*

Seeing her extreme state, Fatima decided to take a chance. She offered to be a surrogate. Fatima asked Yetunde if she could give her a chance to make her a mother by having Bade's child. The naive and desperate

Yetunde agreed to the plan and went on with the plan behind her husband's back. Bade discovered Fatima had gotten pregnant for him through IVF: Yetunde and Fatima used his leftover sperm that was kept in the clinic to make a baby without letting him know.

"You must have lost your god-damned mind, Yetunde. How could you do such a thing without letting me know?" Bade complained.

"She's pregnant, darling. What we have been seeking for all these while, she has done it," Yetunde replied. She couldn't understand why her husband wasn't happy.

"But you're not the one pregnant, are you? You allowed a househelp to use my sperm to make a baby, and you're not bothered by it?" Bade questioned.

"We agreed to make the baby mine. The baby is ours," Yetunde insisted.

"Don't you know that Mama and Fatima planned to use your kindness to get you into trouble? Are you that dumb? Don't you know she was sent on a mission to replace you in my life? Because you haven't given birth, Mama used her to get what she wanted," Bade confessed. But it was too late. He should have warned her when he had the chance, not when she's duped and used.

"You should have told me that? Why now? All I

wanted was to have a child, your child! I don't care if she has her own mission or purpose, but as long as I have my baby delivered safely and sound, nothing will worry me no more!"

"Do you think she intends to give you her baby?"

Not long after, Fatima became the only daughter-in-law she knew and the only one her son married. Mama also pressured Bade to take Fatima as a second wife, as the mother of her future grandchild shouldn't stay 'outside'. She even pressured and bullied Yetunde, who got swindled by them to accept and allow Fatima as the second wife with the excuse of *'Ori omo lon pe omo waye'* (a child could bring forth another child).

In the midst of the problems caused by his mother, Bade got into an accident on his way to make things right. He heard from the doctor who performed the IVF for Fatima that the process hadn't been a success, yet Fatima managed to get pregnant, which was suspicious as Fatima hadn't informed Yetunde. Fatima was pregnant. Unfortunately, before Bade could clear that up, his fatal accident claimed his life.

Yetunde's mother-in-law blamed her for his death. A few months later, Yetunde was sent out of her husband's home. Fatima took her place.

~~~~~

One fateful night, a mild pain gripped Yetunde's stomach. At first, she thought it was diarrhoea, but as the pain grew, she noticed she was bleeding. She was

BOUND BY FATE

rushed to the hospital. Her sweet neighbour took her to the clinic only to be informed to prepare the baby's stuff.

"But she was never pregnant? How could she be in labour?" the confused neighbour asked.

Yetunde never showed signs of pregnancy. Her stomach wasn't round, except for her weight gain, nothing had changed.

"There are people like that too. They may never show, but she is exactly nine months gone, and the baby is due. Kindly get us the things on this list." The nurse gave the neighbour a piece of paper. "Please hurry."

During the long strenuous labour, Yetunde recalled the last night she had with Bade was the one that happened before he got into a car accident the day after. It was a magical moment for the two, Bade had promised Yetunde to make things right, but he never mentioned his findings to her and told her to be vigilant.

For the night Yetunde's son was born, heaven rejoiced, and she called him Bade in honour of her late husband, who'd given her the best gift in the world. He made her a mother as he had promised. Yetunde now understood what Pastor Gbemileke saw in the vision about her saving her husband. With joy in her heart, Yetunde went home with her baby after spending a week in the hospital. It wasn't an easy birth, but worth it.

Two months passed, and little Bade was growing fast under his doting mother's attention and care. Bade's parents came knocking on her door to make peace with her. Mama had learnt her lessons. Not only did they discover that Fatima was not pregnant, but she and her boyfriend planned to get their hands on the properties that weren't theirs.

"My daughter, forgive me. I know I have wronged you. I have said things I shouldn't have said to you. I called you names and belittled you. I can only ask you to please forgive me," Her mother-in-law pleaded, holding onto her leg.

Yetunde, still hurting, wanted to send them out of her house and life, but little Bade kept crying in her arms. It could have been a sign from her late husband to remind her to let go and include his family in his son's life.

Yetunde allowed her mother-in-law to hold little Bade in her arms while she shed joyful tears.

OLUWATOYIN MAGBAGBEOLA is a Nigerian who's passionate about storytelling. She's driven and motivated by African literature and poetry, and most importantly, loves the element and art of her culture. "Being an African is my identity, and I'm super proud to be a Nigerian," she'd usually say.

She hopes to inspire others to read and explore her imaginative mind.

She also writes about African history, food, lifestyle, and culture for the Afrovibe magazine.

MY HEAD IS MY INTERCESSOR
Omobolaji Olofinnika

First Incantation:
I pay homage to Olodumare; creator of all things.
I salute the supernatural beings that inhabit the heavens,
And the four hundred and one gods that hold the earth in their grasp.
Ajagunmale, the chief priest of heaven,
Orunmila, the chief priest of earth,
Esu, custodian of Ase, power of creation,
Greetings.

BOUND BY FATE

I salute the great mothers who reside in Olofi.
For he who enters a house without greeting its inhabitant,
The same is likened to a thief.
I salute the heavens and the earth,
May I never incur their wrath.

As I stand before the Circle of *Egbe Orun* and witness the anger and hatred plastered on their faces, faces that held my earliest memories of happiness and then recently featured in my worst nightmares, I push away the foolish notion that there is any way I can come out of this unscathed.

Here, I have become the proverbial dog that has entered the den of a tiger to challenge its authority. Yes. The same dog that was left bathed in the pool of its blood.

Over the years, I have dreaded coming back here, back to this place where at a time, I thought that joy began and ended. This very place where I played, laughed and made merry with those whose eyes now scream murder at me.

Everywhere was white-plain now, bright like daytime, but without the sun or any luminary characteristic of the earth — a sign of how serious they make of the matter before them. And everyone around was here, the hundreds of the *Egbe Orun* forming the Circle, with the seven elders at the forefront. In the hundreds of years I have been here, the circle had only ever been formed twice.

Kirijo stood not far from me, pointing accusations as he made his case against a certain Monkele, the maiden who was once betrothed to be his wife. Fire spat from his eyes, ears, and mouth like *Koso*, the god of thunder. Whenever Kirijo looked my way to emphasize a point as he shouted 'Monkele this', 'Monkele that,' most of the Circle 'ahhhed' in response to his accusations, turning death glances at me, if their glares could kill, I would be dead twice over already.

Monkele.

That should be me.

But I am not that person anymore. How do I explain that to them? How do I tell them that the Monkele they knew was dead? That I hoped I would never again hear that name, or at least not for a long time. How had this even come to be that I am here once again? I had taken all the right precautions and made all the necessary sacrifices to *Esu*, the god of trickery and mischief, to hide me from their sight. But here I am, where I least wanted to be.

A tense silence dominated the atmosphere as Kirijo finished speaking. His entire body was now blazing with the fire of his rage as he stared fixedly at me, eyes piercing deep into my soul with accusations and a thirst for vengeance. The broiling wave of rage I saw in his eyes shook me for a moment. I wanted to run away from him — from here. Whatever have I done to cause another to hate me so? But I force myself to hold his gaze.

"Monkele, what do you have to say for yourself?" Yamu, the youngest of the seven elders, asked. Her voice was like a thunderclap ringing loud in my ears for a second. I knew I alone felt that as no other person amongst the hundreds of *Egbe Orun* forming the circle scrunched their face as I did under the brunt of her sound attack. This was Yamu punishing me in her way. My heart sank for a moment as the import of her act dawned upon me. They had judged me even before they listened to my side of the story.

I heaved a deep breath and stepped forward, walking to the circle's centre where all would be bare.

"Why did you not return at the appointed time?" Yamu inquired with the same ringing thunderclap I alone heard. Although I was somewhat prepared for it, it still caught me unaware for a moment. I scrunched my face for a second as I stared into Yamu's slender, otherworldly face. It was like I was staring at a stranger, not the elder I used to be on close terms with. It hurt a lot. Yamu had been a very close friend.

So, why did I not return at the appointed time? The wrong question, I thought. Why did I not go to the family I had chosen before this same Circle?

Now, that would have been a better first question. But it is not so unusual amongst us to do that. We can always change wherever we wanted to go at the last minute, provided we come back at the stipulated time. I would have to start from the beginning, and time is not a problem here; we have a lot to spare.

~~~~~

Second Incantation:
Divination for Omo Asode, Omo Aroko, and Omo Asawo.
These three came from the same heaven
They made the promise before going to earth to return in seven days
The three mothers of these children went to get a reading from the same priest
Only one made the necessary sacrifice
They were told to only name their child and not hold a big ceremony
The other two mothers used the money meant for sacrifice for a big ceremony
During the naming, Egbe orun called the children home
When they got to Omo Asawo,
He was able to send them away because of his mother's sacrifice.

My name, Kokumo, means 'this child will die no more'. And no, I'm not an *Abiku*. Personally, I hate *abikus,* those wicked group of spirit children who take so much joy in bringing tears and sadness to the lives of helpless mortals by coming into their lives again and again as babes, only to die and leave them in sorrow before reaching adulthood. But this part of my story begins with one of them.

I am an *Emere*, another group of spirit children different from the *Abikus*. Emere's either come into the life of mortals for two reasons: to help or bless the families where they are born or, to curse and cause such families untold hardship for reasons ranging from the evils they had committed either in their present or past lives, or the sins of their ancestors.

I, who they call Monkele, used to be one of the good *emeres* whose life mission was to bring goodness to the life of mortals. I have lost count of the number of families I have brought goodwill and affluence to, working from behind the scenes to grant them good fortune, and it never gets old to see the smiles of happiness on the faces of these mortals —although there might be sad when my appointed time reached and I left. But unlike the Abikus, we Emeres don't return to the same family after death, and we don't stop them from having other children. We just do our thing and leave for good.

I arrived from *Ikole-Orun* - the third heaven - that day for Ololade, the woman whose family I planned to make my abode on this fateful mission. It was late at night, and another woman was already in the labour room at the hospital when I got there. I know not what led me to the labour room even though the woman I sought was not yet set to deliver. Maybe it was fate; perhaps it was pure curiosity. But on reaching the room, there was this woman, Ibidun, lying limp on the bed with a face pale and devoid of colour, and making no efforts to push despite the doctor and nurses' pleas.

Looking at this woman from the spirit dimension was much more different. The negativity I saw her embroiled with hit me hard and raw, breaking my heart into a million pieces. In this woman's great circle of the Egbe Orun, I saw a life submerged under a mountain-load of grief, despair, angst, and hopelessness, making me wonder for a moment what type of destiny and *head* she could have carried from *Ajala*, the potter and maker of heads.

"Go! Prepare the operating room!" The doctor turned to one of the nurses, who hurried out to obey his command.

Anger surged through me as I looked even deeper and saw the Abiku firmly lodged within the woman's womb and staying fixated on the spot. I could see that this was supposed to be his last rebirth into her life, and he wanted to take her with him, this time to the seventh hell.

Great Circle of the *Egbe Orun*! If I could, I would

have wept for this woman who seemed to have gone through so much and was now being led to her death by the very fruit of her womb, which was supposed to be a blessing unto her.

It was no battle as I jumped upon this Abiku in a fit of rage, tearing at him. He quickly made his way out, for he was weaker than I was, fleeing fast without even a backward glance. There and then, I decided to come forth to earth through this woman, Ibidun, and to bring her all the happiness I can to make up for her life of suffering.

One more weak push from Ibidun, and I came out with ease, surprising even the doctors and nurses who were already making plans to resort to the caesarian section.

"It's a girl," a nurse muttered as they brought me closer to her for a look.

"A girl?" Ibidun asked in a voice that was no more than a whisper, her face filled with shock and disbelief until she looked down between my thighs. The shock remained on her face even as she fell back on the bed into a dead faint, tired from the strain of the protracted delivery.

Circle of the Egbe Orun! In this, how have I done wrong? For amongst us are there not two: the good and the malevolent? And do I, who you all know as Monkele, not stand for good? Are we not given the authority to bring upon mortal men whatever they truly deserve? For me happiness and goodwill? Is that not why *Olodumare*, the god of creation and all that exists, made the good a little above all the other powers so that his mortal creations might not suffer forever under the yokes of the evil ones?

I saw where I was needed, and I went without even a prior background check. That might have been my greatest mistake, not fully understanding the situation before I went in. But I, whom you all know as Monkele do not regret my decision. Not one bit. A leopard is not shy of his spots; neither do I regret my intention for wanting to do a good deed as my nature compelled me to.

So was I born into the family of the Ogunrindes in a hospital at Ile-Ife, in a busy city district, only to later find that my mother, Ibidun Ogunrinde, had only come to Ile-Ife to trade and fell into early labour and that my new family was based in Ayegun, a small farming settlement far off from the nearest town.

It was already too late to withdraw, not that I planned to do that so early nor could I even if I wanted to, for strong-powerful magic held me bound to earth like a living elephant to its tusks. Ibidun after being afflicted by the *Abiku* five times, I had engaged the services of a very powerful wizard who with magic sought to prevent the child from dying this time, only that I have taken that child's place.

I arrived on earth, lost. My powers were cut off from me and I lost touch with the heavens and the supernatural. That was why you could not find me even when you said you searched, and I could not find the wizard who had done this to me, not when I couldn't ask my mother about it without drawing suspicion - and she was the only one who knew who had helped her do this.

So I made up my mind to bring her so great a happiness that her heart would be full of love for me, for that was the only other time the portals to heaven and the supernatural become wide open to point a beacon on those of us who are lost—through the intense feelings broadcast by our loved ones and the successes of accomplishing our duty—allowing the *Egbe Orun* make contact.

So began my new mission—to make mother happy!

Mother was sickly, a broken thing not unlike our old transistor radio, which was held together by swaddling lengths of binding tapes and rubbers to stop it from falling apart—and that transistor radio was the electronic appliance we had in our otherwise sparse hut. She was weak from the strain of farm work, the incessant child loss, and the lack of love.

Bada, The man whom I came to know as my father, wanted nothing to do with us, condemning us to a hut at the edge of his compound while he stayed in the main house with the two wives he married after mother and their seven children—

although mother was his first wife. Only her strong will and the herbal concoctions of Baba Ewenje—a very knowledgeable and powerful herbalist on the outskirt of our village—kept her living as long as she did. And I would go there every other morning to get her herbal concoctions to keep her body from totally breaking down.

Great circle of the *Egbe Orun*! In my hundreds of years as a member of this very circle, I have never tried so hard to make someone happy as I did my mother, only to fail so woefully. It was like the case of someone throwing eggs at a mountain again and again, only for the eggs to keep breaking apart and have not a single effect on the hard, rocky surface. How hard I tried to make my mother happy, even if for once. But everything was for nought…

Being the most hardworking and obedient daughter anyone could ask for didn't do it for her. Being the brightest student in every one of my classes and bringing home awards every other day only brought weak, forced smiles to her face, and being awarded a scholarship that saw me through secondary school when she couldn't afford it didn't bring that happiness I needed.

Circle of the great *Egbe Orun*! How broken could one be that happiness was so far from such a person? This was my poor mother's reality. She was a woman scorned and neglected by the man she loved; reduced to hard farm work to source her next meal even though her husband was a man of great wealth according to the village standards, and her weakened body barely supported her. I don't think I ever saw her laugh in all the years we spent together, not even a single smile reached her eyes.

By the time I received a scholarship to study in the States for my tertiary education, my mother was gone. Dead. She died when I was thirteen - a few weeks before I graduated from secondary school - on her farmland as she was pulling cassava stumps. Worse still, she died alone with no one beside her. A passing farmer saw her body hours later and called attention to it. Her death marked me a total failure in what mattered the most where she was concerned. I couldn't make mother happy. Not even once.

I wept, *Egbe Orun*. I cried so hard for days that my eyes ran dry of water, and the next thing that would have trailed down my cheeks would have been blood. I railed at the heavens for letting mother choose such an unfortunate destiny. I cursed at the earth for swallowing her body. And then I turned to my father, who cared less for her death and cursed at him for breaking her and not showing her the slightest bit of love when she needed him the most.

But then, life had to go on.

Barely six months after my mother's death, I landed in the United States of America on a fully funded scholarship to study pharmacy and a family ready to take me in, for I was still underage. By then, I had forgotten anything about coming back to the third heavens, *Ikole-Orun*, resigning myself to full life on earth, for I could not take my own life. At the age of twenty-six, I had already completed both my first degree, M.S.c, PhD, and several other degrees to boot and become a professor of pharmaceutical sciences.

By this time, I was now working as a clinical pharmaceutical scientist in one of the biggest pharmaceutical companies in the United States, while on the board of numerous international health bodies due to my numerous accomplishments. This would lead me to how I found myself back in Nigeria where another chapter of my life took root, even after I made a vow never to return to the land of my shame since I had nothing left for me there.

~~~~~

Third Incantation:
This is a song by Owiwi, the lone night watcher.
Singing in mystic tunes under the dark skies.
It shouts a warning to those who walk the night.
A telling of the coming of the morning and brightness with it.
Then comes a time when one becomes two.
It dances.
A dance of generations past.
Etching upon new bodies marks of its presence.

BOUND BY FATE

A new seed sprouts
blossoming like fresh flowers
Two become one once again.

Great circle of the *Egbe Orun*! This new chapter started when I met Olawale.

The pharmaceutical company I worked for was hosting a four-day convention in Nigeria, so I was tasked to lead the team since it was supposedly my home country. This was how I met Olawale. It was on the third day of the convention. I was leaving the venue, worn out, with only thoughts of a cold bath and sleep when I got back to my hotel room, and there he was, struggling to reach me through the heavy security detail. I could never mistake his tribal marks or the thick Oyo-laden intonation with which he called out my name.

In my excitement headed for him through the security men and drew him into a tight hug before their bewildered faces. It was like I had found my family.

Olawale was Baba Ewenje's youngest son with whom I shared a lot of sweet memories. We had hit it off those times when I was younger and I went every other day to Baba Ewenje's place to get my mother's herbal concoctions. At the time, I had found my love for nature, medicine and healing, plants, roots, and the mysteries of natural herbs for the first time.

I usually assisted Olawale in the numerous tasks assigned to him as the youngest child and helper of Baba; picking out leaves and washing them, grinding and pounding herbs, and fanning the fire where pots of herbs simmered over the stove; and by the time I was nine, I could find all the necessary herbs needed to prepare my mother's herbal concoctions and do so perfectly on my own without any help. But I never stopped going to Baba Ewneje's, who saw my love for his work and taught me so much alongside his children. That began my journey as a pharmaceutical scientist and my love for finding cures.

The Olawale I met that day was a broken man. My heart bled as he told his story, and I broke into tears from his struggles in my hotel room. It turned out that after Olawale graduated from the University where he studied microbiology, he went on to set up a herbal medicine company with his knowledge of herbal remedies, and the company began to grow geometrically before disaster struck.

His wife and best friend duped him of all his wealth, with his wife dropping a signed divorce letter before leaving for Australia with a child he always thought was his but later turned out to be his friend's. He had come to the convention hoping to be one of the few upstart pharmaceutical companies that would be given a grant before he saw me and reached out, and both he and I knew he wouldn't get the grant - this convention of ours had no interest in herbal medicine.

Great circle of the *Egbe Orun!* Here was my childhood friend, broken and sad. Should I have left him without stretching a hand of support? Of course, I couldn't. That would have been against my nature. I decided to assist Olawale with funds since I had the financial capability. We partnered to form a new company, and very quickly, our company became a household name, with our herbal concoctions sought all over the world.

Circle of the great *Egbe Orun*! A feeling like nothing I have ever experienced before began to encompass me whenever I found myself with Olawale. I began to laugh more, to feel more at peace, to feel more fulfilled, and whenever I was not with him, I felt suffocated, like something important was missing from my life. When Olawale later asked me to marry him two years and seven months later, I did not hesitate to drop all I had going on for me in the United States to move down to Nigeria and become his wife. We had two children, a boy and a girl. I am about to have the third when Kirijo suddenly found me and brought me back here without warning, without my consent.

Circle of the great *Egbe Orun*, I declare my innocence on this trial, and I push a motion to bring Kirijo to justice for bringing me back here without my consent, taking me away from the best thing that has ever happened to me in my hundreds of years. I push the motion to be released back to earth to this new life I have found for myself, to stay where my heart has found peace and every good thing that comes with it.

Gasps of shock spread around the Circle as I come to a stop, their eyes boring into me in surprise.

I hold my ground.

"Child, do you understand what you ask?" one of the seven asked after a long time.

"Yes, I do," I replied tersely. It meant that my immortality would be stripped off me, and I would die a true death here in *Ikole Orun* when I do on earth. I wouldn't be able to be reborn into the spirit world ever again. I didn't mind that. I would do anything to go back to my loved ones.

A containment field appeared around me without warning, throwing me into darkness as the circle took the time to discuss and contemplate my case. I waited patiently for the long hours it took them to reach a consensus, and when the darkness was finally lifted, and I saw their sombre gazes and the smirk on Kirijo's face, I knew something was wrong.

The leader of the seven elders, Udamigui, took a step forward. Her long black hair flailed behind her as an unnatural wind rose, her brown eyes becoming crimson red like a blood moon.

"Our very existence is predicated on rules. Rules which you have now broken," Udamigui began. "We might have forgiven if you had chosen to come back, but your lack of remorse is even more unbecoming. We, the Circle, hereby find you guilty and have chosen to sentence you to death."

A soft cheer resounded amongst the circle, and the look of utter glee on Kirijo's face was not lost to me. For once, since the beginning of all these, my body quivered in fear. Was this how I would end my journey? What would happen to Olawale and my children back on earth? If I could, I would shed torrents of tears and plead to the council to retry my case. But there was no hope of that. The council was supreme, and they never went back on their judgments.

The seven raised their sceptres and pointed them at me as one, releasing arcs of darkness that surged towards me to obliterate me from the face of the earth.

"I reject your verdict!" a voice boomed just as the arcs of darkness were about to reach me and blow my spirit into nothingness.

The darkness goes off immediately.

Surprised, I turn back to check who it was that had such effrontery and power to stand against the council of the *Egbe Orun*. Blinding light struck me for a second, burning my eyes, and when it cleared I saw him. It was Ori, the god of destiny. His old wizened face was grim as he slowly made his way to the centre.

"Ori, what is this about?" one of the seven elders asked in a show of false bravado.

Ori kept mute till he arrived beside me.

"It's all alright, I'm here," Ori assured, smiling.

~~~~~

Fourth Incantation

A man's head – ori - is his intercessor.
When I wake in the morning I hold my head,
For a man's head is his intercessor.
I pay homage to Ori, the god of destiny.
Superior is he amongst the gods,
For only he reached Apeere—Perfection.
A divination for mortals on a journey to earth,
Should you not worship Ori more than the other gods?
For Ori is your true sympathizer
- even as Olodumare sympathizes with you.
Let not my legs lead me on a journey without my head,
Ori, leave me not to my own devices—ruin,
For a man's head is his intercessor.

There was a tense silence as everyone watched Ori, waiting. Although the Circle of Egbe Orun, like all other spiritual beings, are not subject to Ori, even they had to show reverence towards him as they were a part of the streams of destiny.

"I will make it short, for I am a very busy person,"

Ori finally said, breaking the ice. "I would tell a story." He paused for effect as everyone hung on his words, and then he began:

"Back when the gods walked the earth, a young orphaned man was taken and sacrificed to an *Ebora*, an evil being of the forest. His betrothed on hearing the death of her beloved, threw herself into the sea to kill herself and follow him even in death, for their love was very strong.

Yemoja, the great mother of the seas saved her, hoping to make her one of her children, but the woman had lost the will to live without her betrothed. Moved by her love, Yemoja granted her a boon. The great mother of the seas brought the woman to me, and I wrote a new destiny for her to be reborn in a new generation and find her true love again.

Several centuries went by and they were both reborn, the man as a hunter, and she as a princess. Theirs were a love for ballads. Circle of the Egbe Orun, I only took my eyes off them for a minute, and before I looked back, a certain spirit had tampered with their destinies and taken the woman's spirit with him, wiping her memories of past lives and making the Egbe Orun turn her to one of their own.

It was the man's turn to commit suicide this time, and even Orunmila, who was walking amongst men as an Ifa priest, could not change his mind in the end. How fate works.

Orunmila came to me this time on behalf of the man, and although I wanted to deal with that spirit for tampering with my work, I held back, letting things play out. It was harder to bring them together the second time as the woman was no more mortal, but I would not be Ori if I couldn't do it."

Ori stopped his story and turned sharply to Kirijo.

"How dare you thwart me twice!" Ori barked at him; his voice rang out like an explosion, shaking the whole atmosphere with its intensity.

Kirijo's eyes widened in fear for an instant as the sound wave blew great waves of air around him, and then he suddenly began to disintegrate into nothingness from his feet to his upper body slowly. His head disintegrated last, with his mouth opened as if he wanted to say something.

There was a tense silence as we all looked on in fear.

"I will be taking her. I am done here," Ori concluded like he didn't just destroy someone before The Circle.

Ori touched my shoulder even as I still opened my mouth in shock, and we were suddenly transported to Olofi - the conduit between heaven and earth.

Was I the woman in his story? And Olawale too? But I had no recollection of such.

"Wha- wh- w-?" I turned to Ori, lost and not even sure what to say.

Ori touched my forehead, and my vision swam. I suddenly saw as a rush of memories filled me. Before I became a member of the circle of *Egbe Orun* I was an average maiden betrothed to the love of her life; and there was Olawale being taken and sacrificed to the *ebora*.

Shock made me speechless as I noticed that it was my mother, whom I had tried so hard to make happy, who was the *ebora* at the time. Our meeting was just another rebirth of her life as a human now.

Then the memories changed again and I was a princess. And there was Olawale beside me, bringing me so much joy and happiness to last three lifetimes before Kirijo came and whisked me away.

"Whenever you go on a journey with your legs, never forget your head," Ori said softly after a while. Then blinding light.

"Wha-" I tried to adjust myself to the light, taking a moment to blink and see through the haze. I raised my right hand slowly to rub my eyes, only to hear a loud squeal and a clatter of something dropping. When my eyes finally adjusted to the light I was on top of a bed in a white room with several beeping machines.

"Yo- You a- are awake!"

It was then I noticed the nurse on the floor by my left, seated on the floor with broken vials around her. I was in a hospital, on earth? Where was Ori? I looked around warily.

He was nowhere to be seen.

Gone.

I could barely keep my emotions in check as I waited for Olawale. I couldn't believe I had finally made it back. The doctors and nurses still looked at me in awe, like I was some sort of miracle.

According to them, I had been in a coma for seven months. I had passed out during childbirth for no known reason, leading them to carry out a cesarean operation to deliver my twin girls, who are currently safe with their father. I had fallen into a coma for five long months since then, confounding the doctors and the specialists that later came to check on me, as they found nothing wrong with me.

I wanted to shout at them that I was only gone for some hours, six hours at most. And then I remembered that time worked differently between the worlds.

The door banged open as Olawale barged into the room. He rushed to my side at a speed of a cheetah to draw me into his embrace. I could not be more at ease, more fulfilled as I am in his warm embrace. He began to cry so mournfully that I joined him for the long minutes he cried, going on even after he stopped.

"Thank you for not leaving me," Olawale said, pulling himself away to stare deep into my eyes. Overwhelmed, the tears began to fall from my eyes again.

BOUND BY FATE

I pay homage to my head, to Ori, the one who had given me a chance to see my love and be loved once again. My head is my intercessor.

TRAUMA
Adekola Temitayo

Ayo Olopon is probably one of the oldest local games in Nigeria and has been in existence amongst the Yoruba people since time immemorial. It is called *ayo olopon* in Yoruba, o*ware* in Twi, *okwe* in Igbo, *ise* in Edo, and so on. The first player begins by moving seeds from his right-hand side to the opponent's side.

Baba Sayo was just like this game of interest. Maybe God has moved the seed to his household again. It is a blissful evening in front of Baba Feyi's house, men of

BOUND BY FATE

his age gather to play *Ayo Olopon* when Sayo suddenly appears, looking furtively over her shoulder.

"*Baami, Maami* is about to put to bed. Sisi Toke and Mama Dami have taken her to the hospital." Sayo trembled.

Baba Sayo jumps up leaving no formality, - it is like a moment of heebie-jeebies for Baba Sayo who was shaking like a leaf as he jumps on his *okada* with his daughter, Sayo, behind him and zooms off.

The fear of labour and delivery seems to be normal, natural, and surprisingly even helpful to have. Sayo looks at her father, his eyes were wrinkled in fear. She suspects a lot would be going on in his mind.

If you have seen *One Born Every Minute*, you'll probably have a pretty good idea of what goes down during childbirth. When you are told to push like you are doing a defecation reflex, when contractions were like a muscle spasm, and every scream of pain sounds like death calling. Although it was not new to Mama Sayo, she is relieved when the doctor said:

"Congratulations! It's a boy."

She beamed.

Traditionally, an African woman is not woman enough if she cannot bear children, especially a male child. Being a mother brings enough joy. The rewards heavily outweigh the sacrifices women make during their nine months of pregnancy; I can't just imagine the position Mama Sayo has after childbirth. It's difficult to describe how God's power works and the indescribable joy she feels.

Baba Sayo has been caught up in the fear and the anxiousness of expectant fathers, who eagerly await the outcome of their jewels. Baba Sayo Jumps up and hotfoots towards the Doctor that was talking to a nurse.

"What about my wife? Hope everything is okay?" Baba Sayo asks, sounding worried.

The Doctor chuckles as he replies, "Mr Ademola, congratulations. Your wife has delivered a bouncing baby boy."

Baba Sayo can't retain his overflowing joy after hearing 'a bouncing baby boy'.

The Doctor cautioned him about disturbing other patients as he received greetings of congratulation from the people waiting to be attended to.

There's an intense attachment between Sayo's parents; the way they smiled at each other, looking at their cute little man.

On the other hand, Sayo was overwhelmed, looking at her baby brother in her father's arms. While Sayo gushes over her brother, her father flatters her mother.

"The apple of my eye, just take some rest, let's me see the doctor," Baba Sayo finished tenderly.

~~~~~

BOUND BY FATE

Traditionally, a naming ceremony is held to give a child an identity, it is the time to recognise the child by name, for it is by our names that we're acknowledged as an individual, a unique and separate person.

Presenting their child after eight days, Sayo's parents invited everyone to the event. People from different walks of life are seen in colourful dresses to share in the joy and support them as Baba and Mama Sayo undertake to help, with love and guidance, the fullest unfolding of the personality of their new baby entrusted to their care by God.

Baba Sayo was well dressed, wearing ironed starched guinea attire, and welcoming his friends and his caucus from Ayo joint. Even the Okada Association crews were present. One could say that the child brought *ese ire* to their home. After the birth of his new child, the chairman of the Okada Association gave Baba Sayo a position in the Okada Association committee.

Mothers have a lot of wishes on the naming ceremony: I hope my child looks on today and sees a parent who had time to play. Mama Sayo lapsed for seconds and soliloquized. She can't just express the joy in her when she is looking at her new baby. Women with *afafeyeye*, glide the lily of makeup and her *gele* in a vaunting manner. She also welcomed her friends from all walks of life and her friends from the tailor association.

Families and friends are all seated, Baba Sayo and Mama Sayo are also seated on either side of the Pastor. The Pastor starts with an opening prayer of thanksgiving to God for the seed He preserved, watched over and turned into a matured baby, and his

Protection of the mother and the child through the process of delivery. A couple of praise songs, the Pastor shares the ceremony's importance and references the significance of the water, salt and honey, which Baba Sayo has already provided. The Pastor asked Baba Sayo to publicly announce the name. Then the Pastor turned to confer on their newborn child.

Traditionally, African names often have unique stories behind them. From the day or time, a baby is born to the circumstances surrounding the birth; several factors influence the names parents choose for their children. This saying in the Yoruba language - *Ile la n wo ta to somo loruko* - The background of a child is important before we give a child a name. Baba Sayo has been keener because he has been promoted in his place of work.

He names the child *Ayodele* meaning Joy has come home. Ayodele is a unisex name for a baby whose birth brought happiness.

After the naming ceremony, the child will be fed a teaspoon of water and honey. The salt may be referred to as something the child will grow to appreciate when he becomes 'the salt of the earth' as a born-again believer in Christ's body.

BOUND BY FATE

After the final prayer for the child and parents, the bowl or plate of honey is taken around, and a drop is put on the finger of all the presents, who will suck the honey and pronounce a blessing on the child. Different gifts in different sizes from different people were given to Baba and Mama Sayo. Then, Baba Sayo formed a caucus for refreshments, a party after party day in Agboola's compound; Sayo also enjoyed her day to the fullest.

~~~~~

"At birth, You are a carbon copy of your mother."

Ten years later
One would certainly say Ayodele was just a male version of his mother or just a reflection of his mother with his looks and his way of doing things. Ayodele is now in JSS 1 at Cetta's High School. It is time for the second midterm holiday.

Night had fallen, and everyone was in bed except Ayodele, who sat alone in the sitting room. A body of water settled inside his eyes like a lake and slowly rolled down his cheeks like rivulets. He was unhappy, helpless and hopeless. He felt thoroughly abandoned, like a stone at the bottom of the lake, as he recalled his parents' reaction to his midterm test results.

'*Olodo!* Your mates are scoring As'', 'Take a look

at your sister's results!', 'Can't you just read like your sister?, 'Or are you just dull naturally?, 'Maybe you should learn to be a mechanic?', 'Because I can't stand this anymore!', 'I am tired!'

His mother's admonishing words echoed in his head over and over again. And each day through the years, he'd throw his school bag at the wall and scream, "I hate school! I hate books! Why is it always like this?"

His mother without delay rushed to him from her room.

"What's wrong with me?"

"Why am I different?" Ayodele mumbled.

Mama Sayo knew that it would be a big mistake to talk about Ayodele's test. She'd carry him, pat him, take his hand and look at him kindly.

"Nothing is wrong with you, my baby. I am sorry I shouted at you," she said remorsefully.

After some cajoling Mama Sayo managed to pat him to sleep.

It is the sole purpose of a parent to protect their child. When a child gets hurt or disheartened, the parent feels the pain tenfolds. Mama Sayo wished she could take Ayodele's pain away. She was unable to sleep; she hummed to herself from time to time.

Baba Sayo on the other side of the bed snores like an apparatus that produces gas. You can't blame him; working in the sun and rain just to provide food and shelter for his family and make them comfortable is not an easy task - The quality of fatherhood can be set in the aspirations, hard work and goals he sets for his children.

Mama Sayo needs someone to hash out her worries too. She gently pats Baba Sayo to wake him up.

"Baba Sayo, wake up, I want to talk to you," she said solemnly.

"Mama Sayo, why are you still awake?" Baba Sayo asked, trying to clear his eyes and sit upright on the bed.

"I am worried about Ayodele's education."

"I have tried my best to make him understand the importance of education," Mama Sayo said affirmatively.

"I know you have tried your possible best. I just pray and believe he will catch up very soon."

"When, Baba Sayo? When?"

"You know how many schools enrolled him before he got to secondary school."

Baba Sayo mildly holds her. "I know, Mama Sayo. You have to take things easy and wish for the best."

"I think Agboola's compound is one of his problems. Maybe the environment is too much influence on him," Mama Sayo suggested.

According to the saying, "It takes a thief to catch a thief."- Mr Agboola is a gentleman but once it comes to the issue of some of his crazy tenants, he goes wild because he believes they just want to outsmart him.

Agboola's compound can be described as a bedlam, crazy, nuthouse in the neighbourhood - full of different junkies, and bizarre attitudes - The prayer warrior, Sister Tomiwa, just be thankful she is not next door else no quality bedtime for you. Baba Dami and his family can relate to this. Sister Tomiwa can pray from morning to morning non-stop, and woe betides you if you complained.

The tipsters, Tunde and his gang. Tunde, popularly called "*Tunapa*" by his boys. Tunde and his boys have been arrested for different atrocities. They even changed Mr Agboola's name to "*Agbos Baba.*"

Iya Bisi and her daughter are another case study in the compound. The other tenants don't want to come across these people. They can borrow everything you have including utensils and ingredients and the annoying thing is they do not have anything for you to borrow. A big-time bombshell when Bisi asked Sister Ruth to borrow her new undies. 'Please, help us, a friend in need is a friend indeed,' is Bisi and her mother's slogan.

Sister Ruth, the incognito, you never know whether she is home because her door is always shut. You only get to see her once in a while.

The other tenants wonder whether they are living in a guest house or whore house, Sisi Toke and her crews have visitors every time and call themselves Ladies Of Pleasure.

If you're wondering how Mr Agboola gets to know what happened even if he wasn't at home when the incident occurred, Okun is the mole. Okun is just thirty-three but he is the oldest tenant in the compound. Okun has lived all his life in Agboola's compound. His father passed on and Okun inherited the title "*chief tenant.*" Mr Agboola treats him like his personal assistant.

...And much more tenants in Agboola's compound.

"I think he needs to go back to the hostel," Mayo Sayo suggested.

"Mama Sayo, have you forgotten that Ayodele was sent home from the hostel because he smashed a broken bottle on his classmate that called him *olodo.*"

"But..."

"No, but... come here," Baba Sayo said mildly, hugging her. As he turned off the light, he whispered, "Everything will be fine. Let's sleep dear."

~~~~~

II
2000 – 2005

Waiting for your exam results can be stressful. Panic,

guilt, and fear will be in conflict with your capacity as a student. Ayodele was seated in his corner as the class teacher read the report cards from the last position in the class, number forty. Ayodele was surprised as his name wasn't mentioned.

"Ayodele, thirty-seventh position," the class teacher exclaimed, shocked

It was a mixed feeling for Ayodele. He opened his report card and saw A1 in Fine Arts and a lot of red ink. Although red ink was not a new thing to him, the only blue ink placed a radiant smile on his face.

A moment of an indistinct sound, murmurs, among the students as their class teacher announced the new student. Ayodele's seat partner got the first position in the class. His mates couldn't comprehend what they just heard because AJ's attitude gave them the impression that he didn't know anything. They sometimes regarded him as a sad boy.

Feranmi, on the other hand, could not believe that the person he detested the most in the school was now his contender. He boiled within himself as he imagined his father scolding him after seeing his report card.

"Second position! How come?" Feranmi cried. "How will I explain this to my father?"

"Don't be too hard on yourself," Daniel, one of his friends tried to calm him down.

"Daniel, let him be," Alao interrupted. "I am just coming from the staff room, where that *I-fight-lion-boy*'s name has been the talk of the town for them.

They said he passed all his exams with distinction. They just back-numbered my friend's name. Do you know how many competitions the school begged him to participate in this term because of his last term's performance? So, one ugly boy just entered this school and outnumbered everyone, feeling fly."

Alao snared at AJ who was sitting in his corner looking at his report card look. Feranmi was still boiling when the driver assigned by his father arrived to pick him up.

~~~~~

The classroom was still congested with some students. Some are lamenting over their grades, while some are rejoicing.

AJ was arranging his books in his school bag, getting ready to be going home. A small piece of paper was dropped on his desk.

The note read: *Thank you for teaching me my Fine Art theories. Why are you always sad?*

AJ glanced at the question and immediately ignored it. A drawing of him with deplorable eyes dropped on his desk. Still, he was dead silent.

"Why this mood?" Ayodele asked with an anxious expression.

He was showing a keen interest in knowing why AJ was not happy. "Perhaps, maybe he's just a sadist," Ayodele soliloquized.

Suddenly, AJ let out a big heavy sigh," If you are not rushing home, can you follow me to a lakeside?" AJ asked.

"Of course," Ayodele replied without obliging. Ayodele picked up his report card he drew AJ's face on and packed all his books to his school bag, and followed AJ.

AJ returned to his place of comfort just down the street from his father's house.

"The serene environment of this lake grants me the escape I need from reality most times. My familiar escape never lost its exquisiteness, which is why it was the perfect cure for any stressful time in my life," AJ muttered.

Ayodele nodded as if he was listening. He was still busy gazing at the beautiful white birds that flew over his head and the stunning pink and purple sky that appeared too gorgeous to be real. The wind brushed his hair scalp, swaying the trees back and forth, making him feel cool and happy. The beautiful white birds, stunning purple and pink sky, the shallow blue water, and loud grey ducks never ceased to amaze him.

"How come I don't know this beautiful place?" Ayodele asked inquisitively.

"This beautiful place is owned by a French man. He bought this land when he discovered that the lake and the beautiful birds around will be a great advantage for his amazement park project, although this place was a forest then. Only the Oligarchs and French pals have the pass," AJ explained.

AJ offered Ayodele a pineapple juice he ordered from the bartender at the entrance. Ayodele was sipping his pineapple juice while AJ was facing the shallow blue water firmly.

"I am not what they call me. I am just an introvert," AJ spoke softly.

"Introvert?"

"Yes, Introvert."

"An introvert is a person with qualities of a personality type known as introversion, which means that they feel more comfortable focusing on their inner thoughts and ideas, rather than what's happening externally. And that is why all of you cringe around me."

"Uhm, Why are you an introvert?" Ayodele asked, a little confused.

AJ pondered, took a sip of his pineapple juice and said, "My full name is Ogunaike Aja Malomo." Ayodele's eyes glittered like a sparking light, shocked and wondering why a parent will name his or her child, *Aja*."

"According to Yoruba tradition, if a woman gives birth to a child and the child dies before becoming an adult, such a child is called an *abiku* especially if the death occurred at childbirth – it's believed the child keeps reincarnating to torment his or her parents.

If perchance, the woman gives birth to a child that survives, such a child is usually given names like *Aja* meaning dog, *Malomo* meaning, don't go again, or *Kashimawo* meaning, let's be watching him or her.

My mother gave birth to six children before me, and all of them died. I managed to survive: That's why my father, a stickler for tradition named me Aja and Malomo. My father rejects all non-traditional medical care."

AJ willed away his tears.

"I suffered a lot of health traumas when I was smaller. Dehydration, frequent infections, swollen hands and feet and other things. My parents believed that the gods were punishing them for not adhering to the *Ifa's* omen about their marriage as Ifa warned them that they were not compatible."

Ayodele sympathetically held AJ's hand.

"It's okay." AJ smiled and withdrew his hand. "When I was five years old, I was taken to my hometown, Ibadan. One of my father's old-aged brothers, with *abaja* marks laced on his face, suggested that I should be given a tribal mark and my mother should carry a sacrifice to appease the gods and bike's spiritual realm.

I cried, and screamed, holding my mother's blouse firmly and begging, 'Mummy, please stop them. I don't want a tribal mark, I will be fine. Please.' I felt the sharpness of the *Abe* blade. Blood covered my face, groin and thigh, streaming unceasingly. My mother did nothing but stand beside me, sobbing and lamenting.

On our way back from Ibadan, we had an accident and I lost my mother. The following year, my father remarried. Since then, my father has taunted me. He blames me for my mother's death. I started my primary school education at the age of seven. Although, I am still battling with my health and my father's derisive words.

On a fateful day, I was coming back from school angry after a classmate called me an *abiku* and was nearly hit by a motorcyclist. The name of the motorcyclist was Mr Francis Lopez. He is a French man, also one of the workers on this lakeside. Mr Francis Lopez was also grieving over his little girl that passed away; he lost his wife during her delivery.

Later, Mr Francis and I became friends. He brought me to this lakeside, handed me one of his entry passes and gifted me a small video camera which he brought from France. He later took me to his chalet at the back of this compound, where we usually meet when we want to see each other. Without my father's consent, Mr Francis took me to the hospital for a medical check-up.

'Be brave enough to heal yourself even when it hurts,' were Mr Francis's first words to me when the doctor confirmed I am a sickle cell carrier. He has been like a father ever since.

Sickle cell anaemia is one of a group of disorders

known as sickle cell disease. Sickle cell anaemia is an inherited red blood cell disorder in which there aren't enough healthy red blood cells to carry oxygen throughout your body."

Ayodele sniffled and wiped his eyes.

"There's no cure for most people with sickle cell anaemia. But treatments can relieve pain and help prevent complications associated with the disease. A lot of people were generally ignorant about this medical issue especially if they are bigoted to their traditional beliefs. So, if anyone with an AS blood genotype marries an AS, there is a high probability that they would give birth to a child with the SS gene.

After the doctor's concise words about sickle cell anaemia, I was full of rage, angry, full of aversion and hatred at my bigoted father. All I can think of is the pains and sufferings have gone through as a kid.

How people out-placed people with tribal marks. Since then, I became a prisoner to my tension. I only open up to Mr Francis Lopez."

Ayodele hugged himself; he was dumbfounded and shuddered from time to time.

It was a perfect day for walking; the paths were resting carpet of golden leaves. AJ and Ayodele walked around the lake.

"How do you manage to know everything?" Ayodele asked. "How do you possess the level of intelligence in your education?"

AJ chuckled and stroked Ayodele's arm. "No one is an island of knowledge. Everybody has his or her uniqueness."

"Why am I a slow learner? Why do I find it difficult to digest things into my coconut head? Sometimes, I feel I am naturally dull," Ayodele said, shaking his head in a worrisome manner.

"Hey buddy, you don't have to beat yourself at this, every child moves at their pace. I believe you will catch up."

"But, I am trying..." Ayodele huffed. "Trying hard to make my parents proud but it's just impossible to catch up," Ayodele bewailed.

"There is nothing like a mission impossible, that is why it is a mission," AJ said affirmatively, "I think to build a child's self-esteem, parents, teachers, and guardians need to focus on what the child can do. At least you are not as bad as you see yourself, at least you can draw the gloomy AJ and can be ahead of Alao and Simbi in class," AJ teased and tickled Ayodele.

Ayodele twitched and burst out laughing.

~~~~~

Mr Francis suggested that Ayodele should see an educational psychologist after AJ explained Ayodele's enduring disposition to him.

"You are dyslexic," the psychologist diagnosed

and recommended a therapy session for Ayodele. How sad they could not afford it. AJ in a prone state, plead with the Psychologist to recommend books on dyslexia to him.

AJ studied very hard in the community library about dyslexia - meaning, symptoms, causes and measures that should be taken against it. He created games and methods Ayodele can learn and understand. He also created a pokey game - some words that don't just follow rules, they need to be learned by sight- visual memory. They also played a game called *give-and-take*, where they exchanged views on some topics and their past experiences. Ayodele shared his experience with Agboola's compound while AJ shared his experience with the annual event of the *Ogun* celebration his father hosted every year.

They also took some lovely pictures and videos with AJ's small video camera at the lakeside.

~~~~~~~

As the years passed by, AJ helped Ayodele to build up his literacy levels. He also helped him to maximize the potential latent and expand the possibilities so that he can tap into the amazing creativity held in the dyslexic mind.

As Albert Einstein once said: 'Everyone is smart, but if you judge a fish by its ability to climb a tree, it will spend its entire life believing it is stupid'. *That* is why AJ propelled that to build Ayodele's self-esteem, he needs to focus on what he can do, which is drawing.

Mama Sayo had beaten Ayodele and nagged at him several times for drawing on his school books. Even after his sober mood and after a lot of red inks in his school work, he drew AJ's sad face on the back of his report card.

Things are different now that they are in SS3. Ayodele improved as he helped his mother with her fashion illustrations and was better organised although he still had difficulties with spellings. He helped AJ get along with some students.

AJ, on the other hand, has gained ground through the years because of his intelligence. They aren't teased as much as before in junior section, just Feranmi and his caucus that became a blustering fellow to them. Just like a rack for cattle to feed on, AJ and Ayodele got intimidated by Feranmi and his caucus expects Daniel who used to caution him. Sometimes, he paid Alao, who repeated SS1 twice and Alao's backbencher stubborn classmates to bully Ayodele and AJ.

~~~~~~

A school assembly is a gathering of all or part of a school for any variety of purposes, such as special programs or communicating information on a daily or weekly basis.

The timekeeper rang an emergency bell for the students of Cetta's high school to gather together at the assembly ground.

As Mrs Yaya, and the principal, stepped forward to address the entire school on the reasons for the alarming call.

"Good afternoon, Cetta's Bright. The noblemen and women standing beside me are representatives of Atod Magnum Opus. They are here to invite us to their annual Story Telling Competition titled "The Orange Storytelling Competition." Their mission is to provide educational opportunities and gifts for the students. Form Applications are opened to all senior and junior secondary school students as you can get yours from your class teachers for just three thousand naira," she stated optimistically, as the school assembly was dispatched later.

In the latter part of the day, AJ got back from school and found his nonchalant father alone at home. Seeing that his father was slightly drunk, he became quite weepy; he had to quietly drop his school bag, and cautiously creep out to avoid his father's taunting words that occurred anytime he took his *ogogoro.*

Mr Francis was AJ's last hope to get the Orange Storytelling Competition application form fees as there are no mutual dealings between him, his stepbrother and his stepmother. Mr Francis has been a surrogate father to AJ. Sometimes, it eats out AJ's heart because what he'd ever wished for was a good relationship with his father.

AJ sneaked out of the house to Mr Francis's chalet.

He recapped Mr Francis's kind words: 'I love you, boy.', 'I'm proud of you.', 'Well done, my boy.', 'I know you can do it. You're a success.'

AJ informed Mr Francis about the competition and his results.

"You messed up but I know you'll bounce back in that subject."

Tears filled AJ's eyes, already missing him; Mr Francis had been confined to a bed by illness for some time.

"Je crois en toi mon garçon. Je sais que tu gagneras le concours. Ne t'inquiete pas pour moi, tout ira bien," Mr Francis muttered out words slowly, showing an expression of assertion and advice.

"Je vais," AJ affirmed.

Mr Francis managed to sit upright on the bed. He held out his hand to get his wallet and gave AJ three thousand naira from the remaining three thousand two hundred naira in his wallet.

~~~~~~

It was a perfect summer day for a competition. The school management had sent out invitation messages to all the parents. Baba and Mama Sayo dressed in Yoruba attire. Sayo, who was now in 200 level at Olabisi Onabanjo University was present.

AJ in a dispirited state did not doubt his father's

absence. He had invited Mr Francis who strained himself to be at the event just to give him moral support.

Feranmi's father was highly welcomed. Not just as a parent but as one of the highest-ranked navy officers in Nigeria.

Before the final round of the Orange Storytelling Competition, the school had invited the students who had paid for the application form to the first level that was conducted on the school assembly ground. After some compensation, the final twenty participants were selected: Fourteen students from the senior section and six students from the junior section.

Three judges and Mrs Yaya sat on the podium. Feranmi and Ayodele were instructed to sit in the first row with some other students while Daniel and AJ were in the last seats in the last row. The judges were provided with a large printed sheet that comprised of names of the participants. The participants will be rewarded with marks based on their choice of story, facial expression, language, confidence and body language.

Mrs Yaya welcomed the parents and announced the Orange Storytelling Competition and also wished the participants good luck. Then, one of the representatives of Atod Magnum Opus announced the names of the participants.

The first participant was a junior secondary school student, followed by Feranmi, who narrated his story with a good performance. He ended up his story by giving his father the accolades, 'My father, my superhero.'

AJ sighed and wished his father was there. All he had ever wished for was to see his father embrace him. He glimpsed at Baba and Mama Sayo at the back.

Ayodele also narrated his story and gave some accolades to a great friend and appreciated his parents' support.

AJ's name was announced and he felt anxious.

"God does not need a bowl of words only a go of faith," AJ wandered in thought for some seconds and he hoped Mr Francis's enthusiasm was infectious enough for him.

He entered the stage and viewed several students looking at him with great contempt; his eyes suddenly caught a glimpse of an old man wearing Ankara attire, sitting at the end.

"Dad," he mumbled. Still surprised, and wordless on the stage, a beaming smile etched his face, marked by an intense joy, seeing his father for the first time in his school.

He began visualizing his story from a little innocent kid that was tagged *Abiku* and the bigotry of mutilation, with the flow of expression, he started narrating the traumas, sufferings, and how individuals and friends made jest of him.

"What many called *Abiku* those days in many cases has been found to have had sickle cell anaemia. The act of marking the face is inhuman. The belief of marking the face as an inoculation against the disease should be abolished," he spoke poignantly.

The hall was tensed, strained to stiffness, aroused of emotions... Suddenly, the microphone went off. Feranmi rolled his eyes like a guiltless being; not tainted with sin. He had already paid one of the technicians to insulate the microphone once it was AJ's turn. AJ was unable to finish his anecdote.

~~~~~~
2005

At the end of the Orange Story Telling Competition, Mrs Yaya shared her appreciation with everyone for the success of the competition.

"However, there could only be one winner, with so much deliberation between ourselves, final decisions were based on how the story had challenged us the audience, academically, psychologically, and socially…"

"Oyela! Baa ba f'e mol'oju ariran," a windy voice said.
"Oyela," AJ's father mumbled.

The voice in the wind became a man, in his right hand held a powdery white substance retrieved from the *ado* tied around his neck. He began to chant: *"Iwaju opon ifa ogbo eyin ogbon ifa ogbo Olumu l'otun Olokanran l'osi adia fun orunmila nijo ti baba agbonmiregun sokale bo lataafin Eledua Arinurode fun ni adiye Ifa ni t'omo araye ba p'adiye je nko Eledua ni ko m'eyin dani, O le yin nii dakuko."*

The man stopped chanting and gave AJ's father some of the powder substance to rub on his face.

"Oyela! Baa ba f'e mol'oju ariran," the man repeated.

"Oyela," AJ's father replied and watched his late wife's spirit vocally express grief over his effortless, careless behaviour towards their child.

The man warned him to take good care of AJ. He also added that AJ was a good luck charm and the pate of success to his family.

"Our winner is AJ Malomo Ogunaike," Mrs Yaya declared openly.

AJ's father regained consciousness after hearing his son's name openly proclaimed as the winner of the competition. He had wandered off in thought for some minutes about the medium's oracle.

Feranmi was marked by a sensation when his name was announced as the third position. The second prize was won by Daniel.

AJ was thrilled to win even after he was unable to finalize his anecdote. He urged his father and his surrogate father to join him on stage. He was thrilled.

He hugged his father tight and whispered, "I love

you, dad."

After the prizes and bonuses were given to AJ, the sponsors offered him a scholarship and he will be their representative at the state storytelling competition.

While Mrs Yaya congratulated AJ's father, AJ's body fell to the ground, the warmth of life stolen by the cold embrace of death, blood rushing out of his nostril. There was an undue hurry and confusion among the audience. His chest lay still under his father's hand, no flicker of life, a sure-fire sign that he was dead.

Mr Francis was numbed with shock and almost knocked unconscious by the heavy blow. Baba Sayo held Ayodele tight as he yelled his friend's name.

AJ's father's eyes were wide open, shimmering with tears. There was an expression of hurt and guilt in his eyes as he remembered his blithe of unconcern, careless, heedless, nonchalant attitude towards his son. He mourned bitterly as he recalled his son's final statement; 'I love you, dad,' and the soothsayer's prophecy about his marriage to AJ's mother.

~~~~~

It was no child's play the day Ayodele lost his friend to the sickle cell disease. Silence sank like sad music in his heart and descended on his soul's pitiable layers. Tears rolled down his face, he promised himself to establish a non-governmental organisation to create awareness on sickle cell disease and also ensure that sickle cell disease warriors get access to quality health care on time. He also prayed and hoped Mr Francis should be relieved of any form of trauma after his surrogate son's death.

~~~~~~

Dyslexia
2020

An effulgent day, it is October 8, World Dyslexia Awareness Day. It was an amazing day at the annual event with different talks and games.

The month of October has been a work time for the Dyslexia Nigeria team. Events are organised to create more awareness and enlightenment for people about Dyslexia. The Non-Governmental Organisation has set up an annual Dyslexia Dialogue: Unmasking Dyslexia. The Leader made the initial introductions, and then the master of ceremony invited the MD of AJ Foundation. An NGO that focuses on creating awareness of sickle cell disease and ensuring that SCD warriors get access to quality health care. Also, the presence of several artists and a lecturer of African philosophy were acknowledged.

Claps echoed from the audience which was made up of several secondary schools the non-government organisation invited over for the annual events. as Dr Ademola of African philosophy collected the microphone. He greeted everyone, then beaming, he started;

"When I was told I was going to be one of the chief speakers of this special occasion, I was so happy. Over time, we have seen so many scenarios in our school systems.

We see children, young and promising, anxious and delightful, but one thing labels them. They seem to be different; they learn differently, and their brain seems confused. We often call them *Olodo* in Nigeria, but are they dull? What could be wrong? Why do they learn differently? Why?"

Dr Ademola paused, glancing at everyone in the audience and then continued. "So many why's. But what if it is not their fault? What if they are sick? What if they have dyslexia?" Dr Ademola asked and paused dramatically.

"Dyslexia. Dyslexia is a specific learning disability that is neurobiological in origin. It is characterized by difficulties with accurate and fluent word recognition and by poor spelling and decoding abilities. Dyslexia refers to a cluster of symptoms that result in people having difficulties with specific language skills, particularly reading. Students with dyslexia often experience difficulties with both oral and written language."

Dr Ademola encouraged his audience to ask questions. A young girl from Celta's High School raised her hand,

"Yes," Dr Ademola gestured to her.

"Is dyslexic curable?" the girl asked.

"Dyslexia is a neurological condition caused by a different wiring of the brain. There is no cure for dyslexia and individuals with the condition must learn coping strategies."

The young girl nodded.

Dr Ademola nodded as well and continued, "Research indicates that dyslexia has no relationship to intelligence, individuals with dyslexia are neither more nor less intelligent than the general population.

In a school where many teachers are not knowledgeable about this condition, students with dyslexia may be considered stupid or lazy."

One of the reporters at the event asked about the causes of dyslexia.

"The exact causes of dyslexia are still not completely clear, but anatomical and brain imagery studies show differences in the way the brain of a person with dyslexia develops and functions. The causes of dyslexia are neurobiological and genetic. Individuals inherit the genetic links for dyslexia. Chances are that one of the child's parents, grandparents have dyslexia.

With a proper diagnosis, appropriate instruction, hard work, and support from this NGO, family, teachers, friends and others, individuals who have dyslexia can succeed in school and later as a working adult."

A young boy timidly raised his hand and asked,

"Uncle, how do I know if someone has dyslexia?"

Dr Ademola move closer to the little boy and patted him on the head. "Consider seeking consultation from a specialist or doctor if someone observed some dyslexia questions like, 'do you read slowly?', 'do you have trouble learning how to read when you were in school?', 'are you comfortable reading out loud?', 'do you often have to read something two or three times before it makes sense?', 'do you omit, transpose, or add letters when you are reading or writing?"

Dr Ademola moved back to the podium as he explained the measures that could be taken.

"If children who have dyslexia receive effective phonological awareness and phonics training in kindergarten and first grade, they will have significantly fewer problems in learning to read at grade level than those children who are not identified or helped until 3rd grade. Children with dyslexia should be treated with love and understanding. LOVE is the keyword here, parents, teachers, guardians, family members, and friends of any dyslexic patient should understand that they didn't choose to be dyslexic and the more reason we should help them get better together. Since dyslexic patients learn slowly, we need to constantly engage them, show them practical definitions to terms."

Dr Ademola adjusted his glasses and added, "Please note, being lazy in school or showing less attention to academics is not a sign of dyslexia, it is laziness!"

Everybody laughed.

"A child might just be lazy to learn. Find out properly before you conclude and when you do, don't stop there; help them become better. Thank you."

A round of applause followed after he dropped the microphone and hot-footed to his seat.

~~~~~~

III
Present-day
2021

September is National Sickle cell awareness month, designated by congress to help focus attention on the need for research and treatment of sickle cell disease.

AJ Foundation is a nongovernmental organisation created some years back by Dr Ayodele Ademola. The NGO focused on creating awareness of sickle cell disease and ensuring that SCD warriors get access to quality health care.

In September, the NGO encouraged everyone to be a part of the national effort to increase awareness about sickle cell disease and sickle cell traits.

"Individuals and organisations can join our efforts to bring attention to sickle cell disease by engaging elected officials for proclamations, hosting awareness events, distributing educational information to dispel the myths about sickle cell disease, and lighting public spaces and buildings," Dr

Ayodele Ademola said optimistically at a radio interview.

"Sickle cell anaemia is one of a group of disorders known as sickle cell disease. Sickle cell anaemia is an inherited red blood cell disorder, in which there aren't enough healthy red blood cells to carry oxygen throughout the body," Dr Ayodele discoursed.

"What are the symptoms of sickle cell anaemia?" The radio host asked.

"Signs and symptoms of sickle cell anaemia usually appear around five months of age. Signs and symptoms can include anaemia, episode of pain, swelling of hands and feet, frequent infections, delayed growth or puberty, and vision problems.

Sickle cell anaemia is usually diagnosed in infancy through newborn screening programs. If a child develops some problems like, fever, pale skin or nail beds, yellow tint, signs or symptoms of a stroke.

Both parents must pass the defective form of the gene for a child to be affected. If one parent passes the sickle cell gene to the child, that child will have the sickle cell trait.

With one normal haemoglobin gene and one defective form of the gene, people with the sickle cell trait make both normal haemoglobin and sickle cell haemoglobin. Their blood might contain some sickle cells, but they generally don't have symptoms. They're carriers of the disease, however, which means they can pass the gene to their children," Dr Ayodele Ademola explained softly.

Dr Ayodele also provided well-furnished answers to the questions sent in by the people listening to the radio station. He also advised and intimated people about preventive measures for sickle cell and reproductive options.

ADEKOLA TEMITAYO is an independent thinker. He holds a philosophy degree from Olabisi Onabanjo University. He has an insatiable desire to write fiction. Temitayo uses black and white ink with gripping and red-hot intensity, leaving a lasting impression on the lives and hearts of men.
Adekola Temitayo's heartwarming fiction explores the African identity of young and new adults. His stories are full of themes and proverbs. He wrote and published The Lost Course (A play). which has been used in schools since 2018 and is also part of the Oyo State Supplementary list of books for the Junior class of 2021-2023. The Cataclysm Of July Thirteen (A play). His works are also displayed on a variety of online literary platforms.

PURPLE JADE
Irinyemi Esther T

Aramide

Aramide checked each cake on the table before picking one for a scheduled delivery on the Island. If her parents were alive, she would not be delivering cakes at this stage in her life. She would probably be in class, fantasizing about her dream job or a boyfriend, but life hadn't given her that privilege. In her paraphrased version of the Bible verse: 'Anyone who does not provide for their relatives, and household, has denied the faith and is worse than an unbeliever. So, she's had to work to survive and see her teenage brother through school.

Ayofemi, her brother, was the evidence that she had been making progress for the past seven years. It had always been both of them mostly, no relatives or family to speak of.

Her first assignment for the day was to deliver a cake to a V.I.P. client, and she had been told not to bother with checking in at the agency but to head straight to the bakery. As she picked up the cake for Mrs Abayomi of Fourth Estate, Ikoyi, her cell phone trilled impatiently from her pocket. Aramide sighed as she put the cake back on the table.

"Hello ma," she said, after she'd picked the call and seen that it was Mrs Banks, her supervisor, on the line. "I'm already on it."

"Get over here quickly and pick up a package for Miss Nina," Mrs Banks replied.

"I'll on my way now… yes, I'll be there by ten-fifty-nine sharp… yes ma." Aramide replaced her phone, picked up the cake and headed out to her scooter.

Tina, Aramide's colleague, was at the entrance with the package in her hand when she got to the delivery agency.

"It's about time you got here. The annoying lady has been calling for her parcel non-stop," Tina rapped, referring to Miss Nina.

"Madam informed me this morning that she's

expecting it by eleven."

Aramide nodded and collected the parcel from her.

"That's what is in the book, but you know what Miss Annoying is like. God help you," Tina said.

She mouthed, "Amen," and waved briefly with her free hand as she went.

Tina watched Aramide exit the building. Aramide was her friend though three years younger and single, but life had been tough on her; the adult sacrifices she had been pressed to make had brought out the kind of maturity that only deepens with suffering and a wealth of sensibility that would have been uncommon even in a person twice her age. It was sad - but not all too surprising, Tina supposed. *Ah, well, we all have our own problems.* Tina smiled and went back inside.

How nice it would be to own a home in this estate, Aramide thought, admiring the scenery as she rode by the houses after being checked in by security. She'd been to the estate a lot of times to make deliveries to the families living there.

"Angels assigned for today's blessings. Can you just give me a home here?"

She smiled childishly. This was her first delivery to this particular client. This was usually Merissa's route, but she had to take up the job when Merissa called in sick. Ara was supposed to return home early enough to prepare to resume at House of Tebi, her second job, by one p.m.

Today had been one of those days when her job at

the delivery agency and at the bakery intersected. And speaking of home, she felt the need to call her brother and find out if he had gotten any update from the school portal. She prayed silently that he would get admitted into university this year. It was always rough and depressing each time he got rejected in the past three years. Now, he was losing hope. She had been the one urging him on while juggling two jobs to save up and see him through school. He was her hope for a better life one day.

"Wow!" Aramide mouthed, looking at the house before her. It was gated, huge and magnificent.

The owners must be swimming in money.

She rode her scooter through the wrought-iron gates, which had automatically opened for her. She saw a girl in uniform, probably a maid, walking towards her as she stopped. Suddenly, Aramide felt her heart begin to beat uncontrollably, and a shudder went through her body. Just then, a red sports car drove past her on its way out. The driver wore sunglasses and looked at her briefly before driving off.

"You don't ride in without being told to do so, ma," the maid murmured a bit sternly.

Still a bit thrown, she said, "Sorry for my mistake. I thought the gate was opened for me. I came to deliver the cake," Aramide replied, looking at the cake sitting pretty inside her basket and then back at the snob-faced maid.

"It certainly was a mistake. The guard must not have seen you somehow, or he would have stopped you. I'll take it from here. We don't want our house tainted by outsiders," the maid said.

Our house? Aramide smiled, knowing too well that the maid was trying to take advantage of the rare opportunity to prey on someone she perceived was weaker than herself. "You need to go learn some better lines if you really want to insult someone. That is something a four-year-old would say," she retorted, handing the maid the cake.

The maid had a scowl on her face.

She got back on her scooter and turned to go but stopped and looked at the maid.

"There are probably cameras watching, right? And there would be evidence that I delivered the cake to you in good condition. Handle it with care."

She drove off without looking back to make sure the maid didn't sabotage the cake. She hoped the maid wouldn't. That would be bad, and she could lose her job if the maid decided to lie against her.

"Stuck-up housekeepers who think they have arrived," Aramide said to herself. The trip to Miss Nina's home was uninteresting after the unpleasant encounter. Outside the estate, Aramide felt the same shiver of inexplicable excitement. She looked up and noticed the same red sports car driving out past her. This time around, all the tinted windows were up, and the car sped off without her catching a glimpse at the driver.

Why was she having such a feeling? She wondered. Ignoring what just happened, she rode in towards the security checkpoint. Got a visitor's card and rode towards Nina's apartment. She parked her scooter outside and picked up the package.

She greeted the guard posted outside the apartment building, who was all smiles, as she went up the stairs. It was a decent building. She found Miss Nina's door open, but she politely pressed the bell button and was told to come in.

Miss Nina was in the sitting room talking to a lady way more beautiful than she was.

"Your services are always poor. Now I'm late for my function," Miss Nina said angrily.

Shee surreptitiously checked her phone and saw that it was just ten-fifty-nine a.m. She had learnt to keep calm and not argue in such situations. As the saying goes, 'the customer is always right'.

Miss Nina stretched out her left hand as she asked, "Can I have the dress now?"

She gave Miss Nina the parcel, which was quickly opened and looked over.

She glanced at the pretty lady who hadn't spoken a word since she got there; she was busy with her phone.

"You can leave now."

She left immediately. It seemed like 'the annoying lady', as Tina called her, was in a good mood today.

Probably due to the visitor, her true colours were concealed. She was usually worse than this.

All she had to do now was ride home and then to work, but she had to call her brother first. She picked up her phone and dialled as soon as she was outside the building. He picked up on the first ring.

"Seems like you've been waiting on my call," Aramide said.

"I wanted to call you. I'm short on cash," Ayofemi said from his end.

Aramide wondered how, and on what, he might have spent his money on. "So quickly? What do you need it for? There was food in the house when I left this morning, and besides, I gave you your allowance of five thousand last month."

"Sis, I used it for school stuff. I'll explain when you come home," Ayofemi replied.

"We'll see what happens when I return today. Take care." She hung up. *These days he has been asking for more money. God help me!*

Sighing, Aramide powered her engine and drove off. She really had to create time to have a word or two with her brother. They had not spent much time together since she got her second job. She didn't know what he was up to these days. "God, show me the way and help out Ayofemi concerning his admission," she prayed silently as she rode out of Miss Nina's neighbourhood.

Aramide

Ayofemi felt ashamed, he had been lying to his sister of late. If only the business he had gone into had worked out. He wondered what had made him agree to Rasque's idea.

"Guy, anytin for us?" Rasque asked as he walked in without knocking.

Ayofemi turned to him. "I don't have any cash at all."

Rasque made himself comfortable on the only couch in the room.

"Your sister no give you money?"

Ayofemi nodded as he sat on the bed in the one room apartment.

"Me self neva see anytin o, everywhere dry. Guy wetin we go come do?" Rasque asked.

"Must we do business? Maybe God doesn't will it," Ayofemi moaned.

"Don't even say that. You know there are always risks and from time to time we have been enjoying the benefits. You wey been already chop your JAMB money. Abi you wan spend the whole year being unproductive?" Rasque asked.

Ayofemi shrugged. "I could just lie to my sister that I wasn't given admission."

Rasque laughed. "You be oponu - correct mumu."

Ayofemi ignored him, he was already fed up with the whole thing. The business Rasque had introduced *him to had not only failed to make a profit but had also virtually lost all the money he had. He promised himself then that next year he would work hard and get into the university like his sister wanted.*

"So what should we do now?" Ayofemi asked, hoping Rasque wouldn't give him another one of his stupid ideas. He knew Rasque was going to get him in trouble one day.

"That is what you should have first asked me," Rasque replied, sitting up fully now. "Okay I talked to one of my niggas and he agreed to introduce me to this quick-money business."

"Hope it doesn't involve stealing? Guy, I know you," Ayofemi said apprehensively.

"Guy, make I land first. It's an easy business," Rasque said boldly. "All we have to do is to sell products and deliver packages, like your sistah."

"Ok, what are we selling?"

Rasque smiled, seeing that Ayofemi was interested. "It's s'cafe," he replied.

Ayofemi burst into laughter. "Seriously? Or you are kidding?"

"Do I look like am a joker?"

"Wait, is it wholesale or what? Because guy you wan burst my kidney. How are we going to hit our target of two hundred thousand for this year?"

"Kai! You dey form street boy, you no no anything. This is a different kind of s'cafe. In fact, let's go now! The more time we spend here, the more money we are *losing," Rasque said, rising.*

"Wait, guy! This s'cafe we want to sell, how much are we going to make in a day?"

Rasque answered, "Five to six thousand. And when we add nilo and smoke to it, we will make more, and before you know it, we will become rich."

Ayofemi was suspicious. "All these names you are using…"

Rasque cut him off, "Let's just go first."

Ayofemi followed his friend, having no idea where they were off to.

"Any leftover cakes today?" Peace asked Aramide, who was at the counter with Sonia.

"Don't think so."

Sonia groaned. "Today wasn't nice at all. No handsome guy to drool over and no cakes to drown in."

"Get yourself a boyfriend and stop drooling over boys," Peace responded.

Sonia hissed at her. "Seriously, we know you've got a guy; you don't need to chuck it at we singles' faces."

She chuckled. "Who are the 'we'?"

The two girls focused on her.

"What?" she asked.

Peace broke the silence. "Seriously, tell me you have found Mr Right?"

She puckered her brow. "No, I haven't. Is there a

problem, girls?"

The two girls looked at each other conspiratorially.

"You can't tell me at the age of twenty-five you would rather go back home to your brother on a Friday evening without going out or having someone to smooch with?"

"For real, you are still single when Peace has a boyfriend," Sonia said, ignoring Peace's sudden glare.

"You guys are making too big a deal out of this," she said, starting to feel attacked.

"Hmm, you need prayers, girl. Will see you girls tomorrow. I have a date with my guy tonight. Was just waiting to find out if there was any free cake today. Goodnight." Peace left without waiting for replies from the girls.

"What's she feeling like?" asked Sonia.

She just nodded.

"You senior dat girl Ara. How far? Why don't we both go out and catch guys tonight?" Sonia suggested.

"No, thank you. I'm not interested. Also, I have to stop by a friend's place tonight," she replied as she walked out from behind the counter, trying her best to escape Sonia's claws.

"You need to get a life, girl."

"I have one already. I don't need to go searching for another," she replied as she walked outside. She pushed their discussion to the back of her mind. There was a lot she still needed to achieve. What guy would want a girl who was only a liability anyway? And besides, there was her brother to worry about.

Sonia felt annoyed, though at no one in particular. She just wished some good guy would give Aramide a single rose. She loved the girl like her big sister. It was a shame that guys were blind to the good, sweet girls like Aramide but had bright eyes for girls like Peace. She hissed. She might have to resort to arranging a date for Aramide.

Anna, Aramide's friend, sat on the sofa in the living room wearing only a tank top and shorts, having a conversation over the phone.

"Why shouldn't you write with a broken pencil?" Anna asked, smiling when someone knocked on the door. "I'm coming!" She opened the door to let Aramide in, still on the call, while Aramide took a seat.

"That's not the answer. Keep trying," Anna said, laughing as she returned to her seat opposite Aramide.

"'Because it's pointless', that's the answer. I'll call you later. Kisses."

"Wasn't sure you'd be home tonight; thought you might be out."

Anna dropped her phone on the couch beside her. "Yes Ara, my plan was to go out with friends to Traffic Bar, but monthly flow decided to spoil my fun." She pouted. "What made you come check up on me?"

"Just thought of you. Dropped by to check if you decided 'no parties or outings' for once," she said jokingly.

"For where? Girl, this is how we get clients, more clients, huge investment coming in, then promotion!" Anna stood up. "Should I get you food or just a cold soda?" she asked, walking to the kitchen in the two-bedroom flat apartment.

For a twenty-four-year-old banker, Anna was living a comfortable life. Especially since she joined the marketing department. She had met friends and some big boys on the island who couldn't resist a pretty-faced, model-body girl like her. Anna was ambitious and didn't mind playing dirty to get what she wanted, but she was a sweet girl and Aramide's friends since secondary school - since they were kids, in fact. Her parents had taken Aramide and her brother in after the tragedy.

"Won't mind having them both, I'm famished," Aramide shouted to Anna in the kitchen.

Aramide wondered why she still lived in one room when all the girls she knew lived in flats or BQs. Maybe she should budget for a self-con after Ayofemi has settled down in school. She was still deep in thought when Anna came back in. She thought she heard her name.

"Did you say something?" Aramide asked her friend.

"You went to la la land... get the stool jare!"

She mouthed 'sorry', pulled the stool beside her sofa and placed it in front of her. Anna placed the tray with the dish and drink on it and sat down.

"What got you thinking?"

Aramide mentioned the inverse of her thoughts: "Femi's admission."

"Oh! Which school was it again?"

"LASU," she replied and sipped from her drink.

"I'll find out if I can get someone to help out," Anna said while tapping away on her phone.

"Ok," she said and began eating the meal.

Jamal

"You can't shock a Yoruba man and not expect his jaw not to drop," Jamal joked as he grilled the chicken breast with I.K. by the pool.

"As in, Tade can't do without being an idiot sometimes," Tebi, the pretty girl relaxing on the pool lounger, said.

Everyone laughed.

"Well, Tebi, I give the best memes," Tade retorted.

"If she doesn't like it, I do," the exotic beauty sitting on the love swing said; she was Jamal's girlfriend.

"Bestie mi, thank you jare! You know when children feel they have sense like their elders, they start to talk anyhow," Tade said, smiling.

"You are de one talking the nonsense."

"You are talking like tin dat do not have good experience..." Jamal added, supporting Tebi with a funny voice.

"Who wants more?" Tade broke out suddenly with

a laugh as he picked up the *Martell Blue Swift* from the ice chest.

"You guys should take it easy on the poor boy," I.K. said as he used a tong to gently flip the chicken.

"I want!"

"You that have been attacking me since."

"Thank you," Evelyn mouthed as she got her cup refilled by Tade.

"The Bible says, forgive and forget."

"Children will always be children," Jamal added in support again. Tade poured in Tebi's cup as they laughed.

"Jamal, your cup…" He scratched his head and smiled sheepishly as he remembered. "My bad."

"You want to give our newly reformed Reverend Father alcohol?" I.K. exclaimed.

"See why I called the guy an idiot?" Tebi smiled into her cup. "Even though I still like him…"

At this, everyone cooed, "'Awwwnn!"

Jamal was silent.

"Like a puppy," Teni finished.

Tade's jaw dropped.

"See his mouth," Jamal said with a grin.

"I don't have your time now. So, Evelyn, would you mind the honour of drinking on your guy's behalf?"

"Bring it on!"

He topped her off. Just then, Mrs Abayomi came strolling toward them with a uniformed maid in tow who carried a serving bowl containing Coleslaw.

"Maami!" Jamal cried while Evelyn and Tebi both went to give his mother kisses on the cheek.

The maid put the bowl on the table and stood aside while the girls returned to their seats.

"I'll be going to the groom's parents' home, my presence is needed there," Mrs Abayomi said excitedly.

Jamal didn't get his mother these days; always fussing about their family friend Chike's wedding, which wasn't until next month. She had gone so far as to order a cake for them for God-knows-why. She had also been asking him when his wedding to Evelyn was happening. He cleared his thoughts away to focus on what his mom was saying.

"I have a fabric I'm supposed to pick from your mom's store. I've been trying to reach her because I won't be able to make it to our appointment."

"Oh," Tebi checked her phone, "Should I call the store for you?"

"There's no need for that, Mommy."

"The maid can help you pick it up. What is she paid for?" Mrs Abayomi insisted, chuckling gleefully; she felt a certain happiness anytime her son's fiancée called her 'mommy'.

The maid did her best to keep her face impassive.

"I will pick it up for you, Mom. I'm heading in that direction anyways," Jamal said.

"Oh, that's solved then." Mrs Abayomi smiled at her

son. "See you two later." She waved at them and left with the maid.

"I will go with you, Jamal. I just remembered I need to stop by my bakery in the complex."

Evelyn had a scowl on her face. "Call an Uber or hitch a ride with Tade. My boyfriend is not your driver."

"I will take you, Tebi," IK said.

"Since I'm going to pick up something for mom in the same building already, I will take her." Jamal set out the disposable plates on the table while I.K. dished out the coleslaw.

Evelyn had a nagging feeling about Jamal and Tebi. The girl was way too close to him. If she didn't come from wealth like they did, Evelyn herself would have shunned and avoided her like the plague.

"You have to drive me down to my friend's apartment then since you are going that way."

"Who?" Jamal glanced at Evelyn; he hated his girlfriend's guts sometimes; she acted like she owned him and could order him around or bend him to her will and whims.

"Peter," Evelyn responded, hoping to get Jamal jealous; Peter was a known flirt.

"That is a different route."

"I'll call an *Uber*," Tebi suddenly piped in.

"That would be better," Evelyn retorted.

"You are coming with me, and that's final." Jamal looked Evelyn square in the eyes before walking away.

I.K. whistled. Tade and Tebi held their lips pressed together.

"How dare he walk out on me?" Evelyn hissed, gave Tebi a look and went after Jamal.

"Well, I can't say I'm surprised. That's Evelyn." I.K. focused on the grilling.

"Don't blame yourself, Tebs. That's how Eve's mood swings are, she'll get over it." Tade tried to cheer her up, seeing she'd already started brooding.

"I caused all this."

"Says who? You didn't cause anything."

Then they all went silent. If it was up to I.K., he would have ended Evelyn's engagement to Jamal. She would be the end of him. Tebi sipped from her cup, and Tade watched the sizzling meat from his seat.

Jamal and Tebi were at the parking lot of the complex, which housed House of Tebi bakery and Tebi's mother's Nigerian fashion store as well as a host of other businesses. They had not spoken a word on the ride over. Tebi had finished whatever business she had at her place, and Mrs Abayomi's package was sitting in the back seat. Jamal's hands were gripping the wheel while Tebi looked out the window. Jamal broke the silence.

"So, I guess I'll drop you off at your house."

"You aren't going to visit your friend?"

"Changed my mind."

And just like that, he had that inexplicable, 'electric feeling' come over him briefly again. He'd been having this strange feeling on and off for some time now. It put his whole body on alert and set his heart racing. It was as though there was something urgent he was missing with his eyes and had to search for. Tebi was staring at a staff member who was walking in, probably returning from an errand, then stopped all of a sudden on her way in, turned around briefly and then went through the doors. Jamal had not seen her.

Tebi finally turned to look at him. "Can I ask you a question?"

Jamal nodded.

"Do you love her?" Tebi asked softy, hoping to get a straight answer.

Jamal sighed and further tightened his grip on the steering wheel. "Duty is more important than love."

"You mean you don't love her?"

This time, he met her eyes. "Are you ready to go home?"

She frowned. "You can count on me, Jamal. I didn't return from Dublin to come watch my friend suffer in a controlling relationship," she said, squeezing her palms in a tight fist to contain her anger.

"I will drop you off then," he said, turning on the ignition.

"I hope you wake from whatever spell you've been placed under."

Jamal ignored her and drove off.

Aramide

I had that strange feeling again, and that same red car was in the parking lot. What's happening? Am I being stalked?

Aramide was lost in her thoughts as Sonia watched her walk through the front door.

"Did something bad happen?"

"No," she said, still apparently thinking.

"I hope not. Hey, I think I actually saw my Prince Charming today!" Sonia was suddenly all smiles.

Aramide looked at her. "For real...? Come, when are we going to hear about your success story instead of boys all the time? If you'll excuse me, I have a job to do, and I'm not going to stand here and listen to talk about boys - not even men!"

Aramide left, leaving Sonia confused.

"Did I say anything wrong?" Sonia murmured to herself, feeling insulted. "It's my fault, I'm the one trying to share gist."

Jamal

Jamal walked into his bedroom to find Evelyn sitting on his bed, busy with her phone. His room was quite elegant. Straight out of a home décor magazine. It had been redecorated by his mom before he'd returned from Singapore. Themed grey and white, it even had a faux fireplace. His guitar hanging on the wall.

"I assume you're here for a reason." Jamal began to

unbutton his shirt.

Evelyn scowled at him, laser-scanning him from head to toe, slowly.

"You dropped her off even after I insisted you shouldn't."

Jamal said nothing, seemingly more interested in changing his clothes.

"You made me look stupid, Jamal," Evelyn continued.

"That's because you decided to be stupid." Jamal walked to his walk-in closet and threw his clothes into the laundry basket.

"I beg your pardon?! What's come over you? You've changed."

"Now there's a pot calling the kettle black." Jamal walked back out wearing a loose blue t-shirt and loose grey cotton drawstring sweatpants.

Mrs Abayomi wanted to inform her son about how her outing went but stopped at Jamal's door to eavesdrop when she heard their voices.

"Tell me, are you in a relationship with her?"

Jamal stood by his dressing table, looking into the mirror.

"Since she returned, you both have been thick as thieves."

"That's because she is my best friend," Jamal finally said and turned to face her. He'd thought he had found love, even though their relationship was an arranged one. And she had been so loving back in Singapore, but

BOUND BY FATE

since they got back to Nigeria, she had changed.

"I should be your best friend, not her. FYI, I am your girlfriend, not hers. What I want is what you will accept!"

"Ta-da! I'm back!" Mrs Abayomi interrupted, opening the door. Mrs Abayomi had been dreaming of a union with the Cookers for a long time. As far as she was concerned, no matter what, these two had to make this work.

"I had a swell time," Mrs Abayomi continued, smiling at Evelyn, who plastered a smile on her face as though nothing was wrong and then turned to her son. "Guess what?"

"I don't think this is a good time for guessing games, Maami."

"Oh, please!" Evelyn frowned at Jamal then smiled at Mrs Abayomi. "You've got something."

"Yes, smart girl, that's why you are my daughter," Mrs Abayomi said, bending to embrace her. "I got you both a reserved table at Spice Route; I'm sure you've missed those Asian dishes, son. It's a date from me to the both of you!" She smiled, looking from one to the other, hoping her lie wouldn't be detected.

"That's kind of you, Mommy," Evelyn glanced at Jamal, waiting to hear what he had to say. He ought to learn a thing or two from his mother, she thought. "Jamal and I would love to go."

"Okay then, I will take my leave. I have Bible study

later on."

"Alright." Evelyn blew Mrs Abayomi a kiss.

"You should pick up cues from your mom on how to treat a lady."

Jamal walked over to his desk, sat down and turned on his MacBook.

"I'll be leaving you to your thoughts then," Evelyn sighed and got up to leave. *Perhaps a visit to a friend would do me some good right now.*

Jamal sighed and relaxed into his chair after Evelyn left the room. He was immersed in turbulent thoughts. He'd thought he was really in love; it turns out it was all lust and a sense of duty from the start. How did one go about breaking an engagement? Or should he give the relationship hope for a change?

Aramide

Ayofemi walked in, smiling. They had made a lot today, and before, he would be able to save up more than he'd hoped. He crossed the room to sit on the sofa and enjoy the break. The job was dangerous, but which job doesn't have its risks? Before long, he would be able to start providing like a real man was supposed to. He just hoped his sister would continue to be none the wiser. He thought so. Since she was rarely home. She hadn't even asked about his admission status yet. Whatever was happening to him now, he hoped it would last.

Jamal

"Why would Jamal do such?" Miss Nina asked after listening to Evelyn's recount of events at the Abayomi's.

"I suspect he's in love with her. God, I just hate all this!" Evelyn was on the verge of tears. Miss Nina tried to comfort her.

"Calm down, you might just be the one over-thinking things," she sighed. "You're bothering yourself while he isn't."

"Should I involve his parents? Maybe they will talk some sense into him."

"Not at all!"

"Then what should I do?"

"You know what? We'll go out and have some fun!" Evelyn looked at her with a 'bitch, what?' face.

"Yes, to cool down and strategize." Miss Nina smiled at her idea.

"Why can't we strategize now and have fun later?" she asked, not liking the idea a bit.

Nina got up and walked to the television and then turned to face her. "Well, I already have a bright idea, of sorts." She saw the eagerness in Evelyn's body language. "It's simple, you employ the services of a detective."

Evelyn sighed. "That's an invasion of privacy."

"Suit yourself. It's your problem anyways." But Evelyn nodded slowly, with a look like she was seriously thinking. "Now let me treat you to lunch at Hard Rock Café, eh?"

"Okay..."

"Relax girl, you will get your man's attention back."

Aramide

Aramide was riding slowly home. Today, she had finished early and planned on finally having a word with her brother. A jeep drove past her in the opposite direction. She turned when she heard her name from the driver. A guy dressed in a red shirt came down after parking.

"Oh my!" she said, stopping and taking a closer look at him. Deji was her ex-classmate from secondary school.

"Never thought I would see you again!"

"You look good! What's the secret?" she asked after assessing him.

Deji laughed. "I do, don't I? You don't look so bad yourself." She smiled. "I'm actually on my way to a business dinner. Can I have your number? We need to sit and talk."

"Of course."

"You never showed up for any of the reunions." Deji gave her his phone.

She smiled without giving him an answer as she typed in her digits in Deji's phone.

He took back his phone and saved her number. "We'll talk about that when we meet again. Call me."

"Okay."

He embraced her before walking over to his car and waved before driving off.

She watched him go. *Hmmm, if men had a say in people's futures, Deji wouldn't be driving a car and looking this good. The boy that was notorious in class and had been chasing after her back in school then. God be praised!* She sighed, then rode off, faster this time, enjoying the cool evening breeze.

When she got home, she parked her scooter and secured it with a chain. She got to the door and turned the knob, but it did not open.

"Where is this boy?" she wondered. *Thank God I had the spare key.*

"Thank You, Jesus, for bringing me home safely. May Your name be praised," she prayed softly before taking her seat on the sofa. She slipped off her shoes, the cool floor felt nice under her bare feet, fished her phone from her bag and dialled her friend Anna. Anna picked up at the fourth ring.

"Hey girl," she said, stretching on the couch when her brother walked in with a boy in the neighbourhood she had warned him not to hang out with. The two boys were shocked to see her there. Rasque collected the nylon bag from Femi and turned to leave.

"Stop right there!" she ordered, sitting up. "I will call you back Anna, yeah?" She ended the call and glared at the boys. They both looked dusty and overall unkempt. They were also acting weird.

"What's in that nylon?"

"My mother sent me on an errand to get this for her," Rasque replied.

"And why would you be the one holding the bag, Femi?" she asked, not believing a word Rasque said.

"I helped him carry it," Ayofemi replied.

"I see," she said, disappointed.

"My mother is expecting me. I'll have to leave." Rasque took the bag off Ayofemi and walked out before Aramide was even done nodding her permission.

Ayofemi fidgeted.

"Young man! How many times have I told you I don't want to see you with that boy?"

Ayofemi did his best to look innocent.

"See the way you look and smell. Where exactly are you coming from?"

"Down the street."

"And you got all that dust by just walking down the street?"

"I fell down."

"At the same time he did?" she paused. "Instead of you keeping yourself busy by studying, you are following a street boy whose family are known all over the neighbourhood to be miscreants and good for nothing! Tell me where I went wrong?!"

He lowered his gaze.

"Just go take your bath and come sit down. I would like to know if there has been any progress with your admission.

Ayofemi picked up a bucket by the corner and left to fetch water. He exhaled heavily as he walked to the tap.

Aramide admired the skyscraper that was A&J Oil and Logistics. She had a delivery to make here this morning. She walked into the building after being checked in by security and got directions for the lift and floor numbers that would lead her to Mr Jamal's office. She'd never liked lifts because they made her dizzy but she had no other choice as she was in a hurry. She got in with a beautiful lady whom she later recognised as the one she'd seen in Miss Nina's apartment days ago.

"Good afternoon," she said courteously. The lady gave her a smile. *What's up with her not speaking?* "I'm going to the 6th floor…" she said, waiting for the lady to respond.

"Same," mouthed the lady.

She punched the button, and the lift began to rise. She didn't know what happened, but all of a sudden, she found herself being supported by the lady while struggling to keep hold of the large envelope in her hand.

"Are you alright?" the lady asked.

She took some deep breaths as she tried to steady herself. "I'm fine…" She paused to catch her breath again. "…Very fine."

The lady smiled. She brought out some type of candy from her bag. "Take this. It will help. I'm Evelyn, by the way."

"Thank you. I'm Aramide."

"Go on," the lady prompted her.

The candy wasn't sweet, but it was able to calm her a bit. She rested her back on the wall.

"Are you alright now?"

"Yes, I am. Thank you."

"Is everything alright there?" came a voice from the speaker in the lift.

"Yes." Evelyn pushed a button and got the lift rising again. She'd apparently stopped the lift when Aramide fainted. "Okay?" Evelyn held Aramide's hand to make her feel more comfortable.

"Thank you."

"You're welcome."

They were both silent until the ding indicated their arrival. Evelyn mouthed 'bye' to her as she walked out.

Aramide took a few seconds before her hand on the door and then walked to the secretary and introduced herself. After getting him to sign the delivery paper, she turned to leave, but this time, she went down the stairs. It took a lot of time and a little rest along the way, but she made it down and then outside the building, breathing in the air freely.

Just then, she experienced that peculiar feeling again, and she felt eyes on her, so she turned around, searching, and saw a dark-skinned, 'model-physique' guy in a dashing pink suit. He'd just got down from the red car with a briefcase in hand. He stared at her strangely before walking into the building.

Aramide breathed out and then realised she had been holding her breath. She walked to and sat on her scooter for a while to think. Then she remembered she had a date with an ex-classmate later. She started the engine and rode off.

It was mid-noon when Anna got a call from the police station and got the shock of her life. After getting permission from the office, she set out to bail out the brother of her best friend. Her friend who had been out working her ass off without knowing what her brother was up to. She got there and, after pulling some strings, the boy and his friend were released. Ayofemi looked bashful, tattered and bruised. He got into Anna's car while Rasque went with his sister, who had been there waiting but was unable to bail them out. Thank God he knew Anna's number by heart, he didn't want to cause his sister to worry.

In the car, they were both silent. Anna had not looked at him once during the drive, and Ayofemi was dreading her questions. She looked at him briefly, then back at the road.

"Why didn't you inform me or your sister that you wanted to work?"

Ayofemi was quiet.

"I know very well I'm talking to a human being!" She took a peek at her ringing phone. "It's your sister calling."

Ayofemi begged her with his eyes.

She sighed and answered the call via Bluetooth. "Hi friend, I'm driving. I will call you back later...." She went silent for a while. "Sure. That's awesome. And stop by my house after the dinner we really need to talk.... Okay, bye." She ended the call and hoped that keeping the situation from Aramide wouldn't be an issue later.

"I will take you to a pharmacy to clean up your wounds."

"Thank you," Ayofemi mumbled. Anna didn't care for his gratitude. He was like her own little brother.

Jamal

Evelyn walked into the living room. She wasn't happy about her visit to A&J Oil and Logistics. Her conversation with Jamal had not gone the way she had planned at all. He had been cold to her. In the end, he had set a date for them, no doubt as a way of ending their conversation and dismissing her.

"You look disturbed," Mrs Davis Cooker had walked in on her daughter standing in one spot, lost in thought.

"Do I?" She went over and kissed her mom on the cheek. She forced a smile. "How are you, mom?"

"I'm good, but you, what's up with you?" Mrs Davis

Cooker asked, sensing her daughter's distress.

"Nothing, it's just the stress from driving; you know I don't like to drive, especially in Lagos here."

Mrs Davis Cooker looked confused. "And that got you to standing there all this while, deep in thought?"

Evelyn was slightly shocked; she hadn't realised she'd been standing still for that long. "Mom, I need to go freshen up. I have a date with Jamal."

Mrs Davis Cooker smiled, the previous subject of their conversation quickly forgotten. She loved the Abayomi family and thought it would be great to be in-laws. "Your dad made a great choice for you," she said sagely.

"Yes, he did," Evelyn smiled. "See you later, Mom."

Evelyn hurried off to her room while Mrs Davis Cooker smiled and sat down to watch a series on TV.

Aramide

Aramide walked into KFC to meet Deji. She was a bit late. She picked up her phone to call him, but she saw him wave at her from inside.

"Wow, I was beginning to think you would stand me up," Deji said to her when she got to his table.

She noticed he didn't get up to greet her like a normal date would, but she smiled and took her seat. In his defence, she was late. "Good evening."

"Evening, how was work and hope you are very

well?" Deji replied, still smiling.

"Fine, thank you. I'm sorry for coming late."

"No problem. What should I get you?" Deji asked.

"Water would be fine," she smiled.

"You can get water in your house," Deji joked. "Coming here gets you something better than water." He stood and went to the counter.

She looked around her – the eatery was bubbling and then at Deji at the counter. *Would I date him if he asked? Maybe I would say yes.* He was walking back to their table with a tray in his hand. Apparently, he'd decided to carry their food to the table himself. She smiled.

"Hope you like chicken and chips?" Deji put the tray on the table and placed a plate and a bottle of juice in front of her, sat down and set a plate in front of him.

"Thank you."

"You're welcome," Deji murmured and dug in while she nibbled on her chips.

"Can I ask my questions now, while we eat?"

She sipped her juice. "Sure."

"I thought you would have bagged a first-class degree as a computer scientist by now, but I was surprised when I heard you didn't even go to university."

She smiled. "I have some goals which going to a university doesn't allow for right now."

"Really?" Deji asked, surprised. "What? If I may ask?"

"My brother," she said simply.

"Then he must certainly owe you a lot. So, how far?"

"I don't get…"

"I mean, what progress have you made in achieving this goal?" he asked, looking serious now.

"Oh. He is now about to go to university." She bit off a chip.

"That's great. Where is he planning on going?"

"He chose Lagos State University, but we are still waiting for an admission," she said with pride.

"Would you mind if I helped out?" Deji asked.

"Can I get back to you on that?" she replied cautiously.

"Okay."

He was done with his food. "If I offered you an opportunity to learn a professional course, would you take it?"

This was classic Deji. He never cared too much for ceremony or whatever the rules were for proper and polite social engagement. Back in school, he was always bold, daring, and willing to take risks based solely on instinct. Still, she was a little surprised and asked:

"Why?"

"All this time, you have thought about only one thing, neglecting your personal development—I'm sorry, but not sorry to say this." He paused while she frowned at him. He smiled. "This is an opportunity I'm giving you. Let's say I'm being kind because of your kindness to me back in secondary school."

And he had obviously retained the charm that he often used to get himself out of otherwise awkward or sticky situations. She smiled in spite of herself. "Well, I wasn't doing it for any kind of reward or anything."

"Sill, I appreciate. Maybe you should go home and think about it."

When she didn't reply, he left her to her thoughts.

Aramide walked down to Anna's house with her scooter after Deji had dropped her off - and gotten her scooter out of the back of the car - and they'd said their goodbyes.

She was feeling conflicted now. She was thinking about what Deji said. In the car, he asked her if it was a crime to start thinking about her own self and stop worrying so much about her brother. She had always believed that what she was doing was what her parents wanted and that they would be proud of her if they knew.

She arrived at Anna's, and Anna opened the door before she could knock.

"Hey, girlfriend," Anna said, frowning at Aramide, who didn't look happy. "The date didn't go well?"

She walked in and sat on a sofa, still quiet. Anna closed the door and joined her. "What is it?"

"Tell me, as a friend, all that I have been doing, is it a waste?" she asked, hoping for a 'No' from her.

Anna frowned. "Was that what he told you?"

She sighed. "This year has been tough and confusing for me, and now I'm questioning myself if all I've been doing is right."

"There's no perfect human, girl. Everyone makes mistakes."

"Deji is right. Just being a 'good Christian' and churchgoer is not enough, but also letting God have the access to direct one's life is important."

"Okay...?" Anna was lost and muttered to herself. *What sort of date was this?*

"I've been leaning on my own strength and only focusing on one thing when I could have been broadening my horizons with God's help."

Anna nodded. She thought she might like this guy that had got her friend thinking this way.

"So, what happened? You said you wanted to talk."

Ayofemi heard his sister's question and walked into the living room, his head low, dejected and ready to tell her the whole truth.

"What happened?" she asked, surprised to see her brother at Anna's and concerned asked, "Did you get into a fight?"

"Worse than that," Anna said. "Look, Ara, that ex-classmate of ours that told you such-and-such, I would advise that you listen to him because if I tell you what Femi got himself into, you won't believe me."

"Is that so?" she asked him, hoping Ayofemi would

say it was just a fight, but she knew Anna had already confirmed it was much, much worse.

"See, I had to go bail him, and that's thanks to a certain person I know. Your brother was caught selling hard drugs, Ara! To underage kids! And that's no small offence."

"What? Femi!!!"

"That's not all. He also confessed to me that he'd invested his JAMB money. So he has been lying to you all this time. Can you imagine a boy scamming his own sister?" Anna glanced at Femi, still offended by his confession to her earlier.

"Where did I go wrong?" She raised her arms up and dropped them, defeated.

Ayofemi was disappointed in himself. He didn't remember the last time he'd seen his sister look this way. "I'm sorry!" He fell to his knees in tears.

"Are you—?"

"Shut up, Anna! Can you excuse us, please?"

Anna was shocked by the way Aramide cut her off. "Okay… I will leave," she said and left for her room.

"I don't have a word to say to you, but know I'm so disappointed." She let the tears drop. "Where did I go wrong? I've always made you my priority, neglecting my own needs." Ayofemi started to speak, but his sister cut him off with a raised hand. "I don't want to hear a thing from you. We are going home. I will think this through, and you will hear from me tomorrow." She wiped her tears.

BOUND BY FATE

The day had been momentous.

After more tears and less sleep, Aramide finally decided on what to do, but first, she had to call Anna and ask for her forgiveness. She looked at her brother, who was asleep on the bed. She had stayed on the couch. She had to establish that he couldn't be seen with that boy anymore when he woke up. She just hoped he would listen. She had also made other serious, life-altering decisions.

She heard her phone ring, looked at the caller ID, and picked it up.

"Morning Anna, I'm so sorry about yesterday," she pleaded.

"I understand. I called to find out how you're feeling this morning."

"Better. I'll stop by your place later on... Yes, Femi's..." She looked at her brother. "...sleeping."

"Take it easy with yourself, huh? I got to prepare for work. And I'll be back late. I've got bible study in church," Anna said.

"Can you come pick me up for church?"

Anna was surprised. "Won't you be working today?"

"I'm calling in sick."

"Are you sick?" Anna asked, knowing Aramide wasn't one to lie.

"I don't particularly feel good, not good enough to

do any work, anyways," she replied. Also, she had been using her job as an excuse to not go to church on weekdays and sometimes on Sundays. Even Anna, whom she felt wasn't "living right," had the time to attend church services and was also a worker in the church. One truly shouldn't judge a book by its cover.

"I'll come over by five-thirty to pick you up then."

"I'll be ready by then. Have a nice day." She ended the call. Now she just had to call in and inform them she wouldn't be in today.

When there's an opportunity to start over, qa/QA2 one should take it. Not forgetting it's important to examine oneself periodically to be sure of one's continual personal growth.

Jamal

At an exclusive bar, a lady dressed in a red dinner gown is unhappy and drunk but keeps on drinking. She had failed her dad and would be a disappointment to him… But strangely, she feels free. And so, she begins to laugh. She laughs while the other patrons give her funny looks. She doesn't care. She would face her issues tomorrow, but tonight was a night to be reckless.

Jamal sat on his chair in his office, clicking away with the mouse. He was checking out some slides which would be used for his presentation in the meeting with his dad and other shareholders. He remembered his date with Evelyn the previous night, when he ended the relationship. He had not informed his parents, and he was also sure Evelyn had not told her parents because if she had, his dad, Mr Abayomi,2Q would have been on his case already – his mom too. He hoped she did it the right way if she decided to tell them. If not, he would use the envelope he received as his evidence and defence. He had not even brought it up yesterday because he knew how her mind worked. He knew she would find a way to deny that the pictures were from her or that they were, at least, her doing. His phone rang, and he picked it up.

"Hey man," he answered Tade.

"Where are you?"

He sensed something by the way Tade sounded. "I'm at work. Is there any issue?"

"Tebi got in an accident."

"Oh my!! I hope it's not serious?"

"It seems she has been in a coma since last night. I'm at the hospital, and I'm scared. She is going to die without me telling her that I love her."

"She's a fighter. She'll... She'll be fine. Text the hospital address, please." Jamal looked at his secretary, who had just walked in. "I'll call you back, man. Hold on, she will be fine," he said, feeling the weight of his friend's distress as well as his own.

"What is it, Dele?" he asked his secretary.

"Your mom called the office. She said she could not

reach you on your mobile phone."

"Did she leave a message for me?"

"Yes, she did. She said your fiancée is in Chevron Hospital, admitted for drink poisoning; that she is stable now; and that you go check on her."

Jamal sighed. Today was one uneventful day.

"Ok, I'll call her." Dele was about to leave but stopped to pass another message.

"Your father is around. He said, 'hope you are ready for the meeting?'"

Jamal almost laughed at the ridiculousness of the message in the light of recent events, but then his phone beeped, indicating the arrival of a message. "When's the meeting again?"

Dele checked his watch. "Forty-five minutes from now."

He checked his watch also. "Any board members around?"

"Yes. Chief Shonekan, Mrs Bade and your fiancée's father."

He raised an eyebrow at the last one. "You can go."

Dele left. Jamal's thoughts were all over the place, and he had to struggle to put them in some kind of order. He had to tell Dele to start referring to Evelyn's father as Dr Davis henceforth; tidy up and get himself in the proper mindset for the meeting - He had called for it so he had to deliver his best performance to impress the old dogs; and after the meeting he would go over to see Tebi at the hospital.

BOUND BY FATE

Aramide

Ayofemi was home alone when Rasque came visiting. He had been ignoring the boy since the arrest incident, and besides, he was still healing. Also, he hadn't gone out in obedience to his sister's directive.

"Guy, I never see you for some time. Wetin happen? You just got small beating and disappeared as if you had died." Rasque took a seat, looking at Femi, who sat up on the bed.

"Don't you have manners?"

Rasque frowned.

"The door is there for you to knock on, and you can't come in without being invited."

"Hold it there! Me sef get my own house. What's with this manner of a talk? Your door was open, Mr Man!"

"Even at that, you still have to knock," Ayofemi insisted. "What brought you here? Didn't you get the memo? My sister doesn't want you here."

Rasque hissed at what he said. "Forget that one. We are in debt."

Ayofemi looked at him questioningly. "I don't get you."

"The goods we had before the police picked us... the dealer is expecting his cash. These guys don't hear stories."

"How much is the debt?" Ayofemi asked, hoping they could pay with the money they had realised so far.

"See, it's one hundred thousand."

Ayofemi was shocked.

"I know we usually deal goods worth fifty thousand, but seeing the profit we were getting, I decided to top up, not knowing we were going to be busted that day. Where are we going to get the hundred thousand?"

"I have my twenty-five thousand naira. We can join it with your own and give him fifty," Ayofemi said.

"See, you know I'm the one feeding my family. The whole twenty-five is gone. Even if I had it, where are we going to get the remaining fifty?" Rasque asked.

"Ye! What my sister said was right!"

"See, there's a solution. I know another dealer we can get goods for free from. We will get them and pay these other guys in instalments," Rasque said, proud of his idea. "And one of my friends agreed to introduce me to some rich men's children that spend heavily on drugs," he added.

"You are insane! Listen to yourself! Is it because you didn't get injured like I did? And it's like it didn't enter your head what it means to go to prison!" Femi looked at Rasque like he was mad.

"If I was insane, do you think you can stand? Welcome to the streets, bro! Where boys become soldiers. I just came to inform you to be prepared. Tomorrow we are going out. I did not come here to listen to whining." Rasque stood up. "Charlie, me out."

Rasque left.

'God, I'm so in it now.' How am I going to go about getting this money now? I can't tell my sister about this. I can't go with Rasque's idea either. I have to think of something.

Aramide walked into the House of Tebi, planning to submit her resignation letter. She had decided to take Deji's offer. Tina, her friend at the delivery company, together with Merissa, who had finally returned from her sick leave, had agreed to handle her delivery for a month. She believed she would be able to get things sorted out before a month's time and she would be able to decide what to do.

She met Sonia and Peace at the counter.

"I heard you were sick. Hope you are better now?" Sonia said before she had a chance to say anything. "And Peace said you got a guy."

She was used to Sonia by now. "Morning to you too, and thank you, I'm better."

"Morning and good to hear you are fine," Peace said, hissing at Sonia for her manners.

"Morning, Ara. I did miss you." Sonia smiled.

Aramide smiled back. "Is the manager in?"

"He is not," Peace replied.

"Didn't you hear? Madam's daughter is seriously ill so he went to pay them a visit at the hospital," Sonia informed her.

"Newspaper vendor," Peace snorted.

Sonia pointedly ignored Peace while Aramide fished out her phone from her purse.

"I'll call him." She excused herself and went outside.

"What's the big deal that she has to go outside?" Sonia asked, frowning.

"She has to hide from people like you nah."

Sonia laughed. "Really? And not you? Are you not the person that informed me about seeing her with a guy at KFC some days ago, and here you are, sinner preaching to sinner."

"I just remembered I have something of great value to do." Peace walked away.

"What rubbish, its Sonia this… all the time! Everyone is forming innocent…" she stopped ranting when she saw Aramide coming back in.

"I will have to wait for him." She sat on a high stool behind the counter.

"You aren't working today as well?" Sonia asked softly

"No, I'm not. I came to tender my resignation letter."

"Oh!" Sonia was surprised. "You got a new job? Why?"

"I'm going ahead to make something out of my life like you guys have always insisted."

Sonia smiled, though she felt a bit sad. "That's good, but I will miss you… Chai!" She went over to hug Aramide.

"I'll miss you too." Aramide smiled genuinely. She

saw that Sonia held back tears. She was a drama queen but a fine colleague. She would miss this young adult.

Jamal

Jamal walked silently through the park. The park looked deserted, and he was alone with the trees. He had been thinking deeply since his visit to the hospital. The police had confirmed that Tebi and the Taxi driver had been running away from suspected killers. They found evidence of multiple gunshots and bullets on and in the car. Eyewitnesses in that area corroborated the story. Tade was still scared that she wouldn't make it, and he was hanging on by a thin thread. She was to be flown abroad for further treatment.

Going over to his and Tebi's usual spot, it was one of the places that the photos showing both of them together that he had received had been taken, where they sat whenever they came here, he prayed, 'lord, please let her live. '

He had been praying softly for a while when he got that curious, jolting feeling again. He looked up and saw that a lady had occupied a nearby bench, and then he noticed she was in tears. Jamal brought out a handkerchief and went over to sit by her. Up close, he recognised her as the pretty lady he had spotted at random times. The lady didn't look at him at all. He wondered what could be making her cry. They were both silent for a while.

Aramide let the images of the past and all her mistakes play through her mind's eye, crying and letting the tears flow out freely with the memories, hoping she would feel lighter afterwards.

Jamal wondered what pains and demons she was letting out. He held the handkerchief tightly and closed his eyes, hoping the breeze would carry away some of his own sadness.

The evening breeze refreshing,
its current perfect.
Could it take their sorrows and pains away?
These two souls,
ignorant of their compasses leading them
On the same journey,
to the same destination
A lifelong bond.

They felt Zephyr caress their skin.
And a mysterious stream of current wove through them;
Sparking a new beginning
Different worlds mesh
Two threads,
stringing to form a single cord;
Strong enough to withstand the pressure
 and the pain.
It was what forged them in the first place.

BOUND BY FATE

"Here." Jamal passed over his handkerchief to her.

Aramide looked at him curiously. She felt a kind of peace radiating from this stranger. She took it and began to wipe her face.

"Feeling better now?" he asked, looking at her.

Aramide smiled sadly, "If by 'better' you mean 'cheered up', I don't think so."

"Oh…" he mouthed. "Do you mind sharing?"

"Why do you think I would share my problems with a stranger?" Aramide asked, amused.

He smiled. "I'm Alvin."

It was strange how she felt like trusting this guy. "Aramide."

"Ara. What a great name."

"Thank you."

He moved his eyes around then back to her.

"It's the first time I've seen someone else in this park. I come here with a friend a lot."

She folded her hands on her lap.

"I found the place today, or, should I say, it found me."

They both laughed.

"Did you feel an angel pass by just now?" he joked.

"I thought so too," Aramide said.

He couldn't tell if she was serious or was joining in on his joke.

"Are you sure you aren't the angel we are talking about?"

Aramide stared at his face attentively now, with the help of moonlight. She saw that he was handsome, his face was symmetrical, and his dark eyes looked like they were made for comfort. She saw that he had on a black suit - probably coming from work. She also saw that she recognised him.

"Are you done drinking me up?" He smiled.

Aramide blushed. It was rude to stare at people's faces for too long. "I'm filled." She tried to redeem the awkward moment with a clever reply.

"My friend, the one I usually come here with, is in a coma right now, and they say there's a slim chance of recovery."

"Oh!" She felt sorry for him.

"Yeah…"

They fell silent.

"I'm not telling you this so you can feel sorry for me. I guess I'm saying this to say that life oftentimes doesn't go our way, but that doesn't mean it's the end… I feel it strongly inside me that she will survive…" Jamal suddenly became calm and quiet. But before he could stop himself, he suddenly broke down in a series of muffled sobs, letting out the tears he had been holding back.

Aramide took his hand and held it tightly, and he leaned his head on her shoulder, sobbing.

"I lost my parents at the tender age of ten. I had to learn to survive for myself and my brother who was still very young, just clocking six. We had no relatives from either of our parents who could help. They didn't know us and we didn't know any of them. We were only children."

Jamal shed his tears quietly as he listened to her story; Aramide had returned his handkerchief to him. He was the one in need of its services now.

"The only family alive from my dad's side of the family that we knew was in prison. He was a paedophile. We stopped going on vacations to his home after that."

"Did… Did you know any of the kids he molested?" he asked cautiously.

She began to cry fresh tears. "Myself and some other kids."

He felt anger rise slowly in his chest. He sat up rigidly, looking at their surroundings, trying to calm down.

"Is he still alive?" he asked, handing her the handkerchief.

She wiped her tears with the already soaked handkerchief. "He died in jail."

He moved closer and wrapped her in an embrace. He couldn't imagine the pains she must have gone through from childhood. His only hope was that she healed in time.

"My best friend's family took me and my brother in. They were nice and did their best, but soon I had to leave. They wanted to focus on giving their daughter the best training possible. So I had to find a job and support myself and my brother, neglecting my own desires and dreams, and now feel like I've failed both of us…" she cried. "All this time spent busying myself with work and not having the time for my brother, myself or for God."

Jamal didn't know what to say. He just let her cry in his embrace. The wrist chain he wore as a symbol of his engagement unclasped and fell off his wrist.

Evelyn pretended to be asleep on the hospital bed while her dad and mom discussed in hushed tones.

"She has just been an issue. Why would a child refuse the parents' instructions?" Dr Davis Cooker said.

"At least she is recovering. Don't make her hear what you are saying biko nu," Mrs Davis Cooker pleaded.

"When she wakes, I will still tell her. She shouldn't misbehave just because she is your only child!"

"She is your only legitimate child! I don't care about whatever children you have with your mistresses."

"I can see where she gets her character from. Talk to her and make sure she understands that what she did is foolishness!"

"I will talk to her but not for you because I don't want anything to spoil her marriage to that family."

Evelyn cried silently as she listened to them. She had heard rumours of illegitimate children, but now, it has been confirmed. She was turned away from them so they could not see her face. It seemed like they still hadn't found out that Jamal had called off the engagement. She wondered how her dad would take the news. She heard a third voice in the room, and her heart jumped in her chest. Were her parents about to find out now? Mrs Abayomi was exchanging pleasantries with her parents.

Evelyn wished she had died. Mrs Abayomi would no doubt be hurt. She had gone out of her way multiple times to plan dates and dinners for them. She listened attentively to what Mrs Abayomi was saying.

"I've tried reaching him, but his phone has been switched off. I'm scared," Mrs Abayomi lamented.

"I will be going now. Thanks for coming, ma'am." Mrs Davis Cooker frowned at her husband as he left. She walked over to comfort her in-law-to-be. "I'm sure he is fine. Maybe he's somewhere, cooling off because of all the recent events. He had to visit two hospitals in the space of one day yesterday."

"Poor girl... in coma," Mrs Abayomi sighed.

"I heard she is going to be flown abroad."

"Yes, this week. I pray she comes out of it."

Mrs Davis sighed. "Her parents must be devastated."

Evelyn was sad to to hear about Tebi. She wondered what had happened. Was it a motor accident? She didn't like her much because she thought Tebs was her rival, but she felt sorry for the girl. However, there was some small consolation in that Mrs Abayomi did not seem to be aware of the breakup as yet. Perhaps there was still hope. Perhaps all wasn't lost. Not even with Jamal...

Jamal parked close to Aramide's compound. It was quite late when they arrived at her place.

"Thank you for the ride."

"You're welcome... I guess this is a goodnight." Jamal smiled at her, and she smiled back.

"Would you mind if I came around again?" Jamal waited patiently for her reply.

"I wouldn't. If there's more ice-cream involved," she joked, indicating the *Cold Stone* pack on the floor in front of her.

"If that's the ticket, I wouldn't mind buying the whole building."

Aramide laughed. "I have to go; my brother probably is worried about me."

"Ok," he pressed the unlock button. "Goodnight and sweet dreams."

"You too," she smiled, got out and waved at him. He waved back, watching her go in before driving off.

Jamal remembered that he had turned his phone off before leaving for the park. He turned it on and saw so many voicemails from his mom and others. "Oh boy!" He dialled her number, and she picked up after the first ring.

"Where are you, and where have you been, Jamal Alvin Abayomi?! I have been worried!" she lamented.

"I'm sorry, ma, I'm on my way home, driving currently."

"WILL YOU LOOK FOR SOMEWHERE TO PARK AND CALL ME BACK?!"

"I just want to let you know I'm fine, and I will be home soon."

His mom ended the call; she had warned him about driving while talking on the phone. Baring his soul wasn't something he would have done with a stranger before today—or someone who was not Tebi.

God works in mysterious ways. And everything happens for a reason.

Jamal was having breakfast in the dining room. It had been two weeks since he paid a visit to his newest friend, Aramide, and he planned on stopping by her place today. Anytime they spoke on the phone, he left their conversation feeling wonderful. He was falling in love with the girl, but he was treading carefully in order not to send her running from him.

"What's got you smiling?" Chief Abayomi sat down and opened the newspaper on the table.

"Good morning, Dad." He smiled at his dad.

"Morning, son. How was your night?" Chief Abayomi's eyes were on the paper in his hand.

"Your oats will be brought in a minute." Mrs Abayomi walked into the dining area to inform her husband.

"Morning, Ma," he said to his mom.

She kissed his cheek. "I didn't know you were in here. Mrs Davis Cooker called."

He sighed. "What did she say?"

Chief Abayomi watched his son discreetly.

"'You haven't been to visit them!' And 'why?'" she asked as she bent to give her husband a peck. "I told her you have been busy. She admitted that your fiancée informed them that you had been calling every day and that there was no need for you to come over. But I guess they want to see your face."

"Hmm, she should probably listen to her daughter." He wasn't surprised that Evelyn had not told her mom about the broken engagement – heck, he hadn't.

Mrs Abayomi frowned. "No matter how busy you are, find time to take your wife-to-be out!" she said, not noticing the frown on Jamal's face. "Let me check on the cooker. I'll be back." She left.

Chief Abayomi stared at his son, who was obviously lost in thought, for some time, and then he finally spoke: "Is there trouble in paradise?"

Jamal looked at his father but didn't reply.

Chief Abayomi continued, "I noticed you don't have your wrist chain on, and it seems to have gone missing for some time now. Either fix whatever issues you got or end it."

His dad had been observant; he wished his mom was too. "Dad…"

"There's no point brooding over spilt milk. In all

BOUND BY FATE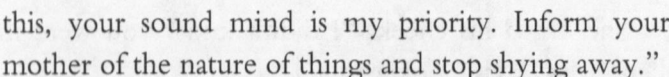

this, your sound mind is my priority. Inform your mother of the nature of things and stop shying away."

"You aren't annoyed or disappointed, sir?"

Chief Abayomi smiled. "Why should I be? We aren't benefitting anything from this. It's the Cooker's who will. You are my son, and you will take your place as CEO someday. All I want is for you to have a healthy mind while running with the vision for the future of the company. A vision you helped fine-tune."

"Oh…" He was relieved to hear this from his dad.

"Here it comes…"

Jamal lifted the paper to his face as Mrs Abayomi came in with the maid who was carrying a tray with the breakfast.

"What are you both discussing?" Mrs Abayomi looked from son to father. The maid placed the tray on the dining table and stood aside.

"Got to go." Jamal stood up. "I'll see you both later."

"Do try to inform her, will you?" Chief said to his son as he started to leave.

Mrs Abayomi blessed her son: "Be safe and do what your father said. Visit Evelyn."

Jamal didn't reply as he left.

"That boy is stubborn sometimes. So unromantic."

Chief Abayomi nodded.

"He got that from you."

Chief Abayomi smiled.

Aramide

Aramide went to visit Anna, who was down with malaria and had stayed home from work. Anna laid on the sofa covered with a duvet.

"So how are the classes so far?" Anna asked Aramide, who was busying herself with her phone.

"It's been amazing. I'm grateful I took Deji up on it."

"Ok." Anna watched her friend, who was smiling foolishly at her phone. She cleared her throat, "Hmm-mhmm."

"You've been acting different…" Aramide looked up reflexively. "…I mean in a good way. Is there something you aren't telling me?"

"You tell me; you are the one seeing the 'difference'."

"Ok. Are you in love then? With a certain guy?" Anna joked.

"What certain guy…?" she smiled.

"Wow! There's more than one? Girl, you've grown wings!"

"You are a pumpkin-head," Aramide replied, laughing.

"If you insult me, I'll go straight to Mommy G.O. and inform her that her Protocol needs discipline."

"Just say you are jealous that Mommy loves me so much." Aramide returned her attention to her phone.

"Me?! You used your charms on her! We who have been attending the church longer than you, and you from nowhere stole her heart."

"You are not serious," Aramide said.

"Ok, pray tell, did Deji ask you out? How long have you been his girl?"

"Are you actually sick or you are just pretending to be?"

"Yes, I'm sick, but I'm not too blind to see the writing on the wall. Maybe you'll be the first among us to get married." Anna smiled.

"Na wa! The malaria must be affecting your thinking." Aramide joked. "And for your information, Deji is married."

"What!? That's so sad."

"Lord have mercy on you," Aramide said while replying to a message on her WhatsApp and smiling.

"But wait. I'm sure it's a guy that's got you smiling. Confess now."

Aramide stood up, ignoring her friend. "I'm in the guest bedroom if you need me." She stuck out her tongue at Anna impishly.

"You cannot hide it for long!" Anna called out to her. "How can you leave a sick person alone, Ara?! Come back here!" Anna was genuinely happy for her friend. Even if she didn't completely know what was going on, she was sure that there was a man involved. "I'll report you to mommy G.O.!"

She did not reply. Anna's friend was a little forward sometimes. She has a friend - a male friend, yes - in her life but not a boyfriend. However, if Alvin asked her out, she knew she would say yes. She smiled to herself and sat on the bed.

Jamal

A lady in a black hoodie wearing dark sunglasses sat on a bench at a table in a local canteen. There is a plate of food on the table. She is waiting for someone. No one pays any attention to her. In fact, everyone there seemed to be pointedly minding their own business.

"Hey, boss." A guy looking very much like a tout sits on the bench across from her. He has hard eyes.

"I brought your balance." She throws a fat envelope on the table, and he picks it up.

"Nice," he said. "Should we continue the job?"

"That's why I'm here in person." She looks around surreptitiously, then back at him. "The police are investigating. You guys have to stop for now. No obstacles currently," the lady says to him.

"Okay. I'll tell the boys."

"I'll be leaving now."

He watched her go, waited for a while and then left as well.

The food is untouched.

A boy ran hastily, trying to cross the street without pausing to look, and got hit by a car. Jamal, a few cars behind, quickly parked his car and ran to the scene of the accident. People had gathered around the boy while the hit-and-run driver sped off.

"Jesu, omo lo mo oh!"

"That driver is heartless!"

"Na the boy run enter road!"

There was a lot of excited talk happening.

"Please, help me carry him to my car." Jamal *motioned to two able-bodied guys who moved instantly. He drove off to their family hospital, which was nearby.*

While all this was going on, a thug was watching from the sidelines with a face that said he was not happy with the turn of events.

Jamal was in his office working on his computer when he got a call from the doctor.

"Hello, Doc, how is the boy?" He put the phone on speaker and continued working.

"He is fine. Just some scratches and a swollen kneecap," Doctor Feranmi briefed him. "We have been able to reach a family member."

"Ok, that's good. I will come by later on."

"Alright, have a nice day."

"And you too, Doc." Jamal ended the call, but just as soon as got another call from Evelyn.

"Hello…" Jamal said when he didn't hear from her.

"Did you hear about the ball in my father's company?" Evelyn finally said.

"No, I didn't. What's the issue?"

"I'm expected to have you there with me."

"For what? Haven't you informed your family about our current status so they can stop expecting such things from me? Don't you think it's long overdue?"

"Please, Jamal, I will do that when the right time comes, but as a friend, please," Evelyn pleaded.

He sighed. "Okay, when is the ball and at what time?"

"It's today, by nine pm."

"And you are just informing me?"

"I'm sorry."

He groaned. "I'll do my best."

"Hope to see you there."

He ended the call. Now he had to cancel his trip to Aramide's. Well, hopefully, he would at least finally get some answers about the pictures that she had sent to him a while back.

Aramide

At the hospital, Ayofemi was sitting up with scratches on his face. He looked down at his hands. Anna sat on a couch by the bed.

"Why are you always looking for trouble? Or is it trouble that is looking for you?"

Ayofemi did not reply.

"I will leave if you don't answer me!" Anna said sternly.

"I'm sorry, Aunty Anna. As I told you, I was being chased by the supplier."

"How did you plan on raising the one hundred and fifty thousand, hmm?"

"These people will kill me if I don't pay up. I'm so ashamed of myself."

"You should be. I have called your sister, and she will be here soon." Anna heard someone at the door. She thought it was Aramide, but the one who walked in was a handsome man. *One I wouldn't mind going out for a couple drinks with,* she thought before she could stop herself.

"Good evening."

"Evening. How may I help you?" Anna asked.

"Erm, I was the one who brought him to the hospital," he said.

"Yes, the doctor told me. I'm so grateful." Anna, relieved, stood up from the couch and went over to the bed. *"Please, have your seat, sir."*

Ayofemi also voiced his gratitude.

"Thank you. I heard what you both were discussing. I'm sorry for eavesdropping…" The man scratched his head.

Anna smiled. *"So…?"* she asked.

"I was wondering if I could help."

Anna frowned thoughtfully as the man looked from the boy's face back to her's.

"Can I see you in the hall?"

"Okay." Anna looked at Ayofemi. *"I'll be back."*

"Okay," Ayofemi said, watching the two adults

leave to talk outside.

Aramide walked in through the hospital doors and towards the reception; when she got the call from Anna in class, she wasn't able to concentrate anymore. She felt guilty as she thought on what the pastor's wife advised her to do, which was getting him engaged in something productive and profitable for himself. She was given directions by the lady there, and she left. As she approached the room, she met Jamal and Anna deep in discussion.

"Anna!" she called.

"Oh, hello, Ara." Anna smiled.

"Hey…" Jamal said, surprised to see her.

"Ara, meet Mr Jamal, our good Samaritan!" Anna said, beaming.

"Evening, Alvin." She smiled.

"Evening. It's a surprise seeing you here. Is the boy your brother?"

"Yes, he is." She looked at Anna, who looked half-confused, half-amused. "I see you've met my friend, Anna."

"Yes," Jamal said, smiling.

"Where is he?" she asked Anna.

"He is inside and doing fine," Anna replied.

"I'll leave you both to talk then. Let me go see the doctor," Jamal said.

"Thank you," she said.

"You are welcome; I'll be back." Jamal left for the

doctor's office.

"Are you alright?" She decided to ask Anna, who was smiling sheepishly for some reason.

"I am. So you know this guy? You both have love written all over you."

Oh my God. "Not now, miss," she replied, shying away from Anna's question. "Let's go see Femi and get the details of his latest misfortune."

"Your brother's issue is dangerous." Anna frowned suddenly, thinking of Femi's problem.

"Really?" she asked, her eyes wide.

"Yes. Let's go in so he can spill the beans himself."

Ayofemi panicked on seeing his sister enter the room. He wondered what Anna had told her.

Jamal

Jamal was resting on the hood of his car and talking on the phone when he saw Aramide walk toward him.

"Hey," Aramide said.

He smiled at her. "Sorry, I forgot. Something came up Evelyn..." he said into the phone.

Aramide rested beside him on the car and looked at the sky.

"I will call you later." He sighed as the call dropped.

"Girlfriend?" Aramide asked.

"Ex."

"Oh." Aramide looked at his face. "Thanks for all you did. I'm really grateful."

"You're welcome." Jamal smiled at her. It was one of the things she liked about him. He didn't ever feign modesty.

"And I heard you plan on paying his debt... and employing him," she said with emotion on the edge of her voice.

"Yup."

"Thank you so much, Alvin. I'm really grateful."

"Are you?" he asked.

"I am! I wish you could see my heart and know just how much I'm thankful."

He wished she could see his own heart and see how much he was in love with her.

"You don't have to, 'Mide mi," he said lovingly. "You know something? I had actually planned on coming over to take you out today."

Aramide smiled. "Yeah? I was wondering when you were going to take me out," she said softly.

"I want to make a confession. I had planned a rosy, romantic stuff... but I guess God had his own plans..."

Aramide listened in silence. "Maybe He wanted me to say it under the sky, with the stars smiling brightly down on us as witnesses."

"Hmm," she barely breathed.

He leaned in close and pulled her to him, enfolding her in his arms. They stood motionless for a moment, in their own oasis of time.

Lifting her chin with a finger so he could stare into her eyes. He kissed her. It was the gentlest, most tender

BOUND BY FATE

contact she had ever had with another human being.

He broke the kiss and laid a finger on her lips to feel them.

"I love you, Aramide." The words came out as naturally as breathing. Then, he waited anxiously for her response. She held his entire being in suspense, just gazing at his face. He waited like a child uncertain of the reaction he would get for something he had done without thinking.

"You took my first kiss today..." she paused, then said, "You first stole my heart at the park but..."

His heart hammered at the "but." *Please, let her accept me.*

"But today, you have it willingly given." She smiled.

And he smiled back at her. Before she could say any other word, he was leaning down to kiss her again. It was sweet, sweeter, and much longer.

The stars in the sky shone brighter tonight. A new love was birthed.

At Chocolat Royal, a café in Lekki, two women sat down to enjoy cake and ice cream.

"So, first he cut off the engagement, and then he didn't attend the ball with you last night?" Nina inquired from Evelyn.

"Yes. It hurts, I won't lie to you, but I've decided to let him go." Evelyn sighed.

"Oh." Miss Nina smiled. "Poor girl. There are many

fishes in the river, my dear."

"Yes, there are, but men like Jamal are rare."

"Hmm, I agree. So, what did your dad say?" Miss Nina licked the ice cream off her spoon.

"That's another issue. I haven't told my parents. I've been avoiding the talk and making stories up for why he hasn't come to visit."

"That's dangerous, girl. You can't hide the truth for so long. It only makes it worse." Miss Nina frowned at her.

"I know. It's just that the right time hasn't come up." Evelyn picked at her cake with her spoon.

"I see… you need a boost, girl. You look pathetic. Is your dad at the office?"

"You know what? Let's forget about my issues and talk about your currently brightening career." Evelyn smiled at her.

"Ok, if you say so…" Miss Nina picked up her phone and quickly tapped out a message to someone. "The model industry has been tough, you know, and it hasn't been easy lately, but thank God for my pretty, innocent face."

They laughed.

At *Small Suya Spot*, Jamal and IK were both enjoying their suya and glasses of Chapman.

"I heard she's out of coma."

"Yeah, I got a call from Tade," Jamal replied.

"He's really tried. Leaving his father's company to

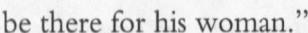

be there for his woman."

"That's a lot of sacrifice."

"Yeah, I don't think I can do that for any woman," IK declared unashamedly.

"That's because you haven't found Miss Right."

"Probably. So, how's your fiancée?" IK stabbed his toothpick into the meat and put it in his mouth.

"We ended things. A while back, actually."

IK smiled. "I knew from the start that this wouldn't work."

"How come everybody did but I didn't?" Jamal asked.

"You were blinded. The police haven't come up with any leads on the incident," IK said, referring to the attack on Tebi.

"About that, I received an envelope containing a picture of me and Tebi before the incident."

IK was shocked. "That's evidence that should be submitted to the police! Wait! Hope you aren't the next target?"

"I don't know. I've been suspecting Evelyn because she thought I was having an affair with Tebi. But I don't know if both things are related. The implications are scary to contemplate if they are."

"Hmm." IK was thinking. "She might have been the target because of that. You know you ought to submit the pictures to the police. I know you probably don't want to put Evelyn in trouble, but then again, she might not be behind any of this. I will put some things in motion on my end while the police work."

Jamal nodded. He knew he could trust IK with stuff like this. He had a lot of connections in a lot of places.

"Will you be going back to work later on?"

"Nah, I'm going to my girl's place."

Amused, IK asked, "Thou hast got a girl, and I knoweth it not?"

He chuckled. "I do. I did. Sorry, bro, you'll meet her one of these days."

"You need to be flogged," IK joked.

"Hello, guys," a lady's voice said.

"Um… Hi," IK replied to her.

"Jamal, hi," the lady smiled suggestively at him. He looked at her, then back at his suya. She was offended but kept smiling. "I saw you and your friend, and I decided to come join you guys. Can I sit?"

"Actually, we are about to leave," Jamal said before IK could speak.

"Oh…" the lady ran her hand through her hair, "Maybe next time then."

"Sure…" IK replied, confused by Jamal's behaviour.

"Bye guys. Bye, Jamal."

He didn't respond.

"Bye." IK said to her and she left. When she was out of earshot, he asked his friend if he knew her. He nodded. Then he asked him why he had been rude.

"I don't like the girl. She has this way of looking at me that makes me uncomfortable. We first met at one of those social function-slash-party things Evelyn's father is always so fond of throwing.

Everyone knew Evelyn and I were together, and yet she practically flirted with me unashamedly. We've met a couple times since then at random - although I suspect she plans these 'meetings' - and each encounter gets more inappropriate and uncomfortable than the last."

"Oh," IK said, noticing the way the lady kept staring at them from her table. "I wonder who she is and how she got invited. Dr Davis' events are usually quite exclusive. Did you ever talk to Evelyn about it?"

"Yeah. She asked me for the lady's name, and I said she never really offered it, and I never really asked. Although she hinted one time that she was 'a member of the family', whatever that means. Let's go, man, she gives me the creeps."

IK laughed. "You've got someone seriously crushing on you."

They both stood up to leave.

"Not a crush. I'd say a stalker. One day, she actually showed up at my place of work for no reason. I was so mad that I almost fired Dele that day! He said she convinced him that she was related to the Cookers and that she had a personal, urgent message for me."

"Ha! I'm sure it was. Damn! How come you're getting all the girls and I'm not?" IK joked as they walked to their cars. He got his car door open. "My regards to your new girlfriend."

"Sure thing, man. I will call you later, bro." He got into his driver seat at the same time IK did. IK honked at him before driving off.

He decided to go home first before going to see Aramide.

Aramide

"I'm done cleaning!" Aramide announced and sat down in Anna's living room to join her in watching the movie.

Anna lowered the volume and looked at her friend.

"I have been thinking…"

She just looked at Anna, waiting to hear what she had to say.

"God is really good. He gave you a man that's not just any man; a wealthy man's son."

"And?" she asked.

"Just wanted to let you know that you can't screw this up. I'm here if you need advice or help on anything but don't screw this up."

She smiled at her friend. "I won't, and thank you, Anna. I appreciate your concern."

"So, what job did he get, Ayofemi?"

She turned to the television. "He got him enrolled in an A-level centre. Femi will be leaving for the centre on Monday."

"Wow, that's the job?" Anna asked.

"Yes, all he asked Femi to do was study, and he would receive a regular allowance like a normal paying job."

"That's nice of him." Anna smiled. "So, does he have friends that he can introduce me to?"

She laughed. She would have made a snide comment about 'Anna and men', but she had noticed that her friend seemed to have changed these days. She considered whether it was because of the good things that she saw God was now doing in her best friend's life (who had started this year not having anything, compared to her). "Very funny!" She dodged the throw pillow Anna threw at her.

"You are not serious! I will ask him myself."

"That's your business."

"You are not nice." Anna feigned annoyance.

"Please let me watch this movie in peace."

And they talked throughout the entire movie.

Jamal

Doctor Davis Cooker walked into his house, furious and screaming for his daughter.

"Calm down. What has got you so worked up, my husband?" Mrs Davis Cooker walked into the living room when she heard her husband screaming for their daughter.

"Did she tell you!?"

Mrs Davis was puzzled. "Tell me what?"

"That she ended the engagement with Chief Abayomi's son."

Evelyn had heard her dad and had come down to the bottom of the stairs wearing a bathrobe. Then she heard what her dad said.

"Is that what Jamal told you?"

Doctor Davis Cooker turned around to face Evelyn. "That is none of your business! All I want is for you to fix it! Do you know what this marriage means to me?"

"So you don't care about me and how I feel?" Evelyn raised her voice.

"It's enough!"

"It's not, Mom. Why me? He doesn't care about us. It's all money, money and more money!"

"Is that how to talk to your father? My 'money' took you abroad to study in Singapore and gave you every luxury you have ever enjoyed and are still enjoying. If I had done half of what I did for you for my other children, I would be more appreciated!"

"Then go ahead and do that!"

Mrs Davis Cooker walked over and slapped Evelyn.

"Mom!" Evelyn placed her palm on the stinging cheek; she was shocked.

"You are a disappointment to me. I wasted my hard-earned money on you!" Doctor Davis Cooker pushed Evelyn aside as he climbed the stairs to his room. "You disgust me."

"You! I will come back for you," Mrs Davis Cooker said to her daughter and ran after her husband.

Evelyn sat on the bottom step. The cat had been let out of the bag. She would not cry, she decided. She wondered how her dad had gotten to know. She picked her phone from the pocket of her robe.

Jamal got a call from IK while he was driving. He told him that he had discovered that Jamal was being followed. So after he had hung up, he changed his plan to take Aramide back to her house and decided he would take her to meet his parents instead.

"Ooh! Let's get something for your parents then!" Aramide suggested.

"Don't worry about getting them anything." He kept glancing at the side mirror.

Aramide had noticed him doing this for some time now and asked, "What's going on?" She looked behind them and then at Jamal.

He looked at her – and just then his phone began to ring.

"I'm driving, Evelyn. I will call you back."

Aramide was suddenly tense as she heard his ex's name. She trusted Jamal and had believed him when he said that their relationship was platonic. They were made for each other; she really believed that. There had been signs. They had both discussed the interesting 'feelings' they used to experience before they knew each other. That could only have been rom God. Right…?

"He knows…? I didn't inform your Dad, Evelyn…… Ok."

He looked at the rear-view and side mirrors and didn't see the black car that he had spotted trailing them earlier on.

"Will you tell me what's going on?" Aramide insisted.

He kept his eyes on the road. "I'll tell you when we get home." At that, she fell silent and was suddenly alone with her thoughts. The least of which was not this particular worry: Will his parents welcome her?

Aramide

Ayofemi was so glad about his turnaround of fortune. At the A-level centre tomorrow, he planned on starting over and making his sister and Jamal proud. His sis had really hit a big one. Now, he looked forward to a future where he would not lack things.

"Lord, have mercy on me and bless my sister's relationship with Jamal. Let it lead to marriage o." Ayofemi smiled. "Amen."

Someone started knocking on the door, and immediately, Femi went to bolt the already locked door to doubly prevent Rasque from waltzing into their house as usual. He waited in front of the door, breathing heavily when he was done.

"Femi, I know you are in. Open up, man!" Rasque called.

Ayofemi did not answer. He instead retreated to the bed to lie down. He had learnt his lesson about bad friends, and he knew it was too dangerous to let Rasque in. Only God knew what he had come for now. He ran off when they were in debt, and now that they were debt-free, he was back.

"Femi!" Rasque kept knocking, and Ayofemi refused to move.

After about a minute of incessant knocking, he left when he realised his friend wasn't going to open up.

Ayofemi hissed.

"No plan of the enemy to terminate my newfound blessing shall prosper."

Ayofemi turned on the television and sat down to watch while he waited for his sister's return.

Jamal

Chief Abayomi watched his son and the girl from upstairs. He watched as she looked around the compound while they walked hand in hand towards the house. He sat in a rocking chair on his balcony. The lady looked different... sensible.

He didn't mind who his son married in the end; all that mattered was that she was able to withstand all that came with marrying into the family and the vision that he had put in place for his son and the company.

His wife, Ajoke Abayomi, would not readily accept a girl that was not from a family at least as prominent as the Cooker's family, but she would come around. He was happy with the way things were going.

The Cooker's were surrounded with a lot of scandal

and all manner of unsavoury rumours. From what he personally knew of the man, all Dr Davis Cooker cared about was aggressively growing his wealth, with little concern for the people who were trampled along the way.

"Hey Dad," Jamal called to his father as he walked out to the balcony.

"Is she the one?"

"Yes sir, the one I told you about. She is in the living room. I came to see if mom was in. Would you mind joining us, sir?"

"Sure I will, she's beautiful," Chief Abayomi said. "Have you heard from Tade?"

"Yes, Tebi is recovering very well, and the police say they're making progress in the search for the offenders."

"That's good to hear. I guess I can go meet my son's girl?" he stood up. The two men smiled.

"Yes, sir." Jamal led his dad inside.

Aramide

Anna was driving with Aramide in the passenger seat.

"Now that Ayofemi has gone, it's time you move into my place so we can stay together as I suggested before."

"I'll give you a response on that later," she replied.

"So, what was meeting the parents like?"

She smiled, remembering Jamal's dad. He was welcoming. "I met his father. I haven't seen his mother yet."

"Oh." Anna steered into the next street. "So was his dad okay?"

"Yes. He said he was happy that I had visited. I feel blessed having Alvin in my life, Anna. His dad wasn't even judgmental about my background. He just encouraged me to continue to make a future for myself and to put God first in all I do."

"Hmm, sounds like a good man. Just hope his mother will be as welcoming as her husband," Anna said.

"I pray so. You know, I have never wanted something so much as I do with Jamal now."

"Hmm… be careful o. I know Alvin is a nice guy, but one still has to be vigilant," Anna advised.

"It's been two months. We have known each other, and I have not seen anything to make me regret ever meeting Alvin." She smiled.

"You are blinded by love; that's why. Should I drop you off here?" They'd reached the training centre.

"Yeah, and don't bother coming to pick me up. I'm meeting with Deji later on."

"Okay, send my greetings to our former classmate-turned-married man," Anna said as she slowed down close to the gate.

"Bye, darling!"

Anna honked at her and drove off.

Jamal

"Chief, why was I not told about the breakup?" Mrs Abayomi asked her husband who was dressing up for work.

"Maybe the two individuals involved did not want to break your heart or wanted to avoid your involvement in their affairs."

Mrs Abayomi sighed. "You know how hard I tried for this relationship to work; I don't know what's wrong with these kids."

"They are adult, not kids", Chief Abayomi corrected.

"I know. It's just that I had so many plans already, and they just went ahead and did what they wanted." Mrs Abayomi sat by the bedside.

"You should know that they also have their own minds. Don't stress yourself, wifey." Chief Abayomi picked up his briefcase. "Just accept what your son wants."

"An orphan with no relatives or worthy background!" Mrs Abayomi cried out.

"Yes. Even if it's a trailer girl he chooses, I'm off to work."

"Chief, you are supposed to join me in rejecting this."

He blew her a kiss and said, "See you later." And then left for work.

"There's been a breakthrough in the search for the guys

who were trailing you the other day." Jamal listened to IK on the phone.

"That's good. Have you informed the police?"

"No, my guys want to handle the lead without the police interference for now. Later on, we will inform the police," IK said.

"Oh… just keep me posted on the details."

"Just keep a low profile for now, and give my regards to your girl until the day we meet in person."

"I'll do that. I plan on proposing soon." There was a long pause on the other end of the line, and a gorgeous lady walked in and sat on the sofa.

"Wow, you are serious about this relationship. Isn't that a little soon?"

"Yes, I am. It feels like I have known her for a long time. Whenever we are together, there's this effortless and natural connection. Also, it's getting to months now," Jamal said, looking serious, while Evelyn sat quietly.

"Hmm, so lover boy, when are you planning to pop the question?"

"Don't know yet. Soon. I will meet with Chike, the newlywed, so we can arrange things."

"Yeah. Alright, gotta go. I'll call you later on."

"Bye." He ended the call and looked at Evelyn.

"It's nice to see you, and to what do I owe this visit?" he asked.

"I need your help," Evelyn said. "I need to go back

to Singapore."

"Okay…?" Jamal paid attention.

"My dad has basically cut me off because of you, and he is making plans to bring his illegitimate children to the house."

Still not getting what she wanted from him, he asked, "So what have I got to do with that?"

"I need some cash to help me start afresh in Singapore," Evelyn said.

He took his time to process what she said. "Ok, if that's what you want."

"Thank you, Jamal… I've missed you so much, I won't lie, but if this is how things have to end between us, I guess I accept it. So… about planning your proposal for your girl, why don't you contact the House of Tebi? They would help you plan the perfect thing."

"Hmm. I just might do that. So, when do you need the money?"

"Within the month."

"Ok. But do me a favour. Could you speak to my mom? You know how fond she is of you. Help her understand that we both agreed to move on from the relationship."

Evelyn sighed. "If that's what you want, Jamal. I will do it."

"Thank you."

"I'll take my leave now. Take care." Evelyn left.

He went back to work.

It's a sad thing how little certain parents cared about their children's desires.

"Where are you coming from?" Mrs Davis Cooker asked.

Evelyn frowned at her mother's question. "I went out to see a friend."

"Does that friend happen to be Jamal?"

"Am I being monitored?"

Mrs Davis Cooker ignored the question. "I heard your father is planning on making one of his whore's daughters marry Jamal."

"Oh," Evelyn said nonchalantly. "Good luck to him, then."

"What has gotten into you?" Mrs Davis Cooker was not a bit happy with the way her daughter was taking this. "Do you know what this disobedience of yours has caused? I won't watch any whore's daughter take what's meant for mine!"

Evelyn clapped her hands. "That's great, Mom. You and Dad just toss me around like a piece of meat... very soon I will leave your house for you." She walked away.

"Come back here, Evelyn!" Mrs Davis shouted after her.

Aramide

Anna and Aramide had just arrived from church, and

they both walked into Anna's apartment. She remembered what Anna had told her in the car on the way over.

"So, when will you be leaving for Ottawa?"

"In two weeks. My mom and dad will be coming here this week." Anna bent down to pull off her shoes.

"Why didn't you tell me mom and dad will be coming?" she asked.

"I told you I would be travelling with them."

"Yes, you did, but it would have been nice if you told me they will be arriving this week."

Anna saw her frowning. "Alright, I'm sorry; at least you get to introduce Alvin to them." She smiled.

"What's it with you and bringing up Alvin all the time?" she asked, pretending to be suspicious.

"Your guy is fine and if you ever decide to dump his ass, just know you're throwing him to me," Anna joked, picked her shoes up and went into her room laughing at her friend who was staring aghast at her.

"Now I know you are a jealous girl!"

"I'm not denying it, girl!" Anna called out.

She answered her ringing phone. "Hey, babe." She was suddenly all smiles and lay down comfortably on the sofa.

"Oh, you can tell? It's Anna. She got me smiling, and you know what about - you…" She continued her conversation with Jamal, laughing, smiling and sometimes frowning at his jokes.

BOUND BY FATE

Jamal

Jamal sat down at the dining table, looking at his phone after ending the call with Aramide. He looked up at his dad walk to the table.

"So, when are you popping the big question?" Chief Abayomi asked.

"Soon. I'm just hoping mom finally comes around."

"She has no choice; she will come around." Chief Abayomi knew his wife was getting closer to accepting Jamal's choice. "So how did the contract signing go with Forte Oil?"

"Actually, we're still on it. There are still some investigations going on, and there are some pending letters," Jamal replied.

"Speaking of investigations, how's the case on your trackers going?"

Jamal looked surprised.

"Did you think I'd gotten too old to know what's happening around me? Did IK give you any updates, and are the police involved already?"

"Dad… I didn't want you to worry. IK says they have the identity of the perpetrators, and the police are now involved. They've been able to ascertain that they're the same group of people who had attacked Tebi."

"That's good." Mrs Abayomi walked in looking disturbed.

"Are you alright?" Chief Abayomi asked his wife,

whose eyes were huge as saucers.

"You guys didn't hear about Evelyn's father's arrest!?" Mrs Abayomi sat down heavily. "The poor girl must be devastated!"

"Did you know about this, Jamal?"

"I didn't know. But truthfully, that man has always been a dubious character." Jamal didn't look shocked or surprised. "He probably finally got caught on one of the money laundering or misappropriation rumours that were always circulating around him. I never really liked him much, to be honest, Maami."

Chief Abayomi was very quiet, taking in what his son said and then turned to walk away.

"Where are you going?" Mrs Abayomi asked.

"I need to find out what he's being charged with." Chief Abayomi left the room.

"Maybe you can call Evelyn and find out from her. She has refused to pick up my calls," Mrs Abayomi said to her son and went after her husband.

He already planned to do just that because he was curious. He checked the wall clock; he had an appointment to go check an apartment this evening that he was thinking of buying.

"There's a call for you, sir. On the landline," a maid said to Jamal. He nodded at her to leave. It should be the real estate agent. It was almost time.

Aramide

Aramide arrived to work at the Delivery Agency. She

came in and saw Merissa and Tina deep in discussion.

"Good morning, girls."

"Morning," they replied at the same time.

"Where is Miss Nina's package?" she asked, surprised to see Tina with nothing in her hands.

"There won't be any delivery to Miss Nina today. She got arrested last night." Tina dropped the news.

"Oh my! What happened?" she asked, shocked.

"They say she was arrested for conspiracy to commit murder," Marissa said. "I'm not surprised though, with the way she behaves, that woman can kill somebody."

"Hmmmmm… I wonder why someone would plan evil against their fellow human being." Since she had no other immediate deliveries that day, she would be around to welcome Anna's parents, whose flight was scheduled to land at Murtala Mohammed Airport by twelve pm. "I guess I'm off then," she said, walking toward the exit.

"Take care of yourself," Tina said to her.

She waved at them as she walked out.

Jamal

Evelyn sat in a café. She had on honey-coloured designer Visor glasses and loose-fitting gym wear to help disguise her identity. She sipped her coffee slowly, waiting. Jamal sighted her as he came in. He briefly assessed her odd look and then proceeded to her table.

"Hi, Evelyn," he said when he reached her table.

She was so beautiful, though, that she could pull off almost anything.

"Hey, Jamal."

"How are you and your mom? I thought you would be halfway to Singapore by now."

"We are coping. I can't leave the country now. I have to help my mom sort out some things."

"Ok... and I heard about your friend... Nina? Not sorry about that though."

"I'm so sorry, Jamal... I was the one who caused it. I was confiding in an enemy I thought was a friend," she said, beginning to sob softly. "I found out she is actually my stepsister." Jamal blinked in surprise. "Yes... she wanted everything that I had..." she finished in tears.

"Come here..." Jamal gave her a hug. At that moment, it didn't matter that they were in public.

After she had been waiting for Alvin in the car for some time, Aramide walked into the café. She did not see him at first. Then she saw him. He had moved a chair to sit closer to a girl who seemed to be crying on his shoulders.

"Maybe she is a friend," she considered, trying to wash off negative thoughts and the horrible feeling of jealousy that was rushing to the surface. Looking closely at the lady, she recognised her as the lady in Nina's apartment and at the elevator. So this was Jamal's ex? She also remembered how kind the lady had been to her that day. She decided to go back and wait in the car.

Jamal saw Aramide leave the café out of the corner of his eye. He let go of Evelyn.

"I gotta go. I'll see you another time," he said.

"Thank you, Jamal," she said to him while he hurried outside the café. "It's a shame that I couldn't keep you," she added after he had left, feeling sad. She sat back in her chair to await the lawyer.

Aramide

"Hey." Jamal entered the car, looking a little guilty.

"Mmm," Aramide replied.

"Yeah… I'm sorry…" Jamal said awkwardly.

She smiled. "For what? You didn't commit any offence."

Jamal smiled at her. *Thank God.* "I forgot to get us coffee."

"Now, that's an offence." She frowned.

Jamal smiled again. "I've got something else for you, though."

"Okay?" She smiled.

Alvin turned the car on. "My mom wants me to bring you home today," Jamal said, manoeuvring out of the parking lot.

"Really?! Stop by the market, then. I need to get some things for her," she replied happily.

"Ok, princess. We'll stop by the market."

"And a shopping mall," she added.

"Let's just go to the palms then," Jamal suggested.
"Ok." She smiled.
Jamal drove off while they talked.

Aramide lay on her bed that evening, happy about how the day had gone. Mrs Abayomi was nicer than she'd expected, and she'd had a swell time with Jamal's family. She'd also taken Jamal to Anna's parents, and they approved of him.

Despite all her shortcomings, she had been enjoying a lot of good and amazing days. She had a date with Alvin the next day at House of Tebi, of all places. Anywhere was good if they were together. He also said he had a surprise for her. She also had been to see her brother, who was doing pretty well and would be starting his exams next week.

God had been good to her.

Jamal

Evelyn sat on her bed. Her dad was in prison. Her mom had always been unhappy in her marriage. She hadn't fully realised it before now, but, in a way, they were both victims.

She planned on taking her mum to Singapore with her after some issues had been resolved. If only Jamal was with her, she could have leaned on him for comfort and his leadership abilities. She'd been too reliant on other people, and it fed her insecurities, which had led to the failure of her relationships. That was over now. She had to learn to depend on herself.

She had been avoiding Mrs Abayomi and her husband. She would meet with them someday, but for now, she would try her best to stay away and continue to move on.

Jamal was also sitting on his bed, staring at the ring in his hand. It had a specially designed stone cut out of purple jade. To him, it was like the connection he had with Aramide – one of a kind. He couldn't wait to make her his wife and to share eternity with her, the end of a dark epistle and the beginning of a new friendship of lifelong bliss.

IRINYEMI ESTHER T. lives in Ogun state, Nigeria, and is currently studying industrial chemistry at Olusegun Agagu University of Science and Technology.
During her free moments, you will find her writing.

YEWA'S IN-DWELLING
Ayo Ore-Ofe

ÌBÙGBÈ YEWA.
PROLOGUE.
'Desperate times call for desperate measures.'

Those were the words Yéjídé used to console herself and gain confidence as she and Ododó trod the uneven path to the shrine.

"The end justifies the means... I'm choosing the lesser evil."

Balancing the pot of Fish in tomato sauce they had brought as *àdìmú* in her left hand, she tapped her friend who was stomping her way in the dark with way more confidence than she could understand. "Ododó, are we there yet? My husband mustn't know I came to this kind of place. His mother already thinks I'm a witch. What will she say if she finds out that I'm going to a shrine?! I might just lose my husband in the quest to have a child!"

"Yéjídé, do you want to have a child or not?" Ododó asked angrily, evidently tired of having the same conversation over and over again.

"You know more than anyone that I want this child. I'm just scared *Òré mi*." The wind howled through the forest as if to confirm her words.

"Let's get this over with then. We have husbands to get back to." Ododó continued walking, dismissing her friend and ending the conversation.

Yéjídé followed her friend through the forest, skipping over trees and thorns biting into the sole of her rubber slippers.

"We're here!" Ododó announced.

The shrine of Yewa, Goddess of Death and Fertility was decorated with red, pink, and burgundy fabrics, red paint staining the rocky ground and entrance of the cave. Smoke and the smell of rotting fish filled the air. Yéjídé fought the urge to gag.

"*Màmá Òrìsà!* Priestess! We're here to ask for your help and the help of Yewa. Hear us out we plead."

As soon as Ododó spoke the words, a shrill ringing started from inside the cave. The Priestess came out from inside the cave, her methodical footsteps jingling with the bells she wore on her feet. She was also adorned in burgundy and pink. She looked ethereal and beautiful, like the Goddess Yewa herself.

"What do you seek?" the priestess asked, her voice boomed, echoing through the forest.

"Children, Màmá! Children," Ododó began, getting on her knees and pulling Yéjídé with her. "We have been married for years and have no children. Our husbands have threatened to replace us. Have mercy, Màmá. Grant us the gift of the fruit of the womb."

"What do you offer?"

Yéjídé placed the pot of fish along with a bag of crunchy peanut balls in front of the priestess.

"You have done well." The shrill ringing began again and the trees in the forest began to shake as the wind howled furiously.

"Ihòhò làgbàdo ñ wo ebè. Igba Omo ló ñ kó jade. Ihòhò làgbàdo ñ wo ebè. Tó bá jáde tán á donígba omo. A ké pé ó Yewa. Òrìsà ikú àti ìbímo Òrìsà Égún! Fun wa ni Ibukun. Awon Omo ré ti kó èbùn wa fún wa l'ébùn omo."

The wind seemed to sense that the priestess was done with her incantations because everything became eerily quiet.

"You may go. Yewa has heard and Yewa has given."

They stood up on shaky legs, turned, and began to

BOUND BY FATE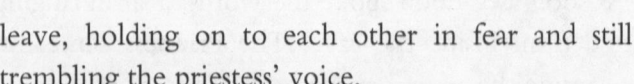

leave, holding on to each other in fear and still trembling the priestess' voice.

"*Dúró níbè!*" Màmá Òrìsà's voice stopped them in their tracks.

"Yewa has conditions. She will give you a pair of children, one for each of you. These children will be one, bound to the same fate. They will flourish apart from each other, but together, they will destroy each other. You might try, but you won't be able to keep them from each other. They will possess the power of Yewa. And when the time has come, Yewa will take them back. They will be yours for a while, but Yewa will claim what is hers. *Awón wònyí ní yóo jé Ìbùgbé ti Yewa.*"

~~~~~~

Being a doctor has its good days, bad days, and annoying days. Today was turning out to be a particularly annoying day for Folárìn Àlàní as he sat in his office.

"*Why can't people just take care of themselves,*" he thought to himself.

Folárìn Àlàní was the best doctor Winfield Hospital had, probably the best in the state. *It's not every doctor that can see ghosts, after all.* He saw them everywhere and every day and had conversations with them. They became his best friends. The good-looking, rich and excellent doctor with a troubled countenance and mysterious eyes.

The ghosts came in various temperaments; the ones who weren't ready to die and spend the rest of the ghost-existence sulking, the ones who were continually trying to live their lives through him, the ones who were just grateful for human company, and the ones who are very annoying and won't stop pestering and talking to him, like this particular ghost.

"You know, I didn't think I'd die in surgery. Why didn't you operate on me? I could be alive now!"

"Philp, I have told you a million times, your surgery wasn't on the list of procedures that I had to do. It wasn't my fault you died," Folárìn replied, exasperated.

"Fine! Fine! But how can you see me though?"

"I've also said that I don't know. I've been seeing ghosts since I was a kid."

"So you're a freak?"

"No, I'm not!"

"Okay, not a freak. A psychopath?"

"What?"

"Oh, wait, you're a superhero!"

"Are you kidding me right now? What do you -" He was cut off by his office door being pushed open.

"Emergency, Doctor!" the nurse cried.

Folárìn jumped up from his seat and started towards the door.

"Wait for me!" Philip shouted, running after them.

Ghosts and hospitals are two concepts that go together.

Every week, at least one new ghost is added to Fola's group of friends. They kept calling out to him as he raced towards the emergency room.

"Someone fill me in," Fola demanded as soon as he stepped into the ER.

"A gang shoot-out at one of the clubs downtown. five injured, two out of the five need surgery, and the other three are being patched up. Three brought in dead."

Yikes!

Folárìn walked further, seeing new ghosts already, trying his best not to make them know he can see them. And that's when he saw *her*.

A young woman, probably in her thirties, with eyes so hollow and dark, they looked like she was staring into your soul. Her skin was light, in deep contrast with the dark circles under her eyes. Yet she looked...*beautiful*. How could someone like her have ended up in a place like a club?

Femi had seen his fair share of pretty women, but there was something about her. Something that felt like a connection. Then she turned her head and looked straight at him. And that connection snapped into place.

He kept staring because he couldn't take off her. It felt like a part of him he didn't know was missing had snapped into place. She must have felt it too because those big dark eyes widened, and she couldn't quite look away also. Their stare-down was broken when a nurse jostled into his side while going to fetch antiseptics.

"Doctor Fola!"

"Uh.. yes.. yes.." he stammered as he answered the nurse.

"The patient over there might need surgery. The x-rays showed she has broken bones in her wrist and some broken ribs also. The other Doctors are busy with the other patients. Could you add her to your schedule right now?"

"I'll do it." *After all, it was her.*

"Alright, I'll prep the theatre."

Fola walked down to her as she lay on the bed, trying to mask the pain she was feeling.

"Hello, ma'am, I'll be attending to you now. Can you please tell me what hurts on each part of your body I touch?"

She nodded.

Since Fola already knew where it was broken, he gingerly touched her wrist, which was already a deep, angry purple. The pain she was trying to hide took over her face as he touched the area on her wrist, and she let out a whimper of pain.

"Stop!"

"Sorry, ma'am. You seem to have a broken wrist and, from the looks of it, some of your ribs are broken too. You'll have to go through surgery. Do you have any family members you'd like to notify?"

BOUND BY FATE

"Can you stop asking questions and just do your job?" she snapped at him. "And stop with the ma'am. My name is Amari!"

Amari... why does that sound so sweet?

~~~~~

Hospitals... Damn hospitals!

As much as Amari didn't want to spend one more minute in this hospital, she couldn't move with a bout of pain slamming her to her back. The Doctor meant to treat her seems more interested in ogling her than doing something about her condition. *Do they pay these people to be useless?*

"Can you stop asking me questions and just do your job?" She snapped at him. "And stop with the ma'am. My name is Amari!" She snapped at him. *Yikes! Even shouting was painful.*

He seemed taken aback by her sudden outburst, but she was too worked up to care right now. She saw them everywhere. The ones who just died and the ones she didn't know. Capone was staring straight at her... *well, his ghost.* The fight at the club had gotten out of hand, and the idiots had gotten trigger-happy. She hadn't gotten shot, but she was sure she got the injuries she had when she was trying to take cover. She'd kill the ones who had survived herself as soon as she got herself fixed up.

Speaking of fixing up...

Amari turned to the doctor at her side, who couldn't seem to do anything to help her.

"Do you even know what you're doing?"

"Of course, I do!" he said, clearly insulted. *Well, maybe he'll be insulted enough to do something.*

"Well then, do something!"

"I was getting to that. If you'd just calm down and let me do my job."

"Don't tell me to calm down!" As soon as those words came out of her mouth, a fresh bout of pain hit her so hard that tears sprang to her eyes. The tears seemed to spur him to action, and he began to bark orders at the nurses. The activities around her became a blur as whatever they injected her with began to kick in, and everything became black.

White walls and the sickening smell of hospitals... hospital... HOSPITAL?!

Amari woke up with a jolt. *How did I get here?* It all came rolling back to her mind. *Painting... The club... The fight... blood.. bullets.... Ghosts... and more ghosts... and then... The Doctor!*

Amari couldn't hide the scowl that took over her face when she remembered the Doctor's annoyingly pretty face.

Not pretty, Amari! Just annoying.

Seeing him across the room had stolen her breath away, literally seeing that she couldn't breathe past the pain in her chest. He stood taller than most people in the ER; it wasn't hard to spot him from afar. And that connection... *What was that?!*

She had forced herself to look away from him, but then he stepped closer and started speaking to her. Even his deep, baritone voice was annoying. Up close, she could see the whiskey-coloured eyes that had held her captive a few minutes ago. She fought not to get lost in them again and focused on the pain in her ribs. At least he knew what he was doing. She could hardly feel the pain now; the violent spasms had now dulled to a faint throbbing.

He had asked about her family, a family she had left twelve years ago. She left and burned her bridges, never to look back. Too much has happened since then. She had grown and built her career as an artist and lived in an apartment too big for a single lady at thirty. She lived secluded from people and rarely socialized except at her art exhibitions. It wasn't that she wasn't beautiful or didn't want to have friends. It was because everywhere she went, she saw *them*. The only time she didn't see them was when she was-

A door opening interrupted her train of thought. *Ha! The doctor again.*

"I didn't know you'll be up. The effect of the anaesthesia should have worn off by now."

Of course, it would have. You don't have any idea what kind of substances my body is used to.

"So, how do you feel?" the doctor asked in a soothing voice.

"Terrible."

"Understandable. It should pass very soon, though you still need time to recover. The surgery was successful, and you'll be -"

"You said you didn't expect me to be up. So, why are you here? To kill me in my sleep?"

"Of course not, ma'am. I-"

"It's Amari," she snapped.

"I'm sorry, Amari. I -"

"What are you apologising for?"

"You seem upset, and I'm sorry for -"

"Don't say sorry. Don't apologise for anything you're not sure is your fault. First lesson, pretty boy."

"Oh, alright. So you think I'm pretty?"

"Stop acting like you don't know you're good-looking. Bet you spend hours in front of a mirror, indulging in narcissism." That drew a laugh from him.

"Besides, I don't know your name."

"Folárìn. Doctor Folárìn Àlàní. You could just call me Fola."

"Right. Fola. You know mine. I'm Amari. Last name's Bankole."

"Pleasure to meet you, Amari."

"The feeling isn't mutual," she laughed scornfully.

"Are you always this snarky?" he asked with amusement in his voice.

"Only on days of the week that end with y. Plus, I

have a special rainbow attitude for doctors with annoying faces who spend time ogling their patients."

"I thought you said my face was pretty?"

Is that seriously all his brain could shuffle out? "It doesn't change the fact that you have an annoying face. It makes it more annoying."

"I don't understand." He seemed puzzled.

"The thing is -"

"Ask her what hair products she uses. Those cornrows are sweet!"

I didn't hear the door open... It's a ghost... wait, ask her? Can he see?

The ghost keeps nudging Fola and prompting him to ask her.

He can see them too!

"Fola. Fola, can you see him?"

The look on his face spoke volumes.

He can see ghosts, too!

~~~~~

If it was possible to kill a man twice, Fola would have gladly wrung the life out of Philip right now. He had asked to follow him into Amari's ward when he was going to check in on her, but Fola had vehemently refused. And now he had to just ruin it all by opening his mouth and making a foolish statement that she apparently heard, and now she was- *hold up... she heard?!!*

"Fola. I asked if you heard him?" Amari asked, staring at him like he had horns.

"Heard who?"

"The ghost!"

"Hi, I'm Philip. Fola's favourite ghost." Philip beamed a smile so bright; it was disappointing that he was dead.

"Fola's favourite ghost? You can see them too? How?"

Folárìn's attempt at saying anything came out as a squeak. *What did she mean by "you could see them too?"*

"Amari. You can see Philip?"

A haunted look came into her eyes, her voice barely above a whisper, "Yes... I can see him."

"This... this is definitely... it's... a side effect. Yes, a side effect of the anaesthesia. You can't possibly be seeing ghosts. I mean, that explains why you're awake when you're still supposed to be under. Right?" He rushed out, begging her with his eyes to confirm his ramblings.

"I'm right. Amari, I must be right. Tell me I'm right."

She didn't say a word. She just kept staring at him with that hunted look in her eyes.

"Fola. How long?"

"How long is what?"

"How long have you been able to see them?"

"Since I was a kid. When I was seven, to be precise." She remained silent, staring at Philip behind him with a resigned look in her eyes.

"Amari, help me understand. How can you see ghosts? Since when? Are you sure this isn't some kind of side effect? Do you feel lightheaded?"

"I do feel lightheaded."

"I said it. It's most likely the anaesthesia. I'll have a nurse come –"

"Fola," she began, her voice halting his ramblings. "Yes. I feel lightheaded, but it has nothing to do with the anaesthesia. I've been able to see ghosts since I was seven too."

"How old are you, Amari?"

"I'm thirty-four."

Fola's eyes widened. *I'm thirty-four, too!* Once again, that connection snapped into place, and the weight of the bond lay heavy in the air and suffocating.

"Uhm, if you don't mind, I'll still need to know the name of your shampoo. Smells amazing!"

"Shut up, Philip!" Fola snapped at Philip.

"Look, Amari, we'll talk about this. I need to wrap my head around what just happened. Get some rest. I'll be back in a few hours."

Fola all but fled from the room.

Amari Bankole can see ghosts.

She can see ghosts like me!

Fola didn't know what to feel or say. He ran out of the room earlier because he didn't want to stutter like a fool. Maybe it was the connection he felt or the fact that for once in his life he felt less alone than he usually did.

It was probably the fact that looking into Amari's eyes, he felt he had known her all his life although he had just met her eighteen hours ago. He felt something with her he had never felt with any other person. It wasn't romantic. *Entirely.* It was like he could finally breathe past the usual lump in his chest.

"You didn't tell me you had the hots for ghost lady."

"Philip," Fola sighed. "Do you ever know when to keep quiet? Why did you even talk to me when we were in her ward?"

"I had an inkling she could see me. I followed you to the room the moment you stepped in. Her eyes immediately met mine, and she was looking at me instead of through me. I had to test my theory."

"And you could have told me! I would have talked to her about it instead of you opening your mouth and babbling on about her shampoo."

"You wouldn't have believed me," Philip said with a smug smile.

He was totally right. Fola wouldn't have believed a word that he said.

"Just talk to her. Get her to explain how she can see ghosts like you. Find out if there's a connection, and

BOUND BY FATE

see what you can do about it. I did it for you, mate."

Fola knew when ghosts began to make sense, there was trouble brewing around the corner. He could sense it also. Especially as a result of the connection. But can he stay away?

Fola crept back into Amari's room after avoiding her for a full day. He felt so ashamed closing the door behind him, grateful the lights were off.

"Don't turn on the lights, Fola," her voice said from within the darkness.

"What?"

"Excessive lights hurt my eyes."

"I mean, how did you know it was me?"

"Don't you feel the connection that snaps into place anytime we're within a few meters of each other? Well, I do. And I know you do, too."

He was grateful she couldn't see his face in the dark and decided sitting in the dark would be the best way to have this conversation.

"How? Tell me."

"Fola, there's nothing to explain. If you're anything like me, you'll know there's no way to explain my abilities. The first time I saw a ghost was when I was seven. I hurt my knee while playing and I had to go to the hospital to get stitches. I was sitting in the injection room because I had to get an anti-tetanus shot.

I remember being so scared. Then I looked up and saw this man. He looked different and had a whitish hue around him. I thought he was an angel, and I asked him if he was one. He looked shocked and told me he was a ghost and asked how I could see him. I didn't understand a word he said, but I kept talking to him.

The doctor walked into me, having a conversation with this ghost, and asked me who I was talking to. When I explained, she looked at me like I was out of my mind or something. When I left the hospital that day, I can still remember the look of terror on my mother's face as she drove us home."

She took a breath and continued, "I've been seeing ghosts since then. I also steered clear of hospitals except when it's unavoidable. But I still see them everywhere. I channelled that energy into art. My agent says I have the most grotesque style she has ever seen. I take it as a compliment," she finished with a chuckle.

"I channelled my abilities into medicine. It helped me understand human life better and irrevocably be a better doctor. It messed up my social life, though. At some point, I started finding ghosts a better company than actual humans. I've lived my life that way for most of my thirty-four years of existence."

"You're thirty-four too?" Amari asked.

"Yes. I'm thirty-four too."

They couldn't decide if their connection was merely a coincidence or if it was something more. But they were both content to sit with each other in the darkness and just be.

~~~~~~

Amari spent two more weeks in the hospital to recover, and each day mirrored the previous days. She woke up to lie on the bed and stare out her window as ghosts sauntered on the corridors, Fola spending every minute he could with her. Sometimes, they didn't talk. Sometimes, they talked for hours. It was nice to have him there even though there was a dark cloud hanging over them that they were both trying to ignore. Thankfully, she was getting discharged today.

Fola promised to see her before she left, but she was hoping he wouldn't show up so she could leave without seeing him. She felt it would be better if she could just leave and never see him again. The connection felt too intense, like there was a bond neither of them could break even if they tried, like the bond would break them if they weren't careful.

She didn't have much to pack except what she had bought during her stay at the hospital. As she was packing her bag, the door opened, and Fola came in. *So much for sneaking away...*

"You're ready to leave." He said it like a statement rather than a question.

"As you can see, I am."

"This might sound out of line, but can I see you again?"

This was why I wanted to just disappear... "Are you saying I should get hurt again?"

"Definitely not, Amari. I meant, can I see you outside the hospital, outside the whole doctor-patient arrangement? Please?"

"Are you asking me on a date, pretty boy?"

He chuckled. "If that's what you'll call it, then yes. It's a date"

"And why? Is it because we share some psychic ability or what?"

"Amari. There's something here. I feel it, and I know you do too. I can't quite put a label on it. But I'd like to see what it is."

"Since you asked nicely, I'd go out with you."

"Thank you." He said with a smile.

"FYI, there has to be food. I don't like public places, and you're paying."

"Yes, ma'am." His smile was now a full-blown grin. *Pretty boy.*

Fola was sitting in his office trying to catch up on work that he missed whilst he spent every free time he had in Amari's ward when his phone rang. *Maami.*

"Hello, Maami?"

"Àlàní Folárìn. Do I have to come all the way to Lagos before you have time for me? What does a mother have to do to see her son these days?"

"Hello to you too, Ma. How are you doing this afternoon?"

"I'm not fine!"

He rolled his eyes, definitely knowing where she was going with this. "What's wrong Maami?"

"It's my son. Next time you see him, please tell him to take a little time to come and see his mother, whom he left in Ogun state. I might just die today and not see my son before I die."

"Ma, you're not dying anytime soon, and I'll come to see you as soon as my schedule is a bit flexible."

"That's what you've been saying all these while. When will I see you *oko mi*?"

"Very soon Maami. A few more weeks and I'm all yours."

"If you say so *oko mi*. How about the other… thing? Do you still see them?"

He contemplated lying to her, but he knew better than to do that. "*Maami*, I'm fine, really. You don't have to worry about me."

"Folárìn, I can't help but worry. I hope someday you'll forgive me."

Forgiveness? What is she talking about?

"Ma. It's okay. I'm fine. I'll tell you if anything goes out of hand."

"Hmm. Alright. Before you say I'm pestering you, I just want to remind you that you're not getting any younger, and you have no wife yet. I'm just reminding you, no pressure."

"Yes, Ma." He said with a laugh in his voice. Only his Mum can use that tone and then say "no pressure" at the end.

"I have to go now, Ma. I'll send some money to you and the usual lady to touch up your groceries."

"I don't want money. I want my son. And some grandkids."

"Alright, ma. I love you."

"I love you, son," she said before Fola hung up the call.

His finger hovered over Amari's phone number as he fought the urge to call her.

She should have gotten home; it has been three hours.

He wasn't joking when he said he wanted to know more about her and explore whatever was between them. He had a lot of questions for her. Some he had asked before but gotten no answer to. Like what was she doing at a club to the point of getting involved in a shoot-out? He stopped fighting the urge not to call her, and he dialled her number. She answered on the third ring.

"Amari Bankole speaking." Amari's voice came through the line.

"That's formal. Considering how you bit my head off when we first met."

"Pretty boy?"

"Did you bite off any other person's head recently?"

"No, just you."

"I'm flattered. Are you home yet?"

"Yes, I got home a few minutes ago. I had to stop to get groceries and supplies."

"Alright. Take it easy though. You still have a few weeks of recovery ahead of you."

"Aye aye, Captain!"

He laughed.

"Hey, Fola, when are you taking me on that?"

"I wanted to go give you a few days to settle down, and then we'd pick the place. Is that okay with you?"

"Yes, it is."

"See you soon, Amari."

"See you soon, Pretty boy."

~~~~~

"Nice choice," Amari said as they walked into the restaurant Fola had picked for their date. He had specifically looked for a place a bit far from town that wasn't crowded and also have good food. He had picked right.

"I'm glad you approve," he replied, smiling as he pulled out a chair for her to sit on.

"Do you always do this to sweep unsuspecting women off their feet?"

"Only for the ones with snarky attitudes."

"I must say I'm flattered."

"You're welcome."

They ordered food and started to eat.

"So," Amari began. "I know you didn't bring me here to eat out of the goodness of your heart. You brought me here to interrogate me. Ask me questions then."

Fola moved around in his seat before finally settling down and saying, "Tell me about your family."

"My family. I'm the only child. My Father died two years ago. My Mum lives alone in Ado-Ekiti. I haven't seen either of my parents in twelve years."

"Why did you leave home?"

"My mother and I don't have the best of relationships. She is too domineering, wanting to know who I'm with and who I talk to. I got fed up and left without telling her. She also forbade me to talk about my abilities. She made me feel cursed. I'm sure that wasn't her intention, but I still can't shake off the memory of the look in her eyes the first time she found out about my abilities.

I constantly send money to her but through a middleman. She doesn't know where I am. I might not even be in the country to her," she finished with a laugh, but he could see the pain in her eyes.

"Enough about grilling me, Fola. Tell me about you."

"Well. I'm an only child, too. My Father is also late. He died when I was five. My Mother and I are really close. I go to see her as much as I can though she lives alone."

BOUND BY FATE

"I never pegged you as a mummy's boy." They both laughed.

"You can say that again."

They fell into an easy conversation about her art and his job.

"Oh, look! We've spent hours talking. We should get going if we want to beat traffic," Amari said.

"Of course. I have just one question. What were you doing at the club when you got injured?"

"I was hoping you wouldn't ask that," she said after a long pause.

"Tell me."

"When I left home twelve years ago, I was looking for something to fill the void I felt. So, I started using drugs. That club was where I got my usual hits, and I became quite familiar with them. I finally quit after a few years and went to rehab. I came out of rehab five years ago and began my art career.

I thought that part of my life was in the past, but Capone, one of the guys at the club, started to blackmail me with some pictures from my past. When I got tired of giving him money, I decided to go and see him. A fight happened at the club, and then we ended up at the hospital."

"Where's Capone now?" Fola asked; his voice was torn between anger and sadness for her.

"He's dead. I saw his ghost at the hospital."

They kept staring at each other, neither of them willing to break the silence.

"Does that make you see me differently?" Amari finally asked.

"I can't see you differently, Amari. Even if I tried to."

Fola asked to see Amari's art, so she invited him over to her studio, which was in her loft. She preferred working from home anyway.

"Nice place, ma'am."

"Oh, thank you. The studio is this way." She led him out of the living room and down a hallway, past several closed doors till she finally stopped at one and kicked it open. The door opened to a massive room that smelled thickly of acrylic paint. She flipped a switch, and the room was suddenly lit up with stage lights and bulbs that lit up the room so brightly that Fola had to close his eyes for a while to adjust.

"The lights are necessary for my art. And since I paint most at night, I need light to be able to balance out the shades and colours on my canvas."

Several canvases and easel boards hung on the wall. Some were scattered on the floor, and the entire workspace was littered with crumpled pieces of paper. A particular piece was set in the centre of the room, and he walked towards it. It was a woman, crouched down with her hands in front of her as if to shield herself from an attack. Over her head, crows flew restlessly, and her mouth was open in mid-scream.

"I see you found the centre of my collection," Amari said as she moved to stand beside him.

"It's beautiful. In a very unusual way. Just like you."

"I don't know what to call it yet. I don't even know if I'd sell it yet. I felt so much relief after painting it. I might just keep it and look at it."

"Your art is amazing. It's not conventional, but it's powerful. The pictures look ready to jump off the canvas. It's divine."

"Thank you for the compliment. Art brought me through one of the darkest parts of my life. Just like your mother has always been there for you, the only thing I had to turn to was art. It's my lifeline."

"Well, you have me now," Fola said, his eyes shining with sincerity.

"Folárìn, you can't promise me anything. You might be saying this because we have some kind of connection, but that's not something to base your feelings on."

"What if I tell you that I have never felt complete till I met you? It was as if something I never knew I had lost clicked into place when I met you. Amari, I won't throw that chance away just because you're scared."

"It's not fear, Fola. Can't you sense it? We're

carrying too much baggage, and if we decide to be together, we might destroy each other." Her voice shook, but she continued, "I know it's hard to walk away. Trust me, I've tried so hard to leave you and walk away, but I can't. So I'm begging you, Fola. Walk away. For both our sakes."

"See, that's where you're wrong. Everything inside of me is telling me to turn away, but I can't. Amari, if I'll be destroyed, then I choose you as my destruction."

~~~~~~

"*Come to me. It's time. Come to me. Omo tí ó jé èbùn. Come to me.*"

Amari jolted out of sleep, sweat coating her back and soaking her pyjamas. She had had the same dream every night for the past week. A woman in pink and burgundy robes called her to come. The pull was too strong; she couldn't stop herself from going to her. She always woke up at the same point in the dream, when she was about to place her hand in the hand of the woman in pink.

She stood up from her bed, went to her studio, and began to sketch the visions she had seen in her dreams. The pictures in her head bled onto the paper in swirls of pink and red and burgundy. By the time she had finished, staring back at her was a beautiful woman.

"*She looks like a goddess,*" Amari said to herself as she sat staring at the picture she had drawn.

Amari stretched her back after hours of painting later that day. She had two weeks to her exhibition, and she was told she couldn't add one more piece to her collection. It was a painting of Folárìn that she tried to talk herself out of doing. The face was hidden behind flowers, but his hands clutching hers were the main focus of the piece. Something she couldn't talk herself out of doing.

Her mind went to the Doctor, and she sighed when the knot in her chest tightened. She had not spoken to him for a couple of days now. After their argument, she told him to leave her house. She remembered his words clearly: '*I will leave, Amari. But know this, I won't stop chasing you. You can run all you want. But I'll catch you.*'

She fought back the tears and decided to take a break. She stood up and went to the cabinet in her studio. She took out a bottle of whiskey she had in her cabinet. She hadn't drunk in seven years, but right now, she felt like if she didn't have a glass, she was going to lose her mind. She poured herself a glass of whiskey and downed it in one gulp.

The knot in her chest seemed to loosen, so she downed another glass. She continued to drink glass after glass when suddenly the room became cold. Cold enough to make her teeth chatter against each other. She felt her presence behind her, and she turned around to see who it was.

The woman in pink. She is here!

She stood up to leave the room, but her knees failed beneath her. She fell to the floor and couldn't stand up. She looked up to see the woman in pink in front of her.

"*Omo tí ó jé èbùn. Come to me. It is time.*"

Amari tried to stop herself, but she couldn't. The pull was too strong. She stretched forth her hand. And this time, she took the woman's hand. And she followed her.

Fola stood outside Amari's apartment to gather his wits. He has given her enough space for almost two weeks. He had to talk to her. Besides, he could not shake the feeling that something was wrong with her. He had a sinking feeling in his gut and couldn't stop himself from driving to her house. After knocking for a while without any response, he pushed the door open. The atmosphere was dense and cold… *like a morgue!*

Alarm bells went off in his head as he ran into the house. "Amari. Amari, where are you?!"

He stopped in his tracks when he saw her lying on the floor in her studio.

"Amari! Amari! No!"

He knelt beside her and held her body in his arms. She felt cold. Too cold.

"Amari? Amari, can you hear me? You'll be okay. What happened?"

A hoarse cry tore from his throat when she didn't answer him. He felt for her pulse.

"No!" He frantically tried to warm her body with his hands and kept talking to her like she could hear him.

"Amari, you'll be fine. I'll fix you up nice. You'll be okay. Please don't leave me. You don't get to leave me."

Tears dropped from his eyes to her face.

"Amari!" Her name kept falling from his lips like a prayer as he rocked her body back and forth.

Amati stood in the corner, watching Fola cry over her body. She followed the woman in pink. She didn't know she was following her to her death. And even now, she knew Fola wouldn't leave her.

He would follow the lady too.

~~~~~

The past eighteen hours passed in a blur.

Finding Amari on the floor... Calling the ambulance... Amari was pronounced dead on arrival...

Time seemed to slow down, and the atmosphere felt suffocating. Fola sat in his office and stared straight at the wall as he had been doing for hours on end.

Amari... Dead...

He had questions. How could she just die? There was alcohol in her bloodstream, but not enough to kill her. He wanted to run an autopsy on her body, but something told him that Amari wouldn't have wanted it.

Why couldn't he see her ghost?

He looked around for her ghost as he left her apartment with the paramedics. But he didn't find anything.

Seeing her body on the floor had done something to him that he could never recover from. He had gone there to tell her to stay with him, to beg if that's what it took. But she had already left him totally. He closed his eyes tightly as he fought back tears, his throat hoarse from screaming her name.

Deep down, he knew that Amari's death would take something from him that he could never get back.

Walking into Amari's apartment hurt so much that Fola almost gave in to the urge to leave. He fought that urge. He needed answers, and the only way to find them was to do this. He walked into her house and straight to her studio. Somehow, he felt the studio held more answers than her bedroom.

He took a deep breath and opened the door to her studio. It looked the same as the first time he saw it. Most of the paintings he had seen weren't in the room any longer, probably with her agent. But just one canvas stood in the middle of the room. It was the picture of a man, his face hidden behind flowers but his hands on display.

The hands looked familiar... *his hands and her hands.* She had been painting them before she died. Grief rose anew in his chest and threatened to cut off this breath. He stood admiring the painting for so long before he couldn't take it anymore and decided to leave.

On his way out, he stepped on a sketchbook that had been laying on the floor, he picked it up, and stopped at the first picture he saw. A woman. A goddess adorned in pink and burgundy. Something inside of him quickened at the sight of that picture.

He needed answers. And knew just one person who could give him those answers.

It's time to go home.

~~~~~

"Oko mì oo." Yéjídé sang as her son walked into the living room of her house. It had been nearly seven months since she last saw him, and to say she missed him was an understatement.

"Good afternoon *Ma'ami.*" Fola greeted her as he prostrated.

"*Didé oko mì.* How was the journey?" she asked, noting that he looked exhausted.

"The journey was fine, Ma. How are you?"

"I'm fine, my son. I'm very happy to see you."

"I'm happy to see you too, Ma."

"I wasn't expecting you till next month. How

were you able to find the time to come earlier?"

"Mummy. I came to talk to you."

Fear gripped Yéjídé, but she kept her voice from shaking as she asked, "What happened, *oko mì?*"

"Ma. I found a girl." Noting the look on her face, he added, "Not like that, Ma. But exactly like that. She was my patient. We had this unexplainable connection, *Ma'ami*. She understood me. She was beautiful, very beautiful. I fell in love with her, Ma. She knew about my abilities. She could see ghosts too -"

"Fola!" Yéjídé exclaimed. "What did you say she could do?"

"She could see ghosts, Ma. But it's all over now. She's dead." Fola ended with a shaky breath.

Tears welled up in Yéjídé eyes as she shook in terror.

"*Ma'ami,* what's wrong? Are you okay?"

"Folárìn. *Oko mì*. I think it's time for you to know."

"Know what, Ma?"

"Listen to me very well, my son. When I married your father, I couldn't give him a child for the first five years of our marriage. It was hell for me. Your grandmother called me a witch, and your father said he was going to take another wife. I was scared of losing my home to a strange woman. I had a friend. She was also going through the same situation. Then she suggested that we go to consult a priestess. I didn't know things would turn out this way."

"What way, *Ma'ami*? Please tell me."

"Òdòdó took me to the shrine of Yewa. She is the goddess of death and fertility. We gave an offering, and Yewa gave us children. However, she gave us a pair of children. Children with the same fate but from different mothers. Those children would be able to see ghosts, and when it was time, Yewa will take them from us. Fola, I think the lady you found is your pair."

Fola was dumbfounded. "It's not possible, Ma. She grew up in Ekiti. It could be another person entirely."

"Folárìn, it's too much of a coincidence to be anything but. The priestess mentioned that we would not be able to keep you apart. Besides, the last time I heard of Òdòdó, she was in Ado-Ekiti."

Fola's head pounded as he tried to absorb all that he had heard. Tears came to his eyes anew as grief struck him again. It suddenly made sense: the crazy connection, the same birthday, the drawings in her sketchbook.

"Ma, by any chance is this goddess adorned in red and pink?"

"Yes. Those were the colours I saw at her shrine. Have you seen her?"

"Amari did. She drew her in her sketchbook. I think she came for her."

Tears fell from Yéjídé's eyes as she took in her son. He looked...*broken.*

"Folárìn. My son. I'm so sorry for what happened. You have to forgive me. Though it was the worst decision of my life, it gave me the best gift I have ever received. It gave me you. Fortune our desperation *oko mì*.

But you have to promise me something. When she comes for you, don't give in to her. Fight, my son. You have to fight her. That's the only way you'll remain with me. Fight, Folárìn. Fight!"

~~~~~

Fola lay on the bed in his room at his Mum's place, still trying to process all she had told him. It all felt surreal. He tossed and turned but couldn't go to sleep.

"Omo tí ó jé èbùn. Come to me. It is time. Come to me."

Opening his eyes, he saw her. The lady in pink. She had come for him. The pull was strong, and he almost gave in. His mother's voice rang in his head. *Fight, Folárìn.* He closed his eyes and tried to fight the pull. But then he heard *her* voice. Amari's voice.

"Come to me. It is time. Come…"

He opened his eyes again, and he saw her face. Amari was standing in front of him and stretching forth her hand. He looked at her and knew then and there that he was going with her. She had indeed become his destruction.

He stood up from the bed.

And walked away with the one who had power over

BOUND BY FATE

him.

~~~~~~

YÉJÍDÉ.

Èsù á fún ni ní fìlà, fí gbá ódidi orí lówó éní.
I knew this day would come.
The day when I bury my son.
He never was mine, to begin with
He always belonged to Yewa. I borrowed him for a while.
Only the blessings of the Lord make rich and add no sorrow.
I thought I could outsmart fate.
But fate has a way of proving its superiority.
I'm beyond sad.
I am delirious.
Know this: no man can change fate.
You either embrace it or suffer from it.

GLOSSARY.
Incantations Translation:
A corn seed enters the heap of soil naked.
It brings forth two hundred children.
A corn seed enters the heaped soil naked.
When it comes out, it has a multitude of children.
We call on you, Yewa, goddess of death and fertility, goddess of spirits.
Give us a blessing, your children have brought offerings.
Give us the gift of children.

Other Translations:
Awón wònyí ní yóo jé Ìbùgbé ti Yewa."- These ones will be the dwelling place of Yewa.

Àdìmú – Offering
Òré mí – My friend
Màmá Òrìsà – Priestess
Dúró níbè – Stop there
Maami – *My mother*
    Oko mí – My husband (a term of endearment mothers usually use to refer to sons.)
Omo tí ó jé èbùn – The child that was a gift.
Dìdé oko mí – Get up, my son.

AYO ORE-OFE is a Law student at Ajayi Crowther University in Oyo State, lives in Kwara State and was born and raised in Kogi state, all in Nigeria.
She loves all things reading and writing.

SCENT OF A FLOWER
Pritie

The feeling of a changing environment came crashing in on Awu strongly again, and her four-year relationship with Joseph came to a halt. It was a new year, and she had made plans as to how her year would flow, but unfortunately for her, her entire plans were shattered because of the ASUU strike. Awu decided to get a job before she sank into depression again, as she did two years ago when she found out that Joseph was sleeping with her best friend, Comfort.

In the midst of her worries and projections, she

received a call from a friend Mr Ayodeji, he said a friend of his needed a personal assistant to work with her at her charity foundation and he recommended her. He asked if she would be interested, and in a blink, a large smile appeared on Awu's face.

Awu jumped at the offer and told him that she was very much interested in the job. He sent Awu's number to the client and told Awu to expect her employer's call soon. Awu waited for almost a week and didn't receive any call; She reached out to Mr Ayodeji to inform him that the lady hadn't called her yet, and two days later, she received a call from Uchechi, the Director General of the Ucy Foundation. They scheduled an interview for the next week, and after the interview, Awu waited for almost two weeks for a response from Uchechi and never got any.

Awu didn't understand why it was so difficult for Uchechi to reach out to her or send the human resources personnel to inform her of an acceptance or a rejection. She reached out to Mr Ayodeji again, and that same day, Uchechi sent a text of an acceptance. They went back and forth over the remuneration of the office of a public relations representative, and in as much as that was not what she applied for, she needed a new start, so she finally accepted the offer and the salary attached to it.

It took a couple of days before she was asked to resume office. She travelled to Abuja three days before her resumption date and stayed with her childhood friend Amokeye, who is married to a 6-month-old baby girl. In the agreement, Awu was to be put on a one-month probation, and based on her output for the month, her salary would be increased by fifty percent, and she would be given accommodation. Awu refused to renew her rent in Choba with the hope that before it expires, she will move into her own apartment in Abuja.

Awu had an early start on her resumption day and arrived at the office at 9 am prompt. The secretary, Grace, took her to the lounge and asked her to wait there until Uchechi arrived. The office building is situated in the central area of Abuja, it has an unforgettable edifice and beautiful interior decoration.

Awu fell in love with the lounge; it had two sitting sections, a seventy-five-inch television, a bar, and a kitchen. The kitchen had a coffee maker, a microwave, and a fridge with beautiful shelves where she already placed her provisions, plates, and teacup should be. The other staff were warm towards her and left for their offices after they had breakfast. They spent time in the lounge with her because Jacob, the cleaner, was cleaning their offices. At eleven am, Uchechi arrived and Awu was asked to join her in her office. The journey from the door to her chair was over a minute. The office was freezing, and Awu realised why the other staff had blazers on; wearing a simple red formal dress, she had no idea she was strolling into Antarctica in an office in Nigeria.

Uchechi scanned Awu from her head to toe before she offered her a seat; she quickly sat down, rubbing her hands together.

"Are you okay?" Uchechi asked politely.

"I am, although it feels really cold here, Ma," Awu replied.

"Next time, wear a blazer. It's Monday, and you are dressed like it's Friday. In this office, we dress formally Monday to Friday and work from nine am to six pm."

"Noted, Ma. It's nice meeting you again, Ma."

Uchechi placed her MacBook and a tablet on her desktop.

Whatever she needed to do on the desktop can be done with the rest, so why put all of them on?

Uchechi called Ramat through the intercom. When Ramat came, Uchechi complained about the internet and told Ramat to call the guy who fixed it to come back and check on it again. Ramat told her that the problem wasn't from the guy's connection but the location of the connection because some offices receive good coverage while some do not. Uchechi got very upset.

"Ramat, you must be very stupid to say that. I paid for the entire internet, and my office can't get good coverage? Bring all the internet routers here now."

"Yes, Ma." Ramat left the office.

Couldn't she say whatever she said politely?

Ramat returned with all the routers, plugged them, and left.

Uchechi was busy on her laptop for a while and looked at Awu with the look of 'Oh, you're still here.'.

"Are you ready to work Awu?"

"Yes, Ma. I am. I also noticed you gave me the position of a public relations rep and not a personal assistant."

"Yes, because Grace is my secretary and personal assistant, and I have Ramat as my executive assistant. I actually need to create a media department, starting with you as a public relations rep."

"That's great, Ma. That means we'll still need an editor, a videographer who can also be the photographer and a media assistant who can also be a reporter."

"Exactly, but right now, we'll need only an editor, and you can joggle the rest. Remember, you have experience in videography and photography. At least, that's what you said during the interview."

"Yes, I do, Ma."

"Great. So, let's see what you can do. I need you to write down your task schedule for the month and bring it to my office in an hour. We'll go through it together so that you can have a map of what you will be doing here. My organisation has done so much, but the world has no idea. I need you to find a creative way to share it with the world."

"I'll do my best, Ma."

"It has to be good enough, Awu; I don't pay people for coming to the office every day. I pay people for working. I don't care if it's going to be a virtual arrangement."

Awu nodded and was smiling when she left Uchechi's office. She met Nonye and Patience to assist her. Patience led her to her office, while Nonye was quite helpful with setting up her system. In an hour's time, Awu got the task schedule ready and went to Uchechi's office.

When Awu knocked on her door, which was already open, she asked Awu to come back later. As soon as Awu arrived at her office, Uchechi called her intercom and said, "Awu! Do not barge into my office again. Always call me through the intercom to know if I am ready to see you."

"It was already an hour, Ma, and you said -"

"Come back in thirty minutes and call me before you barge into my office. I won't repeat myself."

Uchechi hung up. Awu's mouth hung open for some time.

"Naso e dey happen for here? Isn't this the same sweet lady I met during the interview? The same person who gave her an envelope with ten thousand Naira after the interview. Is she this annoying and bossy?"

Awu pondered until the thirty minutes elapsed. She

called Uchechi as she had instructed, and Uchechi asked her to come to the office in five minutes. When she got to Uchechi's office, they talked about the task and her expectations, and Awu promised not to disappoint. After work, Awu joined Ramat. Ramat and Patience live in the same area, but Ramat dropped Awu off at a junction that is close to her friend's house. At home, Awu told her best friend, Amokeye, everything that happened, and Amokeye told her that she might not last at that job because the environment already felt toxic, but Awu was positive, claiming it was 'initial gra-gra.

Awu gradually understood her colleagues, but the job was somewhat of a mystery. She noticed that her colleagues were not happy; they complained about the lack of staff structure most of the time. Her worry was that they were not issued appointment letters, and she told her colleagues that she would have hers and an accommodation after her one-month probation.

Patience had a hard time when Awu arrived at the Ucy Foundation. She was going back and forth with Uchechi, unsure she was needed in the office as her *iPhone 7plus* and MacBook were given to Awu, and since Awu was overwhelmed with the new job and gadgets, she was totally insensitive to Patience's feelings.

Less than two weeks into the job, Uchechi

complained about everything: her writing, her thoughts, her speech, her ideas, and Awu became worried. This is the first time in Awu's career that she felt she was drowning on the job. With everything she did, she was still portrayed as incompetent and sluggish.

When Awu's one-month probation ended, Uchechi called her to her office and asked that she should have a seat. Awu knew something was up. The first and last time she sat in her office was the first day she resumed in the office; since then, she could only stand in her office for almost an hour, deliberating on a project and getting queried for some omissions.

"How will you rate your output for the past month from one to ten?"

Awu thought for a while and said, "Six, Ma."

"That's great because if you had said anything from eight, I would have asked you to leave. I feel you are on a five. I believe you can do more, but I am struggling to understand your competence."

Awu nodded.

"I cannot increase your salary because I feel with your output, I should reduce your current salary. I wouldn't do that because I believe you have potential and as for your accommodation, you need to find a place and let me know the cost. It should be between three hundred and fifty thousand Naira to five hundred thousand Naira."

"Okay, Ma, I'll put in more effort, but Ma, when can I get my appointment letter?"

"Awu, we don't give appointment letters here because someone tried to blackmail the organisation with it. If you do not accept my terms, you can leave."

Awu thought of so many things in a split second and decided to give the job a second chance. "I won't leave, Ma. I just need an appointment letter for documentation."

"Oh, well, Awu. Maybe when you get better at your job, I'll talk to the H.R. to do something about it."

"I'll appreciate it, ma."

"You can leave my office now."

"Thank you, ma."

Awu stood up and left the office heartbroken; the last time she felt this way was when Joseph told her that he couldn't be with her anymore. Awu needed the salary increment and accommodation as soon as possible. She had already sent her things from her previous house to her cab driver's place since her friends didn't have the space to accommodate them; the aim was for him to send them to Abuja as soon as she got a place.

Awu got home and told Amokeye that she would be putting up with her for another month until she found a place. Amokeye and her husband didn't want her to leave. Awu had another month to prove herself, she finally understood the pain of her colleagues. When she told them about her last meeting with Uchechi, they weren't surprised; they told her they all went through the same tunnel, and it had been a tactic for her.

Awu had a couple of projects and had to meet the deadlines. She planned a photoshoot for Uchechi; they had to travel to her hometown for it. It was a long three days, and it was a success not until they resumed at the office on Monday.

While Uchechi complained to her mother about the space they had in the corporate shoot and promised to have it cleaned up after use, Awu, who was holding her half-eaten food in her hand, bumped into Uchechi and froze; this became the highlight of Uchechi's anger towards her.

Awu, who was entitled a traveling allowance of ten thousand Naira, got four thousand Naira. Awu booked Uchechi's return trip from Abuja in the morning and hers in the evening to avoid Uchechi; she needed rest after having two long days.

Awu had another crazy week in the office, but she had the organisation in a magazine. The organisation was ranked third place in the country, and Uchechi still had an issue with omitted information. Uchechi was meant to give some money to the editor of the magazine but never did.

Awu apologized for this mistake all week. Uchechi asked for Awu's *Instagram* handle and followed her online; she wanted to know the kind of information

Awu put out there. Awu didn't have any issue with it. Uchechi was invited for an event, and Awu made the necessary arrangements.

Uchechi arrived, and Awu took her through a long route to the venue, which upset Uchechi.

"Which kind suffer head be this na?" Uchechi moaned.

After the event, as they approached the elevator, Uchechi said:

"Awu, I am tired of correcting you."

"Ah! What have I done again this time?"

Uchechi replied, "This is a very unprofessional response, and I am so irritated about it."

"I'm sorry, ma. I was just joking around. Please forgive me."

Uchechi said nothing as she left for the reception. Her driver, Mathew, wasn't there to get her; Awu had called him several times to be at the reception. Matthew arrived five minutes later, but Uchechi was furious. Mathew told her that he'd been waiting at the entrance where he'd dropped her off.

Every good deed Awu had done for the organisation didn't seem to count for anything. She irritated Uchechi from the moment she sat beside her at the event. Uchechi found it disrespectful and felt Awu should have sat at the back of the hall with other aides and public relations reps to get information about other social events and awards.

She disliked all the pictures and videos Awu took of her, saying they were blurry and made her look fat. They were both to travel to Lagos for a reach-out the next day, and Uchechi told Ramat to book a flight for herself and Grace instead of Awu. Ramat mentioned it to Awu in the office, and Awu told them everything that happened at the event.

The second month was worse than the first month. Uchechi sent a message to Awu at nine pm not to bother about preparing for the journey for the next day. Awu received the message and already knew that there was trouble. Awu was arranging her files and rounding off the task she was given because she knew she was going to be sacked as soon as Uchechi returned from the trip.

One day, while Jacob was cleaning their office, Awu decided to take a picture lying on one of the couches. Nonye climbed the side stool to take the picture. Awu posted it on Instagram with a sub-erotic caption. Uchechi stumbled on them, called Patience and told her to take pictures of the lounge and send them to her. Awu immediately deleted the picture on Instagram because she suspected that Uchechi gave Patience that task because of the picture she took. She told Nonye about it, and her colleagues knew that there would be a storm in the office when Uchechi resumed the next day.

When Uchechi resumed, she didn't talk to Nonye and Awu the whole day but gave tasks to Patience and

Ramat. Awu had been on a project to invite a motivational speaker to meet and have a chat with the children at Ucy Foundation, and the speaker was ready to visit. She had to inform Uchechi about the arrangement. She called Uchechi, who told her to come to the office. When Awu arrived at the office, there was a visitor, and he was holding flowers.

"Awu you are so unprofessional, incompetent, annoying and irritating. I expected so much from you, and the reason why you haven't been thrown out of this office is because of my loyalty to Ayodeji. I don't see myself working with you anymore. This is because I can no longer stand you. Do you understand?"

"Yes, Ma. I'm sorry for…"

"What is it? Keep your stupid apology to yourself."

"Ma, Adenike is ready to visit the foundation, and I want to know if I can make the necessary preparations."

"What are you waiting for? Go ahead and do the needful. Or do I need to be involved in it too since you cannot complete one task yourself?"

"I'll attend to it, Ma."

As Awu was leaving the office, she overheard Uchechi and her visitor arguing over the manner in which she spoke to Awu. Moments later, Uchechi and her visitor left her office, and Awu went to

Patience's desk.

"I think I'll leave this office next month."

"Why nah? Don't mind, madam, she'll calm down," Patience replied.

"No, I'll leave. I don't want things to get worse than this. My second month here is almost a flop, and I still want to do another month?"

"I felt the same way. When you came in, she threatened to sack me. I begged, cried and cried. She then reduced my salary by twenty percent before she allowed me to stay. Maybe you should allow her to reduce your salary."

"Never! I'd rather leave this month," Awu replied. She left for her office, called Mr Ayodeji and told him about everything that had happened. He promised to talk to Uchechi without letting her know he'd been informed.

Two days later, Mr Ayodeji called and told Awu that Uchechi called him and complained about her. he advised that she should be calm, apologise and get to understand Uchechi better. Awu agreed and thanked Ayodeji for his words of encouragement.

Adenike visited the Ucy Foundation, and it was an inspiring and motivational experience for the children. Awu was excited to have completed that task, but Uchechi complained about the graphics that was used to advertise Adenike's visit, 'too colourful'. She told her to check the entire office and find a gap she can fill, then write a position and her preferred allowance. Awu didn't know what to do when she got to her office. She cried and regretted why she came to Abuja.

Finally, she wrote: Media Representative. Two hundred thousand naira was sent to Uchechi.

Uchechi cussed her for her incompetence. Meanwhile, the cab guy in Choba called Awu to inform her that their properties had been taken to the police station by his landlord because his rent had expired, and he had not been around for the past three weeks; the policemen insisted that he pay about two hundred thousand naira to reclaim those properties.

Awu got to the office the next day downcast; her colleagues tried to cheer her up but to no avail. Uchechi's guest came to the office again with flowers, and Patience attended to him. She took the flowers, placed them in a vase, added water, and set it on Uchechi's desk in her office.

Less than an hour later, Uchechi's guest came to Awu's office,

"Hi Awu, how is it going?"

"Not bad, Sir. Good morning."

"Call me, Rochas."

Awu smiled politely and returned to what she was doing before he walked in.

"Awu, do you have a blackberry charger?"

"No, sir. I use a type C charger, but you can ask Patience."

While Rochas was having a conversation with Awu, Grace passed by and winked at Awu, then Nonye passed too and Awu knew she had to dismiss Rochas.

"Please sir, I hope this doesn't sound rude but I'll love to go back to my work."

"Okay, that's fine. I'll be in the lounge. Ucy isn't here yet, and I need to see her before I travel tomorrow."

"Safe trip, Sir."

Rochas observed Awu for some time before he returned to the lounge. It wasn't long before Uchechi returned, and she and Rochas went into her office. They spent a long time in there and stepped out laughing.

It was past lunchtime, and Awu called Jacob to get food from a lady who sells food at the end of the street. Jacob went to Awu's colleagues to ask if they needed food so as to get food for everyone at the same time. Everyone had eaten except Awu. Awu left her office for the lounge at 4 p.m. to eat and met Rochas there.

"Good evening, sir," she greeted him and walked away.

"Hi Awu, see eh, if I didn't care about Ucy, I would have left an hour ago."

Awu said nothing as she microwaved her food, but Rochas came to stand beside her in the kitchen.

"Do you really love your job?"

"Yes, I do, Sir, and I will lose this job if madam comes and meets us having a conversation," Awu said quickly.

"I'll take the blame."

"It wouldn't matter because I'm meant to be here by 2 p.m. and not 4 p.m. I just want to rush my food and leave." Awu knew that Mathew would prompt her about their arrival because it was against the office rule to eat at that time.

"I think you are an interesting person. By the way, I just followed you on Instagram; please follow Rochas Okorocha back."

Awu didn't know the expression to give as Rochas walked away to reveal Uchechi at the entrance of the lounge. Matthew didn't have the chance to prompt Awu; her hunger disappeared immediately.

"Ucy, I didn't know you had arrived," Rochas said calmly.

"How will you know when you are flirting with my staff? Awu, meet me in my office at five p.m."

"Okay, Ma." Awu couldn't move; she had to force the food into her stomach to be able to stomach every stroke of Uchechi's words.

Awu received a WhatsApp message in her school group that the strike was finally over and schools were to resume immediately. This was on a Thursday, and salaries are meant to be paid the next week. Awu was ready to leave for Choba on Sunday, depending on the conversation she'd have with Uchechi at five p.m.

As Awu was walking back to the office, Uchechi and Rochas were coming out of it.

"I'll see you tomorrow, Awu."

"Okay, Ma," Awu replied while Rochas kept a straight face as if he had never spoken to Awu in his life.

Awu told her colleagues about Uchechi catching her and Rochas talking, and she strongly felt that she was about to be sacked from work. She added that the university was resuming and she would be happy to leave the organisation and return to school because she is working under tension and not pressure.

The next day, a new human resource officer appeared and told them they'd be having a team bonding outing the following week. Uchechi didn't have an awful conversation with Awu until the team bonding day. Awu felt awkward; she had dropped a letter of absence for two weeks starting from the next Monday. She mentioned returning to school for her dissertation defence, but she knew she wouldn't.

Awu heard Uchechi through the intercom and hurried towards her office.

"Why have you been avoiding me?"

"Nothing, Ma, I don't want to upset you."

"So you are the *upsetter* in my life?"

They chuckled. Uchechi produced Awu's letter.

"I want you to take this time off to re-evaluate yourself. I find you unprofessional in certain aspects and might have been petty towards you as well, but that is why there is a probation period during employment. The company is having a little financial issue that has affected the plan for your accommodation allowance, but that will be sorted when you return."

"Okay, Ma. I'll like to know if I will return as a P.R.?"

"Yes, you will. I have made provisions to employ some other people to join you. H.R. is attending to it."

"Okay, Ma, thank you."

"You're such an interesting person, Awu, and you deserve another chance."

Patience walked in with a bouquet of flowers.

With a raised voice, Uchechi said, "Patience, if it's from Rochas, just take it away or, better still, give it to Awu. After all, she has been flirting with him."

"No, ma!" Awu gasped.

Patience smiled and handed the flowers to Awu.

Uchechi grumbled. "Na flowers I go chop? I'm not looking for a romantic guy with prospects. I'm looking for someone who is financially capable of taking my foundation global."

Awu held the flower, dumbfounded. It smelt lovely, and she could perceive it without taking her nose close to it.

"Ma. This isn't fresh flowers, and there's a note

on it."

"Awu, I'm done with you. See you at our team bonding later and safe trip to Choba."

'I see that the natural flowers wear off after some days, so I decided to get you something permanent. Love, Rochas,' the note said.

Awu read the note just as Patience walked into her office with a basket of gifts.

"Why are you giving it to me? Maybe madam will love this one?"

"But she doesn't love the guy and does him yeye, so let's share what's here."

Patience and Awu unwrapped all the gifts. There were bangles, chocolates, a set of dark sunshades, a mustard and a lavender coloured dress, and a box that had five hundred thousand naira cash that had a ticket to a vacation in Kigali.

"Patience, we have to give this to madam. I can't keep this. I'm already in a lot of trouble."

Patience took the bangles, some chocolates, the mustard dress and two hundred and fifty thousand Naira. "Let this stay between us. If you don't need money, I do. After all, she wouldn't value these gifts. Her father is a rich politician, so she's used to the *Lavida Loca* life."

"Patience, the gown isn't your size. It's a size fourteen, and you're a ten."

"My sister sews. She'll help me trim it, and I'll use it for a photoshoot. Awu, let this be between us, even if we're asked about it, *biko*."

Awu replaced the ones Patience didn't take in the beautiful raffle basket and went to Ramat's office, got her car keys, put the basket in, her extension socket, her provisions, plates and teacup in the car trunk.

She was ready to sign off from Ucy's Foundation, but for the team bonding, which was quite interesting, there was a whole lot of fake laughter and conversations. The only real part of the outing that she loved was the food. It was expensive and delicious.

After the outing, Awu ordered a taxi. She got all her things from Ramat's car and left. Amokeye saw the basket with gifts in Awu's room and laughed herself out when Awu told her off when she expressed Rochas likes her. As Awu was arranging her things for her journey the next day, she remembered to follow Rochas Okorocha on *Instagram*.

Immediately Awu arrived at Choba, she received a message from Rochas, he asked for her address, and she sent it. She was so busy in school that she wasn't answering her phone and had missed several of Rochas's calls. When Awu got to her friend Quincy's place, she had a shower, ate and got her phone from her bag. She called him back, failing, she sent him a text message.

Awu told Quincy everything, and Quincy insisted, 'If Rochas is nice, give him a chance to get back with Uchechi. ' Awu was indifferent to everything except her dissertation. She had broken down earlier because her properties were no longer at the police station. She didn't know what had happened to them; the taxi driver's number was also unreachable.

Luckily, Quincy had acquired a one-bedroom apartment; it was a bigger space compared to her previous self-contained apartment; she told Awu to stay with her until she could afford a place of her own. Awu and Rochas had begun to speak daily. When it became serious, Quincy sometimes joined them.

After Awu defended her dissertation, she informed Lilian from H.R. at Ucy's foundation that she wouldn't return to the organisation and then Quincy told Awu to dress up for a small dinner party with friends to celebrate her dissertation. Awu wore the lavender dress which had been amended to fit her.

As they got to the venue, Awu exclaimed, "Quincy, this place looks expensive o! Who dash you money to plan dinner for me here?"

"Na see finish dey worry you."

They laughed and walked into the reception where they had to use a lift to the rooftop. While they were inside the elevator, Rochas called.

"Hey, babe."

"Hi Rochas, what's good?"

"Nothing much. I just want you to know that I

cherish our friendship and would like us to take this up a notch."

"Rochas, I'm a bit skeptical because of how we met. I don't want Uchechi's wahala. Let's leave it at friendship and…" As the lift doors opened, she saw Rochas in front of her holding his phone to his ear.

The dinner was far real and better than the team bonding event; they had genuine laughter, lots to eat and drink. Quincy took a picture of Awu and Rochas and tagged them to her *Instagram* story. Rochas saw the tag and added it to his story.

At this time, Awu wasn't fiddling with her phone; it had been in her purse since she saw Rochas. Awu heard her phone ring and answered it without looking at the screen.

"Awu, where's your office phone and MacBook?"

Awu almost choked on her drink as she heard Uchechi's voice.

"It's with Ramat, Ma."

"Okay," she said a while later and ended the call. It was almost ten p.m.

Uchechi can only be making this call if something is wrong, Awu thought just Rochas received a call. Rochas spoke for almost five minutes. In that time, Awu received a call from Mr Ayodeji.

"Hello, boss. Good evening," Awu said quietly.

Ayodeji started laughing. "Awu, so you want to

kill Ucy, abi? You resigned and also snatched her boyfriend."

"What? No, sir! They never dated, boss. From what I gather, they were only having sex, and she never wanted to be committed."

"Ah! Awu, you like him?"

"Yes, I do, but things haven't escalated yet. I can withdraw if you say so."

"Do whatever you want. Just know that Ucy is furious, and for the way she treated you, you have every right to be happy. I'm upset about her pettiness towards you. And finally, congratulations, you're now a aster's degree holder."

"Thank you, Boss."

Awu and Rochas's calls ended almost at the same time, and they both returned to their seats.

Quincy and Opus were worried because the smiles on their faces had disappeared.

Rochas held Awu's hand and kissed it. he looked at her face and directly at her lips, and at that point, Awu knew he was asking for permission to kiss her. Awu smiled shyly, and Rochas held her face and kissed her deeply. It was a very long kiss, and Quincy recorded it on her phone.

"Awu, I regret giving the ticket to Kigali to Ucy. I wish I still had it, but to celebrate our relationship and as far as I am concerned, you are now my girlfriend, let's go to any country of your choosing."

Awu smiles and looks at Quincy as if she's asking for

permission to make a request. "Rochas, you haven't asked me out officially. You have to…"

Rochas took Awu's hands and looked into her eyes. "Awu, I actually did like you from the moment I saw you, but my heart was somewhere else. I am ready to love, cherish and be honest with you, and if God's willing, this can go further from here. Awu, please, will you be my girlfriend?"

"Hmm, when I love, I love deeply. I want you to promise me that you will never leave me or disrespect me because I don't want this care and attention to stop, Rochas Okorocha."

Rochas touches Awu's chin. "I promise you would have nothing to worry about with me. I am a one-woman man. Na you go tire."

"Yes."

"Hmmm, 'yes' what?" Rochas asked.

"Yes. I'll be your girlfriend, Rochas."

Rochas kisses Awu again, this time more passionately, and Awu whispers into Rochas's ear.

"I have the ticket to Kigali."

Rochas face brightened.

"What! Babe, let's go then."

Opus raises his glass, saying, "To love and friendship."

Everyone else did the same and cheered.

SARAH ENO OBONGHA is a Writer, an Artist, and a Public Relations Manager; she was born in 1990 as the first child of her parents. She is a native of Mkpani in Yakurr Local Government Area, Cross River State, Nigeria. Sarah lost her mother at the age of thirteen, and things took a different turn in her life. She spent her teenage years as a mother to her father and siblings. Because of this, she was always more mature and principled than her friends and colleagues due to her position in the family. Her experiences and wishes ignited the flare of writing in her from the age of fourteen.

She is a Master's Degree graduate in Arts History from the University of Port-Harcourt, Rivers State in Nigeria. Writing has been a form of expressing her feelings, thoughts, dreams, and

DON'T FIGHT TODAY!
Foyeke

ONE

Àdìgún walked around muttering in strange tongues as flies buzzed over his jaunty afro. From the busy roads of Orita, his bare feet would smack the floor as particles dropped from his threadbare dashiki with each step taken on his cracked heels. He's in the nine skies today, skipping down the sidewalk while I kept a safe distance behind him. He rubs his stomach and lets out a belch. The air around him clouds in the frosty morning air. I instinctively raise a hand over my nose as the concoction of smells around him darkens.

I checked my time; it was ten minutes before seven a.m.. The stores framing the lanes were awakening slowly, and the cabs were far between. I debated following Àdìgún and simply walking my way to Challenge Bus Stop, or simply stop to wait for a bus. The traffic mostly consisted of corporate-type cars, obviously going to their air-conditioned workplaces. I huffed in indecisive frustration, the harmattan air billowing white before my face. I should have just waited a few minutes before leaving home, but the echoed screams of my neighbour's little child were all I needed to remind me that another minute in the house would have driven me crazy. So here I was on a sleepy Ibadan morning, avoiding a madman while commuting to work.

Àdìgún grew farther from sight. I watched as he kicked an empty cane basket lying on the roadside. A tomato flew out, which he promptly picked up and ate, causing me to shudder in revulsion.

I sighed and began walking, nothing else to do at this point, making sure to keep a distance between myself and this curious wayfarer. I plug in my earpiece and wait patiently for the first sounds of my favourite podcasters to reach my ears. Like a broken tap, it creaks at first, then stops. I checked my phone after two minutes of silence. The SIM icon on my screen read: emergency calls only.

Trust *Glo*, the self-proclaimed Nigerian grandmaster

of data service, to be M.I.A. when you need them the most. I kept my phone in the bag, hoping the service would be restored soon. With *Glo*, you never know; it could be back in a minute or two business days. Moments later, my phone vibrated from the bag; notifications were coming in, then the podcast came on again.

"Perfec....Aahhhhh!" I yelled and skipped several steps back on instinct.

When did I get so close to him?

"Fine geh geh." Àdìgún said to me with a grin, his teeth of many colours flashing at me. I took more steps backward, and he followed. I reached discreetly into my bag for my pepper spray can. What if I sprayed him and he grew ferocious? I looked around and there were people around, but too far from us, and I won't trust them to not just look away.

"Are you not a fine girl?" he asked; his lips curling in a pseudo-posh accent.

Do I respond? Tell him off? He was not known for being aggressive, at least I've never seen him that way. His bloodshot eyes ran over my fit. He pointed at my hair excitedly.

"Bob Marley! Bob Marley is a fine girl," he chanted.

It took me a few moments to realise he was referring to my box braids.

"Ah, yes, yes." I chuckled awkwardly, trying to

sidestep him and make a dash for it.

"Don't you like Mike Tyson?" he asked. A dry cackle followed. I stepped back as he leaned forward and scratched one foot with another.

"You know him? Fight fight," he said, his arms dealing the air with incoherent punches.

"Don't fight, o!" He shrieks suddenly, making me quake in my proverbial boots.

With a dramatic *about-turn*, he walks away, *heheheing*. I look around and see several people observing our interaction.

"Did you hear?" Àdìgún yells again at me. "Or you'll see gbash! Everything scatter-scatter!"

"Oh, mummy is going to love this," I said to myself as Àdìgún finally disappeared into a corner.

But I knew better than to tell her. The next thing would be her driving to my place and sprinkling church water and anointing oil mixture all around my apartment.

It's just another madman talking. Or was it? My mind started to reel. Come to think of it, I almost went knocking on my neighbour's door today when the baby's screams became unbearable. But what could my complaints have done?

"Don't mind him, aunty, that's how he usually behaves," a woman walking up to me said, a huge basket of snails balanced on her head.

I smiled back and offered my thanks.

I wouldn't mind this unusual messenger one bit, but

when you are programmed to overthink things like clockwork, you don't get to have a choice. Whom would I possibly fight today? Office security and his crude jokes? I wouldn't mind whacking my bag on his egg-bald head. Or was it Teni, the virtual intern whose most intelligent contributions at meetings are "noted" but could talk for ages on irrelevances?

I checked the time again; only ten minutes had passed. I realised my earlier chosen podcast had been playing with my earbuds. I switched it off and went back to searching for a cab.

~~~~~~

I ruffled through my bag as *Micra* drivers drove closer to my office. Where is the change? I was sure I put a two hundred naira note in my purse this morning, or was that yesterday? I sighted five-hundred-naira notes, a one thousand note, threw a polyester note aside, but no two hundred.

"Challenge!" the driver called.

"Ówà o! It is here o!" I answered, indicating I was alighting.

"Owo da? Where's your fee?" he asked.

"Mò n bò o. I'm coming." I ruffled through my bag again.

The car parked, still no two hundred naira note.

"Aunty answer us na." The passenger at the front seat complained.

I finally gave up and handed him the five hundred naira.

"Ah, mi ò ní sénjì o. Mo ti só fún yín kí e tó wolé. I don't have change. I told you before you entered."

I huffed, opened the door, and got off.

"See see, giff me my money o aunty. O sàárò o. It's too early in the morning."

I resolved to leave and forgo the change.

"The door slammed as he jumped out of the car.

"Aunty you too look for change na," the passenger at the front seat called again.

"Wo-o! Don't get me angry this morning o, because I told you that didn't have change when you entered," the cab man yelled with veins popping out from his neck. The man was obviously drunk, and the waft of alcohol sickened the air as he spoke.

"Keep the change," I said, repressing the urge to fire back and ask him not to yell at me. And that you don't remember him warning you about change.

"Eseun o, thank you, sister," he said as his frown slipped fast into a grin. The car zoomed off as I entered the office building.

Immediately, I heard him shout from his cubicle room.

"Orobokibo. Fat person," Mr Salisu hailed. I dealt him a glare, but he just kept smiling, his broken tooth giving me an unsolicited window into his mouth.

"Aunty, I'm greeting you o."

"I'm not replying. You did not call me by my

name," I said, a little too gentle than I should like.

"But you're orobo na." He flapped his arms and puffed up his cheeks.

The nerve!

I should give him a piece of my mind, tongue-lash him and warn him off his constant fat shaming language - that is if he even knows the meaning of the phrase. Submitting a complaint to H.R. would be my next order of action. But I wouldn't - the man was too old to be opening gates for me, he was probably older than my father. Seeing him work with his old age like this gives me all the reason to just not be that brat, and today is certainly not the one to start a fight with an old man.

So I walked into the office, casually admiring the logo of Dennard Publishers. Two years after working as an editor, I still take second glances at the simple and perfect construction of the small letter D with an ornate quill in the stem. Was my life so lacking in depth I sought romance in the simplest of things?

The wall clock read 8 a.m. on the dot. The lights were on, definitely, someone else is around. One hour early to the official start of the day meant one hour to pray and let my mind wander. I powered on my computer and checked the schedule for the day. Not too heavy but not light either. The cursor lingered over a particular item on the list, Olajídé.

This particular work brought some immediate migraines. It's been three sessions with the client, Mr Jones, a friend of the founder, and I already wanted to quit.

His story was the result of a Nigerian bred in Britain who makes his way home for the first time and is immediately thrown into the pomp of Òsun-Òsogbo festival.

"Don't you think we need more of a little colour there, Sayo? Africa is quite colourful."

The use of the word Africa was one betrayal you could not forgive. Et tu? Tòkunbò Jones? Even after all the *Twitter* threads sewn against the monolithification of the whole continent. He still referred to his home country as Africa.

More infuriatingly, he pronounces my name the same way American YouTubers pronounce mayo. And every single time I'd gently correct him, biting back a harsh retort: *Sha-yor*! He would get it right at first, then slip back to his original pronunciation. The actual embodiment of pain in the neck.

"Good morning, madam," Teni said as he peeked his head into my door.

"Yes, Teni, good morning," you curtly answer, dreading the chit-chat his simple greeting will eventually slip into.

"I dey, I dey. Anything for the boys?"

I cocked an eyebrow at him. He chuckled, slapped the door and says, "Show me love o, Aunty Sayo."

"Go and tell your oga at the top to show you love. Oya back to your station," I said, shooing him away. "When I walked in and met nobody at the reception. What if it was a potential client? "

"I just went to the toilet na," he said, his hands playfully twisting the door handle. "Oga say we get meeting o… by nine-thirty."

"Okay, thanks for letting me know. Now go back to the reception."

"Ah-ah, you don't like the way you're seeing my face?" I ignored him and redirected my attention to the computer. The silly boy was going to keep me talking for hours if I allowed him. I scanned my schedule again and heaved a sigh. I should certainly get my coffee ready for the long day.

~~~~~

By 9.30 a.m., the conference room was already full of staff members. I watched all of them from the corner of my eye while I scrolled away on *Twitter*. Like the room I was in, my timeline was a mishmash of activities: subliminal posts lacking the '@' button, art pieces, news on wars around the world, cat videos. The room fell silent as the door creaked open. The boss came in with a file.

"Settle down, settle down," he said, waving his hands. His jutting stomach bounced on the table as he tried to sit.

"Good morning, everybody."

"Good morning, Sir," the room chorused.

"I'd get straight to the point."

No, he wouldn't.

"Ehn ehn, Rose," he said, pointing to one of the accountants. "Where were you at 3 p.m. yesterday?"

"Sir, I just went to get a meal, sir. It was a delivery." His eyes did a wish wash over her, then he hissed.

"You just leave your work and do it as if we're here to play. Don't let it repeat itself again."

Everyone knew it would.

"Anyway, both of you should show us the last six-month financial report I asked you to prepare."

"Okay, sir," the duo replied and started shuffling papers.

They soon got into a ramble of numbers and statistics, losing me just two sentences in. With my terrible arithmetic skills and the look that sat on the boss's face, I deduced the numbers were looking bad.

"So, you all see yourself now. Paper is getting expensive, and still, we're not selling."

"Sir, if I may?"

"No. You may not. I'm not done talking," he said, effectively waving Chucks off. "Yes, we'd put more of our books online, but not now."

"Just a question..."

"Will you let me finish?" The last words ended in a long hiss, his eyes popping out wide at the culprit.

"Now, why are you not posting our publications on

social media? Shebi, that's why I employed you youths? Why aren't you all putting your energy into bringing people that have things to publish and sell out publications?"

Maybe because that's the job of a freaking marketing team, I muttered under my breath.

"Yes, Sayo. What do you have to say?"

You had a lot to say. You wanted to lambast him for his continuous shunning of the tech dude. Chucks definitely had a lot of shining ideas, which sometimes he tried to get across to him while he was being too thick-skulled to accept. And what was his grouse with getting an actual marketing team? He kept on relying on the graphics designers, whom he wouldn't employ full time but required to do both book covers and marketing fliers. Why be such a penny-pincher?

I swallowed my breath and simply muttered something about doing better as a collective. He nodded, finally, a confirmation of his thoughts all along. He was obviously sure the languid state of business was not of his own doing. It had to be his staff members that had chosen not to value his company as much as he, the owner, did.

"Sir, like I've told you before, we still have readers of paperbacks, but most people are switching to digital books these days. Unfortunately, this means that we would have to divert a whole load of attention towards publishing online if we really want to break even. And I suggested we create a form of platform for young writers where they can publish a certain number of words for free." Chucks had broken the silence, forging ahead with his idea.

"*Osho free, osho free*! Do you young people want to ever pay for anything again? In our time, we saved up pennies to buy good books. Check my library: Socrates, Karl Marx, Shakespeare, all those classics. Why do you think I started this company? We must let them learn the value of literature and appreciate it."

"Well, Sir, you're not wrong, but we can't keep towing them..."

"We have five books online already, right?" the boss cuts in.

"LET HIM FINISH!" I mentally yell, the words stretching the walls of your closed mouth.

"Yes, sir."

"We'll start small with that. The rest of us should start brainstorming ways to increase sales and get more people to publish with us. I'd send you a graphic of our anticipated releases. Make sure you share it on your social media platforms, okay?"

Everyone grunted, "Yes, sir."

Rose's face from the accounting department was set in a frown; the post which the boss will monitor would cause another theme deviation on her Instagram page.

~~~~~~

I resumed work, willing time to slow down while I ploughed my way through my scheduled edits for the day. It felt comforting, something to easily slip into, reshaping people's thoughts to something more readable. I remembered several of my own works in progress, currently lying in draft, severely neglected. If they could talk, it would be the most chaotic conversation between jilted lovers.

"You showed me the most love, showering me with the best of metaphors as I filled lines upon lines. This wasn't the promise. You said I was going to be submitted with your name boldly written on me! You already wrote an outline!"

And another would say,

"You said I was your best idea. You abandoned these other ones for me, and now you pick another one?"

With all the inventions of man, there should be a sort of technology that you can just connect to your head that translates the creative electric waves firing in your brain and writes out in full exactly what you mean to express. Alas, we're busy reaching for the skies when I can't even get my thoughts down on paper.

I huffed and backspaced. It felt as if the AI gods were listening to me. I had just typed my last thoughts into the sentence of the story I was currently editing. My system clock told me it was already one p.m. Lunch time.

I huffed again and went for my cup of coffee. The appetite for mid-day meals has gradually disappeared after several years of indulging in cold afternoon coffee and crunching on chocolate chip cookies. Did that translate to several wide-eyed late nights, in which I processed all the ridiculous scenarios my brain could muster? Absolutely yes.

I checked my time again. In another hour, I'd have Mr Jones in my office giving me all the reasons why a certain character must say a particular sentence I'd scraped off, or why a certain setting must have dandelions scattered in the air. If I told him dandelions aren't easy to come by in Nigeria, he'd say it's just a make-believe Nigeria where he could imagine whatever he wanted. I'm curious why *ugwu* leaves, pothole-ridden roads or littered streets never crossed his imagination.

I would grit my teeth as he insisted that was his style. And he would bring out book sales stats of other fictional stories he published on *Amazon* and how well those did. He was a science fiction writer quite all right, a dealer in the wanton expanse of what life could be like. Aliens, robots, technology taking over humanity, a new order, humans changing their skin or gaining superpowers - the list goes on. As much as this particular story scratched my senses the wrong way, I still respected his boundless mind and, most especially, his confidence in putting out all the crazies in his head.

I'd rather die than let something of this nature come out in my name. I would rewrite and rewrite as my inner critic bit hard on all my mistakes and inadequacies. My own mind would revolt against the very idea of my work being meaningful.

Surprisingly, Mr Jones was already making confident projections on how well his book would sell. After all, Africa had become a hot commodity in the world's arts market. He has even compiled a playlist of Nigerian songs to be published in the book. It was right off of Spotify's hottest hits. I wanted to show him my own playlist of artists I thought stayed true to their craft despite the commercialisation of music. But what do I know?

The knock on the door was a temperate degree of ominous. I checked my time; it was ten minutes past 2 p.m. already. How did I let my mind wander for such a long time? I thought I just filled my coffee cup and…

All the biscuits had suddenly vanished, and the slight bitter aftertaste of chocolate on my tongue convinced me of my full participation in the sugary meal. I coughed to clear my throat and answered the door.

"Please hold on," I say as I quickly arrange the coffee table for the meeting.

I opened the door and there was Mr Jones, all smiles, as if he knew he was about to wipe mine off.

"Hey, Sayo," he greeted, his mispronunciation unsurprisingly intact. "It's been a week."

He walked in and set his *Daniel Craig*-like frame on the couch without a grunt. The lucky bastard.

"Welcome, sir. Would you like tea or coffee?" I asked, but he leapt to his feet and served himself water from the water dispenser. I wondered how someone could easily slip into being at home anywhere. This was just his fourth time here, and he was already serving himself water without asking.

He let out a long *aahh* of satisfaction and set the cup of the table after exhausting its content.

"So, what do you have for me today?" he asked.

I opened my *Google* docs, and he also brought out his small pad from the large purse and scrolled. The story was an ambitious tale of a shape-shifting young man who is set on a mission to defeat corrupt Nigerian leaders while also looking to capture a girl's heart.

A strong part of me wanted to point out that his hero is too strikingly similar to *Spiderman*. On second thought, I let him have his way with his Osogbo mutant.

"I've indicated changes for you to see, sir," I say as I open the document and settle on my most recent edits.

"I see. I particularly love this chapter. Chapter fifteen, right?"

I nodded in reply.

"The AI-controlled governor's villa. Don't you think that's brilliant?"

I nodded again as I pretended to concentrate on the screen, clicking the keyboard for extra effect, while something in me screamed an effective no.

No, it wasn't brilliant. He did that thing I used to do as a kid, tell the story. He went on about gold doors and white walls, that the governor was fat, and his accent was heavy, and the … A foundational lack of depth. I'd elevated it a little, describing the glow of the golden-plated equipment in the office, as well as the rolling motions of the governor as he greeted his cohorts in a meeting.

"You, you've changed it," he said, looking up at you like a child being told off.

"Well, yes, Sir. I made some minor adjustments." They were not minor at all. My rage grew as I anticipated his insistence on keeping things the way they were because he preferred the easier, simpler style that the target audience would prefer to read. Suds to his target audience.

He heaved a sigh and scrolled the pad in his hands.

"Well, the edits are not bad. But could we retain these." He scrolled some more and finally pointed it to me - the part where the hero confronts the governor.

I pretended to scan over the chapter again, but I already knew it was like the Nigerian states and capital recital. Olajide, named after Mr. Jones' grandfather, was undercover as one of the governor's security personnel. He was to get some files from the governor's personal computer and blow them all up the Skiternet - a futuristic public media where news is displayed in the sky by private citizens. He runs into several problems along the way, like knocking things over and attracting the bad guys' attention, then having to shapeshift into a cat in a split moment, almost getting killed but escaping at the last moment, and then landing inside a secret meeting with the governor and his cohorts.

"I must point out that your job here is not to make the work too stifling. The edited version has to be more interesting than what was initially given to you."

I felt my stomach growl. It was hunger, a deep need to leap from my seat and descend on this creature seated before me and pick at his pink tapered fingers and snap them like sticks.

I switched to the earlier version, which I had edited and read out the specific part to him.

"You're a bad leader, and you deserve to die, but I'll spare you, for now," Olájídé said. The governor and the other men looked at each other, confused.

One of the men shouted, "Who is this fool?"

You better keep an eye on it, Arápá, because I know all your secrets as well! The botched dam construction, your bribes to the Minister of Works! I know everything," Olájídé replied

"Who are you? Do you want me to call my boys on

you?" the governor yelled, his lower lips quivering.

"I am your nemesis," Olájídé roars, and he turns to a lion, causing the men to jump backwards.

"Yes, and what is wrong with that? Isn't it more boisterous, more colourful, and really confrontational as you'd expect a hero scene to be?"

"I... honestly don't really think so, Sir." I hated how the adverbs slipped out like pacifiers to gently stick into his ego. "I think..." you trailed off and began to look for the words, swatting away the brutal suggestions that came to your mind. That the excerpt was childish, a forced attempt at recreating a *Marvel* movie scene. A flowery cliche of a hero's reveal. It's unrealistic that the kid, despite his powers, isn't scared of being in such a dangerous situation.

I wanted to add that he was being a spoilt brat, bent on destroying what could be his breakthrough into the Nigerian market, which he was so little concerned about. I wanted to call him out on his arrogance, then ask him to return to his *Amazon* friends and write something for them; or take his bloody time learning about the culture, translating it, and making it into something more original, rather than this nonsense of stereotypes and clips of popular things he has picked up about the country from Western media.

"I suggest you just leave it. You don't seem to

have anything to counter," he said.

The man lived his entire life in arguments and rebuttals.

"Okay, sir."

I deleted my suggested edit and let it be making a mental note to inform my boss that I would not like my name on any parts of the finished book, not that I expected him to acknowledge me anyways.

The day grew longer with more instances of me offering my thoughts civilly to Mr Jones, and him batting it off with his unspoken resolution that the story remain the exact same way as it came to my desk. Even with minor grammar changes, he insisted that his mismatch of English tenses was deliberate, that his aged grandfather spoke his English in that manner, and thus, that should apply to the other older men in the story, one of whom was a Senior Advocate of the country.

When I was done, the entirety of my head ached, not from doing, but of all the things I should have done, everything that could have made the story better. Watching him ruin what could be good work, at the very least, chipped at my soul.

I wasn't afraid to talk. There was no reason I should have been. except, perhaps, but not too likely, the coloured flashes of a madman's teeth. I could just let him know what he was doing was ridiculous, and that this was my job, and everyone else who has passed their book through me can witness to the tremendous change in their story after I laid my hands on it.

But no, I was fighting myself off for whatever reason. I wasn't scared, of course, and absolutely not. I wouldn't want to appear rude, because that would mean a report to his dear friend, my boss, and I could lose...no! That is not an option. How would I save enough to make it out of the house with my screaming neighbour's child?

~~~~~

I finally got home, remembering Àdìgún again as I hit the shower. I was going to take a long nap after dinner and complete the day. Voila, I've avoided all possible face-offs. By tomorrow, I would have the prophetic clearance to give everyone a piece of my mind. The only other thing to get my attention today will be the Chicken Republic meal I brought from home.

The knock sounded like a knell on my front door just as I clicked play on the Korean series I was watching. I paused, looking at the time and mentally confirming I was not expecting anyone. Opening the door, my neighbour looked tired and worn with the baby on his hip.

"Aunty Sayo, please let me hold your baby," he said, deploying the classic Yoruba tactic of communizing your needs. "I need to quickly buy something from the kiosk downstairs, and his mother isn't home right now," he explained, already thrusting the baby at me.

My mind swiped through its shelf of excuses. And I batted each one away as it all seemed so stupid. I wouldn't tell him my fear of babies, how their evil eyes, which everyone thought adorable, terrified me, how their cries made me want to puncture my eardrums and dive into the lake. I could just say no that I was tired and trying to sleep or that I'm too busy at the moment. But there was no way to refuse to hold a baby without sounding like a total tool.

The kid stared at me curiously. I hoped he would be one of those kids who cried in the arms of strangers. He was not. I wonder why his father would not use the baby carrier. It was just down the stairs; what could he want to buy that he had to drop the child with me?

"Papa," the baby tattled as I returned to the couch where my meal lay. I debated continuing eating but closed the box. The numerous *TikToks* of babies puking on their parents flittered through my mind. I wouldn't trust myself not to chuck the baby if that happened to me. So, I carried him gently like an egg and stared as he settled on my side.

"Da da," he babbled again.

I played the series, something to distract the child while I scrolled through my phone and waited for his father's return. The knock this time sounded like tinkling cymbals. I hurriedly lifted the child and headed to the door. The smell was the first thing that assaulted my senses, then the warm trickle, followed by a loud fart. My stomach was warm, wet, and sticky. My breath came in short spurts as I quickly opened the door.

"I'm sorry. I had to go twice to carry the bags of water. We had run out, and he's been troubling me all day, so I forgot."

"No problem," I lied and handed him the child.

"Oh! "I'm sorry," he said, pointing at your soiled pyjamas. "I just got his pack of pampers too. If you don't mind, I could help you get that dry cleaned. He's been having a running stomach all day and, just like the water, I didn't notice we'd run through his diapers till the last one. I'm so sorry."

I mustered a smile and told him not to worry. I managed to close the door with a gentle click. Then I rested against it. I slipped to the floor and threw a silent tantrum, screaming a soundless scream and hitting the floor with my fist several times. I stomped my way to the bathroom and kicked my couch out of blind anger. It moved the stool on which my laptop was set. Crash! The device landed on the tiled floor and split into parts.

"Fuccccccckkk!" The yell was out of my mouth before you could think of it. "Arghhhhhh."

My common sense said to tone it down, but I could not find it in myself to care anymore. So, I screamed and sobbed and cried, pausing at intervals to yell at concerned people at the door that it was a movie I was watching.

The thought of what my little moment of anger

would cost pinched my insides even more. Fixing the damage or buying a new laptop. Likewise, my meal was definitely gone, as all I could think of was poop. I slapped my head several times, thinking of the fact that I could have avoided the whole misfortune by putting my foot down, not only with my neighbour but with everyone who splashed a little fuel on my residual anger with life today. But Àdìgún's mad laughter will not let me rest.

Not only was my laptop broken, I would remember this nasty poop smell for the rest of today and tomorrow. My appetite is gone. I would probably never see the rude cab driver and his passenger again to give them a piece. Mr Salisu would still call me orobo tomorrow, and my boss would still not listen during the stand-up meeting.

Mr Jones will continue with his badly written story while I watched and fought against my better self to guide him, howbeit with a little more pressure. So much for not fighting, so much for believing the word of a random madman on the street. That was the way of prophecies; they left you with parables and watched you make a fool of yourself.

As I lay on my bed, I recounted the day's activities, just to be sure I had not raised my voice at someone at some point. Or did all my mental yelling and invectives count? Was meant to guard my mind too, against all vexation? But that was exactly what I did. My whole day consisted of battling my own angry thoughts and

BOUND BY FATE

fighting against myself not to act.... Myself.

I asked as the lightbulb went off in my head.

I'd been fighting myself all day. Did I also count? Was the tragedy to befall me for a day's altercation also mean fighting my own person? Is my common sense angry with me now?

I shook my head and turned for the umpteenth time on my bed.

Mortals will do everything to avoid destiny. In the end, we're tied to a fate written by the divine, mad messenger or not.

PEACE AKINYODE is a final-year law student at the University of Ibadan in Nigeria. She also currently contributes as a journalist to Punch Newspaper

She considers herself a growing feminist, constantly learning about gender relations in societies, and believes in the ability of human beings to rethink culture.

When she is not cramming cases for exams, she is either challenging patriarchal views on her blog or ghostwriting romance and crime stories to help fund her chocolate chip cookie addiction.

DEATH DIDN'T DO US PART
Chiamaka Muoneke

Kachi wasn't sure if it was the smell of dry cashew leaves or the harmattan dust, but there was something nostalgic about her maternal grandparents' compound.

She had memories from her paternal grandparents' house because she remembered being there maybe once or twice. It was back when her father was still alive.

They didn't visit often because Dad didn't see the point. His parents were not alive, and his siblings were always too busy to travel.

It had been eight years since he died, and Mum had finally moved on. She was the reason that they were here today. mum had thought it would be great to bring great-grandma to her hometown, as the old woman had been out of touch with reality.

The only people in the compound were Mum and her distant cousins who grew up in this rural part of Enugu and came to visit. Mum's parents were dead too, so the compound was deserted when they arrived.

They had only planned to stay for a week, but because of her relatives, Mum had extended their stay by three more days.

Kachi was grateful for her phone because it was the only thing that had kept her company throughout, apart from the constant bugging thought that she had been at this part of Enugu before.

Perhaps it was all the stories that Great-grandma had told them when she was healthier that gave her all those deja vu feelings every time she went somewhere she thought she had been to before.

Whatever it was, she had to know, which was why she walked up to Mum, who was sitting with Aunty Amarachi, to ask her permission to leave the compound, knowing that Mum would never say no in Aunty Amarachi's presence.

"You don't know this place. What if you get

lost?" Mum asked, concerned.

"I'll just get to the end of the road and come back. I promise."

"Be back before five p.m."

Kachi checked the time on her phone. She had approximately an hour. It was enough time to survey the area.

She started off to the road, taking her time to study the wooden stores and iron gates that she passed by. The architecture looked a lot like the ones at her paternal grandparents' home. It was probably for that reason they looked so familiar.

The road curved to the right to reveal a much busier area. At a corner by the left was a passage, just in between two abandoned shops that led to the main road. It was a shortcut, and people took advantage of it.

She waited until the passage was devoid of people before approaching it. From there, she studied the main road. Nothing about it or the people there looked familiar. She turned back to leave and bumped into a tall, masculine figure.

"*Ndo!*" she let out even before seeing the face. When her eyes travelled to the handsome face, she blurted out, "Sorry", suddenly forgetting that the person might not be an English speaker.

"It's alright," he replied.

"You speak English?" she asked, unsure of why she even cared to know.

"Yes, I do." He smiled. "Do you?" he asked with a

sarcastic tone, and she chuckled.

"It's the only language that I'm really good at."

"That's not good. You're in an Igboland, and you can't speak Igbo? How do you communicate?"

"I don't. I don't talk to a lot of people."

"I'm sorry, have we met?" he asked. His eyes squinted, studying.

"I don't think so. I haven't been here in ten years."

They shifted to let someone pass by.

"Where do you live?" he resumed his questioning.

"Abuja. I assume you live somewhere… not here, too."

"I'm from Port Harcourt."

"Is this your hometown?"

"Yes, of course. I come here with my family every Christmas."

Four boys push a wheelbarrow full of big cartons and try to get it past them.

"We should probably leave this place," the stranger advised.

Kachi followed his lead as he strolled away.

"So, you must like it here," she said, attempting to rekindle the conversation.

"Surprisingly, yeah. I used to hate it here, but it's different this year. I'm not sure why. I didn't even want to come."

"Why did you?"

"My dad persuaded me. I don't know when I'll be here again."

They leaned on an empty table in front of a store, chained to the wooden pillar that held the zinc roof. It was a holiday so most of the shops were closed.

"What about you?" he asked. "What's your story? What made you decide to visit after ten years?"

"My mum thought it would be good for my Great grandma."

"Great-grand? That's a long time to be alive. I don't know if I want to live that long."

"I know, right? She has lost it completely. She has dementia and barely remembers any of us. She only remembers people from her childhood, especially her sister, my great-grand aunt," Kachi narrates. "She says her name randomly, too. My sister and I used to steal her food, and when my mum asked, Great Grandma would blame her sister. It's really creepy, especially since her sister's story was very tragic."

"What happened to her?"

"Great grandma told us that when they were younger, her sister fell in love with a poor man's son, but her parents tried to make her marry a rich man so she and her lover poisoned themselves to death."

"Jeez. That's one hell of a Romeo and Juliet story. Maybe her sister's spirit has been lurking around in your house."

Kachi smacked him on his arm. "Stop!"

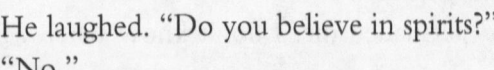

He laughed. "Do you believe in spirits?"

"No."

"So, why are you afraid?"

"Because the very concept is scary. My sister is afraid of Santa and thinks he's not real. She just can't imagine a white man with a white bed crawling into her house from her roof and yelling 'ho, ho, ho!'"

He chuckled.

Kachi continued, "I just don't think that the concept of people coming back to life in any form makes sense, but the thought still creeps me out."

"So you don't believe in reincarnation."

"I don't believe in the supernatural."

"I think reincarnation is more scientific than it is supernatural. We're matter, and matter can't be destroyed. It can only transform. I think that after we die, our souls linger somehow, somewhere, until it comes back in another body."

"That's an interesting theory," Kachi replied, resisting the urge to tell him that souls didn't exist, neither did they count as matter, and that that law of matter only applied to chemical matter.

They fell silent and Kachi couldn't get over how natural it seemed to be so close to someone she was meeting for the first time.

She said, "Strange but I feel like I've known you for a long time, yet I don't even know your name."

"I was just thinking the same thing," he replied.

"My name is Uchenna. Uche."

"Onyekachi or Kachi."

"It was really nice to meet you Kachi," Uche said, staring down at her.

Kachi looked away as she desperately thought of something to say to ignore the butterflies in her stomach.

"I think I should go. I told my mum that I would be home in an hour."

"Can I get your number at least?" he slapped his empty pockets. "I left my phone with my cousin."

"I don't have mine either."

"I'd like to see you again."

"What if we meet here tomorrow?"

"Yes, that's fine. Is 2pm alright with you?"

"Yes, it is."

"Alright then."

"Alright. *Aga m ahu gi ozo.*"

Uche grinned. "I'll see you again too."

"Is that what it means?" asked Kachi.

"You didn't know?"

Kachi shook her head

"Why did you say it?" asked Uche.

"I may have heard it somewhere, maybe from my mum, and it stuck."

"Oh."

"I should go now."

"Of course."

Kachi waved him goodbye and walked away with

her head hanging low so he didn't see that she was blushing.

~~~~~

The next day took forever but finally came. Kachi stood in front of the mirror as she brushed the strands of curly hair that peaked from the front of her head, and packed her braids in a ponytail, then she smeared on clear lip gloss and brushed her eye lashes with mascara so that they appeared thicker. She threw a scarf around her neck before making her way out the door.

"Where are you going?" Mum asked as she saw her. She stared at Kachi, surprised by her outfit.

"I'm going to see someone that I met yesterday."

Mum shook her head. "What if you get kidnapped?"

"I won't, mum. We're meeting at a public place and I'll text you my location."

She knew that Mum could only do little to stop her from going out these days. She was a big girl now. At twenty-two she barely needed Mum's permission for anything, but she asked for it anyway.

"Please, be careful and come back early to pack your things because we're leaving this place first thing tomorrow morning."

"Yes, Mum."

"Also, if you see the mechanic please tell him to hurry up with my car."

Uju hurried down the road until she came to the spot where she was with Uche and saw him there, leaning against the same table and keeping busy with his phone.

"Hello."

He looked up at the sound of her voice and smiled. "I was starting to think you weren't coming."

"Sorry, I had to help my mum do a major cleanup."

"It's okay." He stared at her from head to toe. "You look beautiful."

"Thank you. You look great too." She managed to get to his side as her knees got wobbly.

"So…uh…I was hoping to invite you to lunch…at my place. I told my parents about you."

"Already?" Kachi chuckled.

"Yes." Uche grinned.

"That's lovely. I'd love to come."

"Great. My house is a stone throw away."

He took the lead and she followed. Soon, they were moving side by side. For a while they walked quietly, increasing the tension between them.

"How long are you here for?" asked Kachi, breaking the awkward silence.

"Two weeks or so. You?"

"I'm leaving tomorrow."

"Really? So, I don't get to see you again." He stopped.

"We can keep in touch…Visit from time to time…"

Uche didn't respond. They continue and Kachi

BOUND BY FATE

spots an old cemetery.

"Is that a cemetery?" she asked, pointing to her left. "That's a lot of dead people."

"They're no gone forever."

"Right. 'Reincarnation.'" She made air quotes. "I like your optimism."

"They say if you believe in something hard enough, it becomes true."

"I wish," retorted Kachi. "So, you think everyone has been dead before?"

"Not everyone," replied Uche. "Only those who have unfinished busnesses. They're no at peace, so they come back to finish their…mission."

"But how do they know what it is?"

Uche shrugged. "I guess the universe guides them somehow. Also, we're here." He pointed at his house.

As they walked into the apartment, they were greeted by Uche's parents and his two older brothers who had gathered at the table. There was a variety of food laid out on it to mark the festive season.

Uche's brothers were mostly quiet, but his parents engaged Kachi, asking about her family and the part of the village she was from.

"So, what do you study in school?' Uche's mum asked as she scraped the last bits of rice on her plate.

"I study medicine," Kachi replied.

"That's a great course. You know, the reason

why such professions don't reach their full potential is because of how poor our educational system is. That's why Uche is going to America as soon as our Christmas break is over."

Kachi looked over at Uche as if to confirm what his mother had just said. The somber look on his face told her everything she needed to know.

A sudden wave of disappointment clouded her but she managed to force a smile. It was only after their meal that she had a chance to talk to him in private.

"When are you coming back?" she asked as they sat in a swing chair at his balcony.

"I don't know," he replied.

She tried to hold back the tears that made it hard to swallow, unsure of why this stranger had such a strong effect on her.

"Okay," she managed to say.

"I didn't know that I would meet you. It makes me… confused. I've never felt this way for anyone."

"You're leaving. What does it matter what you feel for me? You don't even know me."

"I feel like I do." When she didn't reply, he added, "I want to."

She intertwined her fingers in his and placed her head on his shoulder.

"What's your dream?" she asked.

"To fly a plane someday. I've always wanted to. What's yours?"

Uche chuckled. "To know what's going on in

Great-grandma's head."

"That's an unachievable dream." Uche laughed.

"What happened to 'if you believe in something hard enough, it'll happen'?" she asked in a mock deep voice.

As she looked up at him, their eyes met, and he lowered his head to kiss her, but she pulled away.

"It's getting late," she said, standing up. "I should go home before my mum calls."

"Speaking of…we can still keep in touch." He pulled out his phone.

She withdrew. "Uche, I don't want to invest in…this…whatever it is, if it's futile. I'm already so sad from knowing we will never see each other again."

"Please, Kachi. I love you." The words flew out naturally. He meant it. And she knew.

She sighed deeply. "I love you too, but I have to go." She picked up her purse. "Goodbye."

"Don't say goodbye."

"Okay." As she walked away, she made sure not to turn back.

At home, she walked past Mum and overheard her yelling into her phone at the mechanic. The mechanic had failed to deliver the car, and Kachi had never been more excited about a disaster. There was hope, after all, that they might just extend their stay again.

"Are we still leaving tomorrow?" she asked Mum, desperate to know.

"What kind of question is that? My job is at stake, and nothing is stopping us from leaving tomorrow."

Disappointed once again, Kachi left to her room and folded herself in bed. Hopefully, she would sleep through the rest of the day and wake up the next day when it was time to go. There was no better way to deal with the emotional turmoil that she felt.

As she was drifting into dreamland, a knock came on her door, and her sister, Chichi, announced that someone wanted to see her at the gate. It was a boy.

Stunned, Kachi got up quickly and rushed to the gate, ignoring her Mum and aunt, who stared at her. At the gate, Uche stood there, holding her scarf.

He shoved his hand forward. "You forgot this."

"Oh. Thank you," she replied, taking the scarf from his hand. "How did you know where I live?"

He scratched his head. "I must have overheard you telling my mum."

"I never mentioned my compound." Or maybe she did but didn't remember. It was the least of her problems at the moment.

"I'm so confused. I must have figured it out myself."

"Yes. Maybe."

"Okay. I guess I'll go now." Half turned, he stopped. "What time are you leaving?"

"6 a.m. Why?"

"Can I come? I'd to see you one last time."

BOUND BY FATE

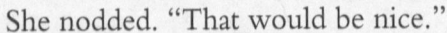

She nodded. "That would be nice."

"Okay." He turned around and walked away without saying goodbye.

~~~~~

Morning came, Kachi almost wished it hadn't. She stretched and forced herself out of bed before dragging her legs to the parlour. Mum was there and so was Chichi.

Mum had just finished shouting at the mechanic on her phone and was folding what was left of her clothes into a small leather bag. She looked up just as Kachi walked in.

"Have you had your bath?" she asked with a tone of annoyance.

"I just woke up."

"Please, go and have your bath so that I can bathe grandma and we can leave."

Kachi opened her mouth to say something but changed her mind. She wanted to tell Mum that she could stay back for a while but Mum was in a really bad mood and the outcome would be brutal. The last thing she would let Kachi do is stay back in the village because of a boy that she met two days ago.

Kachi sighed and made her way to the bathroom. She wondered why the universe had brought her and Uche together if it was so determined to keep them apart. At that moment, she wished that he would change his mind about coming at all. It was all too much.

By the time she was done changing, Mum, Grandma and Chichi were dressed up. All she had to do was wear something and zip her bag, and they would be on their way. As she smeared on some lip-gloss, a knock came on her door.

"Kachi! Your boyfriend is looking for you," Chichi announced.

A bolt of excitement ran through Kachi, causing goosebumps on her skin. She rushed to the door and swung it open.

"Who?"

"That boy that brought your headtie yesterday."

Kachi pushed Chichi gently aside and strode past her.

"Where are you going?" Mum asked as she put on great-grandma's shoes. From her tone, it was obvious that she knew where Kachi was going; she was just daring her to.

"I just want to see someone outside."

"I have been stressed out this past few days while you've been busy playing a love story. We are not taking a flight because of grandma. We're taking a bus. I beg of you, pick your bag so that we can leave. You can see him on your way out."

"I'm sorry." Kachi rushed back inside her room, picked up her bag, then made her way to the door again. "I have my bag. I'll meet you at the gate," she said before leaving.

She saw Uche standing outside, his back facing her, and she ran towards him. He turned just in time to catch her as she threw herself into his arms and hugged him tightly.

"You came," she said.

"Of course I did." He grinned.

Mum walked out of the house, wheeling a box and Grandma's wheelchair at the same time. Uche rushed to help, and it made Kachi's heart drop.

She loved his show of kindness, but she was also losing the very last moment that they had with each other.

As they got to the bus station, they were the last family to buy tickets. Everything from then was chaos. The driver was yelling, the passengers were rowdy and in a hurry, and the luggage attendants were having a hard time fixing people's bags.

Kachi found a seat at the back of the bus, just beside grandma, who sat close to the window. Mum made them sit that way so that Kachi could look after great grandma. Uche appeared at the window. Uju would have leapt for joy if she wasn't overwhelmed with sadness.

"You're still here," she said.

"I'll leave when you leave."

Great grandma looked in his direction and said something inaudible.

"What?" Kachi stared at great grandma concerned as she turned slowly to face Uche.

Great grandma smiled, revealing her teeth that Mum had done a great job at keeping healthy, still saying some words in Igbo that Kachi had a hard time picking up.

"Okonkwo…" she trailed off, raising her finger to point at Uche.

"Okonkwo?" Kachi lowered her head to great-grandma's lips.

"Ay," great grandma replied.

Kachi shook her head.

"Is she calling me Okonkwo?" Uche asked.

"Ignore her," Kachi replied. "Okonkwo was the farmer's son who her sister had fallen in love with when they were younger."

It was the first time that great-grandma had spoken in weeks - she barely spoke these days - and the first thing she did was to call a boy Kachi liked by the name of someone who had been dead for almost a century. It was then that it struck Kachi.

"Oh, my God," she let out, staring at great grandma, who still seemed excited. "Oh, my God."

"Are you okay?" Uche asked, closing in at the window.

Kachi would have remained unmoved in her position, but she needed to tell him before they left.

She lifted her eyes to Uche. "Remember what you said about reincarnation? What if you were right?"

BOUND BY FATE

"I don't understand," replied Uche.

"Okonkwo is my great grandaunt's lover, the one who died with her…"

"Okay…?"

"Great grandma hasn't been seeing her sister. She has been calling me by her sister's name. What if I *am* her sister and you are her lover?"

Uche stared at her, confused. It was a lot to take in at that moment, but it wasn't unbelievable. It explained why he felt so connected to Kachi.

He looked at great grandma, wishing that he could read her thoughts and fix the puzzle that was their reality.

"It makes sense, doesn't it?" Kachi continued. "That's why you knew the way to my house. You've been there before. That's why you suddenly felt at home here for the first time. It's because I came too!"

When the woman in front turned to stare at Kachi, she lowered her voice.

"What did I tell you when we first met? Something about seeing you again… I've never spoken Igbo that well in my life, but it was just there in my memory when I saw you. What if great grandaunt said it to her lover? I said it to you. What if we were meant to see each other?"

Uche didn't reply. He was still at a loss for words; his eyes and mouth widened in disbelief.

The engine revved, and Kachi gripped the seat in front of her as if to stop the car from moving.

"Please, wait!" she yelled before she could stop herself.

"For what again?" a passenger asked with irritation.

"Kachi," Mum called from the other roll, two seats in front. "Are you okay?"

Kachi fought the tears at the back of her eyes. "Yes."

"If it's meant to be, then I guess it'll be," Uche finally said. "Maybe we *will* see each other again."

Kachi nodded. "Okay."

She didn't believe it, but she was hopeful. She took one last look at him as the bus started moving and looked away. She didn't want to say goodbye, and neither did he.

In fact, it seemed just right that they left their statements unfinished because it wasn't the last they would see of each other. It couldn't be.

It was only when the engine picked up its pace that she turned to look at him through the glass. He was staring back at her.

They both stared until they were out of sight.

Ten years already, and the memory of Kachi's last day with Uche still seemed fresh in her mind.

In a few days, she would be in America. She'd been holding onto the belief that she might run into him, even though she didn't even know the state he was in. Maybe, she thought, if she believed enough, it might just happen.

She had turned down every man who'd shown interest in her and was starting to think that she was losing her mind. It was silly to hold onto someone that she hadn't even known, yet she felt like she had, like she couldn't be happy with anyone who wasn't him.

One would expect that at such a mature age, she had grown out of the delusion that destiny was a real concept and fate was fathomable, yet she had held on to both, more than she was willing to admit, more than she could control.

Her encounter with Uche and everything that had happened around the time they met had felt too predictable to be a coincidence. Even coincidence shouldn't be that coincidental.

Great-grandma didn't speak again after their last day at Enugu. One night, she slept and never woke up again. It was almost as though she was alive for a purpose - to bring her and Uche together.

Even the circumstances surrounding her travel were strange. Her mother wanted her to go to the UK for her masters instead of America. 'America is not safe,' she had said. 'They allow anyone own a gun. I want you to go in one piece and come back in one piece. Go to the UK. That's what your father would have wanted.'

Kachi had agreed. Not that as an adult she

couldn't do what she wanted, but she wanted to honour her father. She didn't even have a good reason other than the wild imagination of her younger self for preferring America.

Eventually, she missed the application date for Oxford, which was set earlier than she was informed. She settled for Stanford, not wanting to wait another year to reapply.

"The important thing is that you're going to a good school," said mum after the revelation. "After all, they both end with 'ford'."

Kachi had laughed, more because she was excited about going to America where Uche was. Although, she had to accept that he might not even be there. It's been a decade, after all. He probably moved on and wasn't thinking of her, but here she was.

Mum walked into the room just in time to disrupt her thoughts, and she was grateful for that.

"Are you ready?" she asked, leaning against Kachi's door.

"Almost," Kachi replied. "I just have to pack one last bag."

"Good. The driver is here to take you to the airport."

Airport.

Kachi sighed. It was really time to move on.

~~~~

It wasn't until morning came and Uche sobered up

from his wild night with his friends that he finally decided to check his voicemails from three weeks ago, after he left town for a break. One of them was from his ex-fiancée, Esther, and it wasn't pleasant.

Just letting you know that I met someone new, and he's so much better than you. I'm moving on, and this is the last time I'll try to reach out. But you know what? You're a coward for what you did, and you'll never find anyone like me. Have a great life.

Uche chuckled. "Well, thank God because I don't want to meet anyone like you," he said as he fixed his tie.

They had been together for almost two years before he proposed to her, but he grew cold feet and had to confess that he wasn't in love with her.

She hadn't taken it lightly, and he hadn't expected her to, but he wasn't ready for her reaction. She had caused a scene at the diner where they were and had broken his car glass, causing him to enforce a restraining order against her, not that it had stopped her from reaching out.

The whole relationship had been forced by Esther. He was attracted to her for how closely she resembled Kachi and the fact that she was Nigerian too.

He liked her as a friend, but she had pressed for more. Soon, she wanted a ring, and she made sure to remind him of it every day.

It frustrated him, coupled with his mother's constant nagging about how he was old enough to be a father. Being married to Esther would have pleased everyone.

Everyone except him.

It wasn't the life that he wanted. He wanted true love. He believed in it. In a world like this, it was stupid to, but he didn't care. True love was real. What he and Kachi had felt for each other was real. And that was why he couldn't bring himself to marry a woman he didn't love to fulfil an outdated obligation.

He was going to fall in love the right way, with the right person, even though she wasn't Kachi. There had to be someone who would make him feel what he felt with her. Or at least close to.

He picked up his phone and looked in the mirror as he made his way out the door. It was his first day at a new job and he had to make a good impression.

The drive was only a few minutes long and soon, he was sitting at the airline's Operations Control Centre.

He had quit his job as a pilot when he thought he was starting a family. But, even though his relationship was over, he suddenly didn't want to return to the air. As a dispatcher, he would have more time for his personal life. That meant more time to find the love of his life.

As the first flight prepared to take off, he went outside to watch it, just as the passengers of another plane that had landed started strolling down the airport.

At first, Uche thought he was hallucinating when he

saw a passenger that looked really familiar, but then she stopped in her tracks, holding her box behind her back.

~~~~~

Kachi couldn't believe it. Uche was right there, in front of her. What other proof did she need that she'd been right? That she hadn't been crazy or sentimental. Her feelings were just as strong and intense as they were ten years ago, and her heart suddenly felt lighter. She worried that he might not recognise her and was probably just freaked out by the stranger who was staring at him, but then he started towards her, with quick strides at first, then he was skipping. She laughed-cried, unable to contain her joy.

He was hers in this life and in their first life.

She knew as he got closer, his face wearing a look of joy and sorrow, that he recognised her too.

CHIAMAKA MUONEKE is a nursing student who loves to bring her imagination to life in writing. She writes African literature in multiple genres and has been featured in several upcoming anthologies. As a new author, she plans to publish several books digitally and in print soon. She lives in Nigeria, where she was born and raised, with her family.

Bonus Story

THE WANDERER
Agnes Kay-E

It was the third moon since Ómalichanwa and her de'nnâ, Eriri's arrival in Ónu's compound and the eerie tune only Ómalichanwa could hear still played. Only this night, while Eriri slept, the eerie tune played outside. It had always been during the day.

Refusing to fall asleep, Ómalichanwa stared at the thatched roof, which was weakening at the top. She listened to the eerie tune. Something about it made the hair on her skin stand, almost as if the sound was woven around her. It was hard to resist its pull. She has had the virtue of always following her instinct, and the pull felt like a nudge rather than a shove. The problem was, her instinct gave nothing.

A light and airy voice spoke through the music. *"I have been on a long journey. Can a wanderer find rest in your hands? Can a wanderer find solace in the kindness of your heart? If you can't, I'll sing louder. I have wandered, roamed, strayed, roved, tramped, and moored. I have swum the ages. From dusk until dawn, from sunrise to sunset, sunup to sundown, moons to sunshines, for cycles of seasons, in search of one such as you. Can you hear my plea? I pray you! Can I find solace in your bosom? I beseech you, hear the plea of a forlorn one."*

Ómalichanwa craned her neck and whispered, "Who are you?"

"It is I, the beauty of evolution."

Ómalichanwa slunk back in confusion.

"The metre of experience and the winding path between the sun and the moon, life, and death."

She paused for a while, then asked, "What is your name?"

There was no answer. The night was quiet again except for the chirping crickets and croaking frogs, but the chirping and croaking were different. It seemed like they were taking turns sustaining the eerie music.

A few minutes later, the eerie tune played again, and then the voice spoke; she asked the same questions, but there was no answer. While she waited, she fell asleep, and then the music started once more. This time it was loud but airy, and the foundation of her uncle's hut

BOUND BY FATE

shook. She looked at her de'nnâ, but he seemed unperturbed by the tremors.

Then the voice spoke. "O offspring of Eriri, offspring of Chijile of Ichie's line of the royal family of El'ikenueze. I have crossed miles to reach you. Words cannot describe your wisdom nor silence your power. A desperate one beseeches. Will you not hear its plea? You hold fast to your ideals, but you are gentle and generous. Lend me your heart, that I may find solace. Lend me your sight, that I may concede to the beauty I once beheld. Lend me your hand, that I indeed may find my kindred."

"Who are you?"

"I am yours to command, yours to wield, yours to guide and yours to ordain."

Impatiently, Ómalichanwa rolled her eyes.

"I'm the one to whom a babeling's first exclamation is sublime, the one the grave can't hinder in due season. I am the Witness, to enmity, oath, pain, love. To whom seasons lay their ploy for an arbitrary decision. To whom love settles on the gravity that snares the sun. I ensnare the stars, and the moon begs for a dance. To whom a secret of many moons is disclosed."

"What is your name?" Ómalichanwa asked, more forcefully.

"I am your past, your present, and your future. I need no name."

Ómalichanwa frowned. "Everyone and everything has a name."

"Many are the watchmen but not its antiquity. I am

the beneath and above of living and dying in this realm and beyond."

Ómalichanwa sighed. Her instinct read nothing; this made her more concerned than alarmed. She didn't want this to drag into another night since she had seen her inevitable end. Decidedly, she roused and made her way to the entrance of the hut. As soon as she came out of the hut, she saw a fog, the colour of the moon. She cautiously walked into it. It was brighter inside, with no edges, like being surrounded by bright nothingness. The Ófòr-Oguneli was on the ground in pieces. She knew what to do, but not how to start.

"Follow your heart," the singing voice urged.

She nodded her thanks, unsure whether it was appropriate to say anything. She stretched her hand out to pick up the most significant piece of the Ófòr-Oguneli, and the memories of every past bearer flooded through her. While the memories of each bearer washed over her, her hands stitched the pieces together. She spent a few more hours recalling the nimbus veils of mist. Completing the rites for each nimbus veil, she sent them to their rightful heirs. Most of which she needed to create portals for.

Six nimbuses were missing, four of which were shielded; something seemed to be preventing their return. It cost her hours and a splitting headache, but she was done, and unlike her predecessors, she didn't have long to live. She'd had the privilege of seeing her death but not how it would unfold. Exhausted and sleepy, she still managed to complete the rites of transition. Finally finished, she stumbled out of the bubble of fog and into the hut with the Ófòr-Oguneli.

Just as she was about to lay her head down, she heard the music again and frowned. She had just answered Ófòr-Oguneli's call a few minutes ago. She tapped into the nimbus of hindsight and foresight and saw her death; it was to be by Okpararebisi in a few hours with the help of Nwaneri. The revelation decreed their success. She prayed to the Lord of All for help. For if Nwaneri got the Ófòr-Oguneli, it would be the ending of the Twelve Kingdoms of Evóvuotu and the possible slavery of all living folks.

For some reason, as soon as her head touched the bamboo bed, she fell asleep but still felt awake. The further away she was from the Ófòr-Oguneli, the weaker she felt. Suspicious of her sleepiness, she decided to hold onto Ófòr-Oguneli.

"Greetings," the owl slurred. The owl had god-aura and she knew it had to be Nwaneri; the god-messenger had come to Evóvuotu in the form of an owl.

Ómalichanwa stepped out of the hut. Still drowsy, she leaned against the wall.

"What do you want?" she asked with no hint of malice.

"Give me that sceptre," Nwaneri ordered.

Ómalichanwa gave him a mirthless laugh.

"You shouldn't slight a god, you insolent youngling," he said pointedly, offended that a mortal would act with such irreverence.

Ómalichanwa nodded. She had to tread carefully; Nwaneri's twin was the god of mirth and festivity and was associated with birth, peaceful death, weddings, and festivals. More so, she needed to stall him as she still hadn't located the nimbus of Harvest & Bloom, War & Servitude, as well as four others. She hadn't done the three rites of transition for them.

Nwaneri blinked uncomfortably. He couldn't read her mind nor nudge her because Ófòr-Oguneli was protecting her, and he couldn't understand why. It was just a stick infused with powers. He would need his sibling's help for this, and besides, it was his sibling's fault that he was in this predicament. Sometime soon, Awele would be awake, and that would spell doom for his promotion and diminish his chances of taking Omanma as his bride.

She turned sideways to look at him, only to see black, round eyes staring at her. It was hard to know if he was angry with her. There was no expression on his face. Besides, she had never tried to read an animal's face before.

Nwaneri cocked his head left and right and blinked twice as he communicated with his sibling in the skies.

"There are more where that came from. Enjoy." He said. In a blink of an eye, an assortment of food was displayed on the floor. "I'll be back in the morning for the sceptre."

She squinted as a bright, silvery smoke cloud enveloped the owl, and it vanished. Relieved, she turned her concerned eyes to the Ófòr-Oguneli. In a few minutes, Okpararebisi would realise he was no longer in possession of the real Ófòr-Oguneli. She stalked back to the bed. She wanted to sleep, but the tapping sound kept interrupting her sleep. Suddenly missing Isekó, she sat up.

A loud rhythm called to her also. She closed her eyes in concentration as she tried to trace the unique tapping sound. It was a heartbeat. She tapped into another nimbus to find the heartbeat and discovered it was the babeling in her uncle's second wife's womb, the next Paramount Ruler was about to be born.

She swallowed, but her mouth had gone dry. Her time had indeed come. It was almost time to join her ancestors. She tried to shake off the feeling of foreboding that was about to blanket her mind unsuccessfully and walked out of the hut. As she made her way to her uncle's second wife's hut, she wondered what would have been. She hesitated when she got to the entrance of the hut, but there was no use in the delaying the inevitable.

She shrugged violently, swallowed, and walked into the hut.

AGNES KAY-E is a Nigerian author based in England and the multi-genre author of twelve books, including Blossom in Winter, a bestseller. Her latest is an African contemporary fiction called Unexpected Complications. She is presently working on another Contemporary Fiction. In her spare time, she sings and writes music.

OTHER KEP SHORT STORIES COLLECTION

Ogu & Other Stories
Notes on Love & Other Stories
Rebirth
Flip-Flop
Oops!
Sink or Swim
Loving Nigeria

CONTACTS

Thank you for purchasing this book.
I hope you enjoyed it.
For more, let's meet at any of these places.

Facebook: https://www.facebook.com/kepressng
Instagram: https://www.instagram.com/kepressng
For newsletters: https://www.kepressng.com

ABOUT US

Kemka Ezinwo Press (KEP) Ltd is an African publishing company with the vision of broadening the power of African literary works and compositions. We aim to remind the world that we're avid readers and combat the self-imposed superstition that Africans don't read.

Our core values are Excellence, Collaboration, Discovery, & Generosity.

To launch our official opening, we decided to introduce the KepressNG Anthology prize, a collection of shorts from debut and veteran authors with African lineage. We incorporated our Vision of developing and increasing African literature by making it a competition to select the best story.

The KepressNG Anthology prize is designed for new writers, though not restricted to them, to write stories that they'd hope to read. Our stories matter, and who better than us to tell our stories? Societies change, and the most affected are the young.

The idea of tying the story to a theme is our way of helping new and emerging authors establish a discipline of telling us the story without the faff.

The prose is in short form and not restricted to a specific genre.

There's a belief that short stories are a thing of the past, but most young adults start with short stories. Should we now abandon them in the abyss and or anarchy of the literary formation proficiency?

As an anthology prize giver, we want to reinstate the idea that writing is lucrative if only to the individual's aesthetics, thereby building better mental health and expanding knowledge.

2026 COMPETITION

Attention all writers of African heritage - this is your moment to shine. The 2026 Kepressng Anthology Prize will officially open for submissions on May 29, 2026. Whether you're a published author or just beginning your journey, we invite you to explore this chance to showcase your talent.

Ten lucky winners will:
~Be published in an anthology.
~Get five complimentary copies of the anthology.

This year, the competition features four categories:
~ VINE
~ LILY
~ JUVENILE
~ OAK.

The theme for each category is the same as the title, but it's up to you to interpret it however you wish – literally, figuratively, or creatively.

GUIDELINES

Entry is free and open to all African and those of African descent.
~ Your work must be original, unpublished and not AI-generated.
~Your entry must be in English and fictional.
~ You can submit only one entry per category.
~ All entries must be submitted in MS Word format, double line spaced in TIMES ROMAN font.
~ Your name must not appear in the body of the story.
~ The entry must be between 5,000 and 10,000 words.
~ Your submission email title must be as follows:
CATEGORY TITLE - YOUR STORY TITLE - YOUR NAME (PSEUDONYM).
~ All entries must be received by Midday of October 11, 2026.
~ The winners will be announced six weeks after the last day of submission. (A Change of date will be communicated.)

This is an incredible opportunity to have your work recognised, gain exposure, and most importantly, join a vibrant community of African writers! We can't wait to see your interpretation of these themes.

Send your submissions & FAQs to kemkaezinwo.press@gmail.com.

Good luck.

www.ingramcontent.com/pod-product-compliance
Lightning Source LLC
LaVergne TN
LVHW091621070526
838199LV00044B/883